Praise for *Ra*

"Ms. Galant's collision of runaway reptil
named Heather, and animal rights ac
Hiaasenesque scrimmage." —Janet Maslin, *The New York Times*

"Galant is a gifted storyteller, and she succeeds in making *Rattled* a lighthearted jab at the modern well-to-do." —*Rocky Mountain News*

"Galant skewers everything that's awful about exurbia." —*The Washington Post*

"Galant's modern-day fable is equal parts object lesson and comedy of manners. Each page is injected with just the right cocktail of venom and humor." —*The Star-Ledger* (New Jersey)

"*Rattled* could be characterized as...a tale of manners, but the real fun is that no one seems to have any." —*Daily News*

"Will strike a chord with anyone who has ever done PTA time." —*More* magazine

"Galant, whose witty and topical social commentary has graced the pages of the *New York Times,* nails it with her first novel." —*Library Journal*

"Galant skewers the shallow, striving, McMansion-dwelling suburbanites in this engaging satire." —*Publishers Weekly*

"Snakes, super-moms, and nervous social climbers star in this broad satire of the nouveau riche suburbs of New Jersey.... Entertaining comedic debut with a mild sting." —*Kirkus Reviews*

"In *Rattled,* suburbia is—literally and figuratively—a snakepit, seething with crooked developers, obnoxious yuppies, and a multitude of miscellaneous crackpots. In this wickedly satirical novel, Debra Galant does for the McMansions of New Jersey what Carl Hiaasen did for the swamps of Florida." —Tom Perrotta, author of *Little Children*

"[A] funny, clever book that perfectly captures the mores and foibles of a geographic region in transition. In this case, it is rural New Jersey that is slipping into the past—but it isn't disappearing without a fight. Debra Galant captures the nuances of the culture clash between the McMansionites and the animals and people they are displacing in moments that made me laugh out loud."

—Alice Elliott Dark, author of *Think of England*

"Whip smart, wickedly clever, and very funny, *Rattled* skewers the suburban chic and their Birkenstock-wearing opponents. This book made me laugh so hard I had to put it down. But then I picked it right back up and started howling again."

—Janet Evanovich

"Debra Galant takes it to the new exurbanites with high style and a wicked eye."

—James Kaplan, author of *Dean and Me*

"Hilarious yes, but it is smart like Harvard. Read these marvelous pages and know the perils of the unexamined life...Perfect."

—Dorothea Benton Frank, author of *Full of Grace*

"Reading *Rattled* is like eating a bowl of M&Ms—page after tasty page, just beneath each shiny and stylish surface is the deep flavorful taste you can only get from a talented author who has met the highest challenge of comedy and allowed the reader to savor the sweet treat of her characters."

—Neil Baldwin, author of *The American Revelation*

"Debra Galant's wit and irony are as sharp as a serpent's tooth in this totally engaging, over-the-top hilarious novel. As original as it is inventive, this book will keep you up late into the night laughing at upwardly mobile suburban moms, greedy developers, myopic environmentalists—and even yourself. No one escapes Galant's laser gaze, but then again, who would want to?"

—Pamela Redmond Satran, author of *Suburbanistas*

RATTLED

Debra Galant

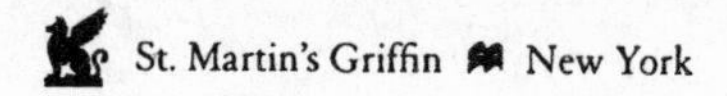
St. Martin's Griffin New York

 For information, address St. Martin's Press, 175 Fifth Avenue, New York, N.Y. 10010.

www.stmartins.com

Library of Congress Cataloging-in-Publication Data

Galant, Debra.
Rattled / Debra Galant.
p. cm.
ISBN-13: 978-0-312-36658-2
ISBN-10: 0-312-36658-2
1. Housewives—Fiction. 2. Animal rights activists—Fiction. 3. Real estate developers—Fiction. 4. Endangered species—Fiction. 5. Suburban life—Fiction. 6. Rattlesnakes—Fiction. 7. New Jersey—Fiction. I. Title.

PS3607.A385R38 2006
813'.6—dc22

2005050000

First St. Martin's Griffin Edition: April 2007

10 9 8 7 6 5 4 3 2 1

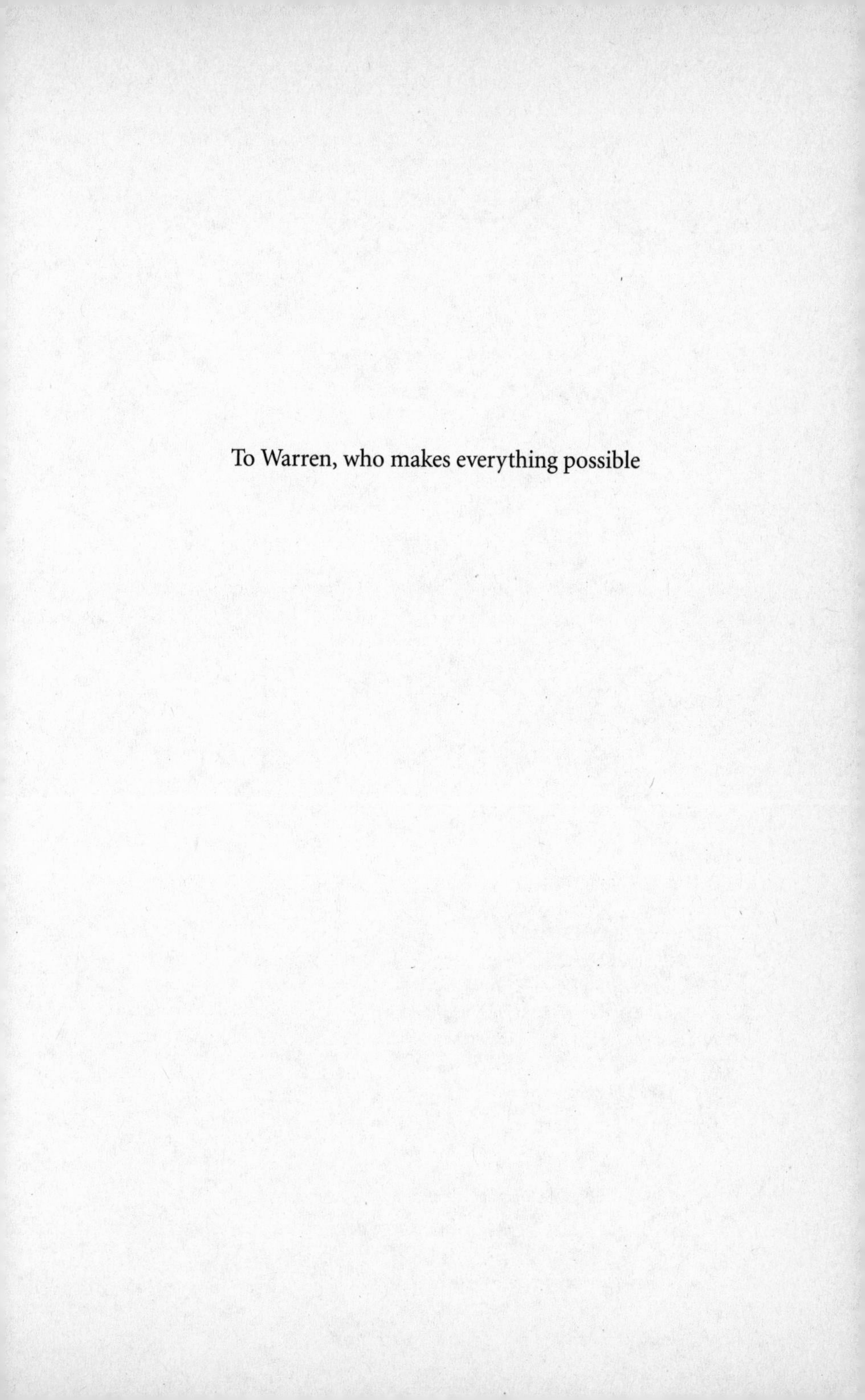

To Warren, who makes everything possible

Acknowledgments

Many people helped me along the way. Thanks first to my agent, Lisa Bankoff, without whose championship I'd never be a published novelist, and to Dori Weintraub, my editor at St. Martin's: your passion for this book continues to take my breath away.

Thanks to all the guardian angels who held my hand until I found Lisa and Dori, most especially to Liza Dawson, Dot Frank, and Neil Baldwin, whose knowledge of the book industry was invaluable.

To my teachers, Alice Dark and Pam Satran, who showed me the craft, and to all my writing friends who read this book in early versions: Allan Ross, Tammy Bakos, Priscilla Orr, Maggie Rohr, Roselee Bloosten, Jenny Milchman, Kalindi Handler, and Adam Philips. Love and special thanks to Sue Kasdon and Lia Schwartzman, who grabbed each chapter as it came out of the printer. To the whole Artists Way gang, especially Dania Ramos and Michael Aquino, you were there right at the start. And to all my readers at Baristanet.com, thanks for always getting the jokes.

Special thanks go to herpetologist Robert Zappalorti, who actually showed me a live timber rattlesnake and provoked it to rattle, to the Pinelands Preservation Alliance, and forester Ronald Farr.

Finally, home. To Margot, the pop-culture expert; to Noah, who could teach story to Robert McKee; and to my parents: I love you all. And, of course, nothing would be possible without Warren, who has honed my sense of humor these past twenty years and brought me coffee every morning.

He that diggeth a pit shall fall into it, and whoso breaketh an hedge, a serpent shall bite him.
—Ecclesiastes 10:8

Adam blamed Eve, Eve blamed the serpent, and the serpent didn't have a leg to stand on.
—Anonymous

Chapter One

All Heather wanted was a nice house. Well, a nice house and a nice lot. A few bushes out front would be nice too. And, of course, good schools. That was important.

There were a few other things that were important as well. The house had to be new, of course. At least five thousand square feet. It had to have a great room. That went without saying. It had to have a two-car garage, minimum. Three would be nice, but she wasn't greedy. And it really had to back up to some scenery, woods or something. Who wanted to pay more than half a million dollars for a house and have to look out at their neighbor's swing set?

None of the other things on Heather's checklist were absolute deal breakers. A basement gym; a master bath with radiant heat, a Jacuzzi, and his-and-her toilets; a marble powder room; a kitchen shiny with stainless steel; a media room with built-in plasma screen and real movie-theater seats; and a vaulted ceiling in the master bedroom—she wanted these things, sure. Actually, it wasn't just a matter of wanting them. It was a matter of dollars and cents. Whatever house they bought, they would—eventually—have to sell. So if only for the sake of resale value, Heather needed these things. Well, most of them. She could make do without a media room if she absolutely had to. After all, the pioneers didn't have plasma TV, and they survived.

And certainly growing up in that pathetic little Cape in Nutley, New

Jersey, sharing an attic bedroom with her sister, Heather had managed without any of life's luxuries. A radiator that produced more noise than heat, a bathroom that wasn't even on the same floor as her bedroom. She'd endured that. It had, as her mother was always saying, "built character." And then there were all those years that she and Kevin had been squeezed into their two-bedroom condo in Woodbridge, with the overwhelming smell of curry seeping in from the Patels' apartment across the hall and the pitter-patter of the not-so-little feet of all six Cosentini children thumping about upstairs.

No, Heather could compromise a little on the new house. They could always add movie seats later.

She and Kevin had fallen in love with this part of Burlington County, and they'd been looking here every weekend for months. The area was perfect: country but not too country. Barns, horses, things like that—but there was also a new mall anchored by a Bloomingdale's and a Saks, and its parking lot was filled with Jaguars and BMWs, so you could tell that successful people lived here. It was a great area, despite the little cracks her mother sometimes made about moving to the sticks. What did her mother know? This was where Heather belonged and the kind of people she belonged with: men like Kevin who were doing quite well in the world, and women like herself with good-enough taste to spend that income.

Most important, though, was that living out here would give Connor a leg up in the world. That was the prize she had to keep her eye on: a successful future for their one and only son, who would be starting third grade in just a month. All she asked was a fair advantage.

So far, though, she and Kevin hadn't found exactly the right house. And Heather liked things exactly right. She prided herself on being an informed shopper, in checking out every possible choice. If you weren't careful, if you didn't do all the research, you could (her stomach clenched at the very thought) make a mistake. But it was August, and if they didn't move pronto, Connor would have to change schools partway through the year. And, well, Connor wasn't exactly good with transitions. She had to think of Connor, didn't she? That was the whole point.

Today they were checking out Galapagos Estates. Maryanne, the sales manager, had told Heather there were a few houses left, prebuilt, on spec. One even had a view of a pond—and they might snatch it up if they were quick. Well, Heather thought, who was quicker than she was? So why was Kevin slowing down?

Their Land Rover stopped in a gravel lot in front of an old general store. It was a small plain white building with lots of signs. An old metal Coca-Cola sign that looked like it was from the 1940s, a big plastic sign for Vineland Farms ice cream, and smaller signs advertising sandwiches, beer and wine, coffee, copies ten cents. In front was a large ice chest and next to that a bench, which was occupied by a man in a feed cap who looked like he'd just stepped down from a tractor. Fairly pathetic as a retail establishment, Heather thought, but not without a certain rustic charm. Maybe they had some apple butter, or jam, something else countryish she could bring back to Kevin's parents, who were babysitting Connor. She prided herself on her thoughtfulness.

"Let me see the map," Kevin said.

"I told you, it's just down there. Maryanne gave me explicit directions."

He ignored her, grabbing the map off her lap. She sighed loudly. Just to let him know. Men. There was no use arguing.

Heather pulled down the visor and puckered her lips, the way she always did when she looked in a mirror. She undid the elastic holding her hair, shook her head, and redid her ponytail. She looked exactly the same as she had before. She assessed herself critically, and—except for the fact that her nose formed a little red triangle, something that happened no matter how conscientious she was about sunscreen—she was not displeased. At almost thirty-five, Heather could, depending on the light, still pass for a high school cheerleader. A good hair colorist: that was her secret. And discipline. You couldn't slack off. If you slacked off, you could gain weight. If you stopped wearing makeup, you'd become plain. They were everywhere, the fat, plain women—behind her in the supermarket, in restroom lines at the movie theater. Powerless, pathetic women whose husbands left them. She checked the mirror often, but it wasn't out of vanity. It was more like a breast self-exam.

"I'm going to get a Diet Coke," she announced.

The general store was a disappointment. No apple butter or jam, although there was Diet Coke. It was just a 7-Eleven with sawdust on the floor, Heather decided. On her way out, she glanced at the man sitting on the bench. He was wearing a feed cap and a plaid, short-sleeved shirt—probably synthetic—and he was chomping away on something that made his cheek bulge in a funny way. The man reminded her of a cow, sitting in a field chewing its cud. "Excuse me," Heather said, with the perky voice she used whenever she needed faster service from store clerks and the people who checked your tickets at the airport. Like her mother said, you got more flies with honey than you did with vinegar.

The man was looking straight ahead, as motionless as a cigar-store Indian.

"Excuse me," Heather repeated. "My husband and I are looking for Galapagos Estates. I told him it was right down there, but he doesn't believe me."

The man just continued to look straight ahead, chewing, as if Heather hadn't just asked him a question. As if, she thought, she didn't even exist. Strange. Well, maybe he was deaf. She'd had a bad bout of tinnitus back when she was in college, after going to a particularly loud Pearl Jam concert, and couldn't hear anything but a hum in her ears for weeks afterward. She still had trouble hearing sometimes. Maybe this guy had that too. She would give him the benefit of the doubt.

Heather was about to turn away when the man slowly leaned over and—still without looking at her—spat out a wad of chewing tobacco. It splashed onto the gravel, only a few inches from Heather's sneakers.

The man on the bench was Harlan White.

He had seen the little blonde get out of the big SUV and walk into the store. He hadn't noticed her here before, but that didn't mean anything. Clearly, she was one of the new people. City slickers with their noses in the air. They liked the way the country looked, but God forbid they should smell manure. People like her were ruining everything with their great big ugly houses, and all those new strip malls with tanning salons and sushi places. The thought of eating raw fish made him want to puke.

Harlan had been warming this bench for half a century. In the old days, there'd been plenty like him, men who'd grown up here, who'd carved their initials into trees as boys, hunted deer, fished trout. Back then, men had time to sit and shoot the breeze. But most of the old farmers had died, and the rest had sold out. And the tradesmen—carpenters, plumbers, roofers, and the like—well, with all the building going on these days, they didn't have time to eat, let alone sit around. Harlan saw them scarfing down sandwiches in their vans, talking on their cell phones at the same time.

Cell phones, Harlan thought with disgust. Plumbers going around like they were the president of the United States waiting on a call from Russia. That was the problem with people these days. They took themselves too goddamn serious.

Harlan was one of the few men left in Hebron Township with property big enough to run a horse on. Not that he had a horse. He had hens. He was an egg man, just like his daddy had been. Only a couple of years ago, Harlan had gone organic. That's what the people in the fancy houses wanted: "organic," "natural," "free-range." Fine. It was like stealing. He could get $3.50 a dozen.

He also hired out as a handyman, doing odd jobs for people in the big new houses. Hell, any man with a ladder and a hammer could make a fortune off those suckers. For all their fancy four-wheel-drives, not one of them could dig himself out of a little snowy driveway. They were as helpless as newborn kittens.

Take the man over there in that SUV, the one the tarty little blonde had hopped out of. Handsome-enough fellow—looked a bit like a young JFK—and just as full of himself too, probably. By the looks of things, he could buy and sell Harlan ten times over. But when a flake of snow fell, this guy would be on the phone to someone like him, someone with a real truck and a snowplow. He wouldn't rake his own leaves either, or even blow them. He'd have people for that too. People to clean his gutters, clean his pool, change his lightbulbs.

Harlan sat on the bench by himself these days. He wished that one of the few old-timers left would come by and talk about where the fish were biting. He wouldn't even mind seeing one of those fat old wives, girls he'd gone to school with, coming in for Crisco. Any old face. Anybody who knew his name. But lately there'd been nobody. In fact, the little blonde was the only person who'd walked into the store in the past hour.

He'd heard her ask for directions, all right. But it was a free country, and he was free to ignore her if he pleased. He felt better after he'd spit. He'd aimed just right. He hadn't hit her shoes, but he'd gotten close enough to send her a little message. Welcome to Hebron Township. Now get out.

A sliver of a smile broke across Harlan's face, like a hairline fissure in a great outcropping of solid rock.

"Did you see that?" Heather said when she got back into the car.

"See what?" Kevin asked.

"That man. I asked him for some simple directions, and he . . . he . . ." Heather started to sputter. "He spat."

"What man?"

"That farmer," she said, pointing at the bench. "Are you blind?" She bent down and began to inspect her white Keds. "I think it was tobacco juice. Yuck."

"Doesn't sound too friendly," Kevin said.

"You think?" said Heather. "Good thing, like Maryanne says, most of the old-timers are leaving."

Kevin didn't say anything. He hated the way Heather quoted people like Maryanne. Maryanne this, Maryanne that. He'd heard it all the way down. What did she think Maryanne was, a fucking oracle?

Heather stopped inspecting her sneakers. Apparently, they weren't stained. Thank God. They wouldn't have to sue the general store. "Maryanne says they all have gas fireplaces," she said. "And guess what? They come with a remote control."

"What comes with a remote control?" asked Kevin. It was hard to keep up sometimes. Weren't they just talking about tobacco juice?

"The fireplaces!"

"Oh."

"Come on, Kev." Heather snapped her fingers. "Get with the program."

He sighed. He hated when she snapped. Some of the same things that had made Heather so attractive as a girlfriend—an undeniable vitality, an unexpectedly sharp tongue—were a lot harder to deal with in a wife. It had been one thing to chase after Heather when she was a cute little ponytailed coed at Rutgers. Quite another to spend his thirties always hustling to keep up.

He slammed on the brakes. There was the sign: GALAPAGOS ESTATES. It was made of logs and featured carvings of animals: a tortoise, a bird, a rabbit, deer. Two pine trees guarded the sign like wooden soldiers. Kevin steered the Land Rover down the curving drive, which was covered with a soft pine-needle carpet. It looked like the entrance to a state park, but for the fact that it ended, abruptly, in a small parking area filled with expensive cars. Just beyond the lot stood a white sales trailer.

There was mud. There was always mud. It came with the territory, because of the bulldozers and the trucks. But Kevin frowned, knowing he'd just have to pay fifteen bucks for another car wash. He wasn't going to let mud cake up on the side of a fifty-thousand-dollar car. Heather rushed into the trailer, but Kevin stopped to survey the neighborhood. A black ribbon of road unfurled into the distance. The trees planted alongside it were tiny, but the houses were huge.

Inside the trailer, which was air-conditioned to the point of refrigeration, was a rack of booklets printed on heavy, flecked, recycled stock. A large map dominated one wall, and a young Asian couple was inspecting it as if looking for hidden treasure. They were being assisted by a vivacious woman in her forties, who pointed to the map with a pencil.

"Maryanne!" Heather called.

The saleswoman nodded politely to the couple and turned toward Heather. "You must be . . ."

"Heather," Heather said. "Heather Peters."

"Just give me a moment," Maryanne said, holding up a finger, "while I help the Lees. Why don't you go check out the model house? It's right there."

Heather flashed a bright smile at Maryanne and took Kevin's arm, walking him out toward the model. But once she got outside, her expression drooped. "Shit," she said. "The Lees are probably getting the lot we wanted."

She was always so dramatic, his wife. "Look, Heather," Kevin said. "I'm sure there are—"

"Weren't you listening? I told you. Maryanne said there were only three houses left."

"Well, now there'll be two," Kevin said. "We only need one."

"If they get the one by the pond, I'll just die. Damn, if we hadn't stopped at that stupid general store, we might have gotten here first."

Naturally. It was always his fault.

But it was a nice house. There was a home-entertainment center built right into the great room, and a nook in the bedroom for his treadmill. The mechanics were sound too. A brand-new, 95 percent efficiency gas-burning furnace presided over a basement clean enough to perform surgery in. No more dungeonlike cellars like his dad's, with boxes everywhere, and crumbling asbestos, and generations' worth of old tiles and linoleum and lawn furniture.

It was fine. Great. Really, they all looked pretty much alike to him. The only thing Kevin didn't like was its name: the Walden. Each house in Galapagos Estates was named for a naturalist or conservationist or something about where they'd lived. There was the Darwin, of course, the Cousteau, the Audubon, and the Walden, named for the pond where Henry David Thoreau had spent a year living simply. Wasn't the house that Thoreau lived in basically a shack? Maybe the name was supposed to suggest raw individualism, but to Kevin it suggested failure. Although the seven-hundred-thousand-dollar asking price was a stretch—now he'd have to make partner at the law firm—he didn't like the idea of living in the smallest, simplest anything.

Heather grabbed his hand and walked up the stately circular staircase, which was topped by a rotunda. The floors still smelled of polyurethane. The smaller of the two walk-in closets in the master bedroom was bigger than the room he'd slept in as a boy. Even the room Connor would get had its own walk-in closet and bathroom.

"Well, what do you think?" Heather asked. She hadn't looked this excited since he'd popped the question.

"It's okay." He meant: owning a house like this would be a fair marker of his economic success, but he wasn't going to start shrieking like somebody who'd just won a refrigerator on a TV game show.

"Just okay? Come here." Heather pushed Kevin into a walk-in closet. She closed the door and pressed him to the wall, rubbing up against his groin. "It makes me hot," she said, her voice uncharacteristically breathy. "And wet." She put her finger in her mouth and touched it to his lip.

Kevin was hard. He felt his breath get short. There was nothing like the possibility of a major purchase to bring his wife's libido out. The best sex they'd ever had was after they'd ordered the French Country dining room set from North Carolina.

He heard footsteps approaching. Kevin kissed Heather full on the mouth before opening the door. He looked down at his khakis, willing the bulge away. They stepped out to find the Lees staring at them. "Just measuring," Kevin said, his face hot.

An hour later, down at the trailer, the Peterses signed the papers on 63 Giant Tortoise Drive, the Walden. It might have been the smallest model, but it was closest to the pond. "Location, location, location!" Maryanne said brightly. The closing would be early September. Perfect. Connor would be able to start the new year at Pine Hills Elementary.

As they drove off, Heather, who seemed to have forgotten about the farmer and the tobacco juice, jabbered nonstop about upgrades, sinks, tile, grout. Kevin nodded. Sex, he thought. Tonight. Maybe his parents could watch Connor just a little longer. He could whip out the cell and say they'd had unexpected delays.

He was so caught up in his daydreams that he had to slam on his brakes to avoid hitting the little woman crossing Route 381, followed by a menagerie of dogs, cats, and geese, all trotting or padding or waddling after her. It looked like something out of a fairy tale. Where she'd come from, he couldn't imagine. It was as if she'd just . . . materialized. And all those animals—what was that about?

As he waited for the woman to cross the road, Kevin felt his heart begin to slow down—had he really almost run over a pedestrian?—and finally his panic turned to curiosity, tinged with annoyance. The woman wore blue jeans and cowboy boots and had white hair pulled into a tight long braid. She was clearly old but hardly feeble; she strode across the road with long steps, her back straight. There was something almost regal in her appearance; her posture hinted that she came from money. But the way she dressed suggested artist, herbalist, or soothsayer. Strange.

"Kevin!" Heather said. "What are you waiting for?"

Was Heather so fixated in grout fantasies that she hadn't even noticed that they'd almost run someone over? As the last of the geese waddled in front of the Land Rover, the old woman began climbing a steep incline, heading toward a small cabin tucked into a glade of pines. It was—what was the word?—*funky.* An old VW Beetle from the sixties, painted lime green, sat in the driveway. There were all manner of signs, stones, statuary, wind chimes, and even a clothesline in front of the house, for God's sake. Very un-Galapagos, he thought.

When the last goose had safely made it to the embankment, the woman turned to Kevin and raised an angry fist. "Why don't you watch where you're going?" she shouted.

Kevin quickly looked away and stepped on the accelerator. "It looks like the natives are restless," he said to Heather.

But Heather was in another world, furiously punching the buttons on her cell phone, holding it up to her ear, then punching again. An automated telephone system, Kevin could tell, and he could feel Heather's irritation working toward a boil. Not that he could blame her. It was extraordinarily annoying these days, to try to reach a human being on the phone. You didn't get people, you got menus. But Heather always acted as if automated answering systems had been invented solely for her own personal inconvenience.

Finally she got through.

"I don't have time to fill out a stupid form!" she snapped at the unlucky person on the other end. "I want to know right now. What's the best rate you can give me?"

Chapter Two

"Damn SUVs," Agnes cursed, watching the Land Rover start off again. The driver looked a little sheepish, she thought. Well, he should. She bent over and whisked a black Burmese up to her chest. "Come here, Clytemnestra," she said, kissing the cat on its mouth.

Clytemnestra was—if Agnes admitted it, which she rarely did—her favorite animal. And that was saying a lot. Agnes had seven animals that lived in her house: two dogs, five cats. She didn't call them pets. That would be too patronizing. The very term embodied a warped eighteenth-century worldview that held Homo sapiens as the master species and the rest as mere lapdogs.

In addition to her seven domestic animals—that was the term Agnes preferred—there were many varieties of fishes, amphibians, birds, and mammals that resided in Agnes's yard. The sparrows, warblers, and wrens she put seed out for (leaving extra for the squirrels), the minnows, salamanders, frogs, and geese that shared her reedy pond, the wounded rabbits and hawks that were brought to her to be mended, and which she tended carefully in cages lined up against the dilapidated greenhouse. She loved all the animals, even the ones that others called exterminators to get rid of: rodents and insects and snakes. It was all nature, wasn't it? Even pests played an important role in the ecosystem. Getting rid of any animal—an angry wasp or a malodorous skunk—was like pulling a thread from the middle of a piece of silk.

Still, even if Mother Nature didn't play favorites, Agnes loved Clytemnestra best.

Like a kindergarten teacher, Agnes counted to make sure all the animals had crossed safely. With all the new construction and the traffic, taking her daily constitutional was getting more dangerous by the week. Had they widened Route 381 again? Luckily, though, all the animals had made it. No thanks to Ken and Barbie in their suburban assault vehicle.

Agnes swung her front door open and let the cats and dogs in before going out to the garden. It was early August, and she was delighted to discover that some cherry tomatoes had turned red overnight. Ripe for the plucking. Her garden wasn't large, but it produced plenty of tomatoes, kale, peppers, and zucchini for a sixty-two-year-old woman living alone. She supplemented her personal harvest with Harlan White's organic eggs. She didn't like Harlan's politics much, but his eggs were fresh and local, and anyway, she didn't have to see him. She left envelopes with cash thumbtacked to the oak tree behind her house. Harlan took the cash and deposited the eggs in the old metal Coca-Cola chest on her back porch.

Agnes plucked a handful of the little tomatoes, left some rotten ones outside the garden fence for the backyard critters, grabbed the eggs from the back porch, and went inside and set the food down in her kitchen. A benign chaos ruled Agnes's kitchen, which served as a fair metaphor for her life. Its red Formica counters overflowed with colanders, teapots, mismatched plates, a yogurt maker, and screen-topped trays in which she grew four varieties of sprouts. Her 1958 Frigidaire was crammed with leftovers in various stages of decomposition. A spider plant dating to 1973 dangled a profusion of great-great-great-grandbabies in front of a picture window. Feeding bowls were scattered across the linoleum floor.

Agnes would make a tomato omelet for one. But first she would check her e-mail.

There were twenty-seven messages.

She deleted the junk mail first. Offers for penis enlargement, orgasm cream, mortgage refinancing, and self-employment deals that would bring in money even as she slept. That left ten. First she opened a note from her friend April, up in Boston. April had grown up nearby, gone to Boston College, and, despite all the barriers to women in business, had become, in her fifties, a manager of a mutual fund that invested only in socially responsible corporations. April had forwarded one of those silly e-mail quizzes—which came with instructions that if you sent it along to seven friends, something good would happen, and that if you deleted it, the world would come to an end. Agnes smiled, amazed that such a high-powered woman would have time for such nonsense.

But she took the quiz. If you were an animal, what kind of animal would you be? Well, now she could see why April had sent it. A cat, of course. Was there any creature more graceful, more exquisitely sensitive?

If you could pick any period of history to live in, what period would it be? Hmmm. Oh yes, the beginning of recorded history, the Garden of Eden—before people screwed everything up.

Describe the house of your dreams. That was easy; she was sitting in it.

Who is your true love? Clytemnestra, she thought. She supposed they meant humans though. Well, of course: Oliver. But he had died seven years ago. She felt a bit guilty that she'd thought of Clytemnestra before her late husband. Her mother had always accused her of caring more about animals than about human beings.

Agnes clicked off the quiz and opened some other e-mail. A notice for an upcoming lecture on fall bird migration from the local Audubon Society. An alert from the Central Jersey chapter of Friends of the Fauna about mistreatment of lab rats at a pharmaceutical company. Then a private message from Leroy Adams, one of the chapter's more radical members, about the possibility of an "intervention" on behalf of the lab rats.

Agnes winced. She could sympathize with those who planned midnight missions to deserted suburban office parks. She felt for the little white-and-pink fluffballs of rodentia who were turned into nicotine addicts or blinded at birth. She'd splattered a little red paint on fur wearers in her day, after all. But she drew the line at breaking and entering. Too dangerous. If she were jailed, who would take care of Clytemnestra and all the rest of her brood? Oliver was gone, and there was no one else.

Agnes scrolled up to the top of the e-mail to see who else had received Leroy's message. No other names. Good. At least he'd used the blind-copy function. Agnes didn't want her name showing up on some Department of Wildlife list of animal crazies.

The last e-mail was from Professor Richard Artemus, and it was labeled "Crotalus horridus. Fall tracking season." Agnes took a deep breath. The timber rattlesnake. If there was one member of the animal kingdom she felt ambivalence toward, this was it. Its Latin species name, *horridus,* told the whole story. Why she'd agreed to help with the radio tracking of timber rattlers, to go out into the field and actually look for the creatures, she couldn't quite say. Her mother must be turning in her grave.

But when it came to animals, she always said yes first and thought about it later. After all, timber rattlers were an endangered species. And you couldn't expect the snakes themselves to prevent developers from clear-cutting the forests and building new McMansions. They needed human help.

It was amazing work that Artemus was doing, this radiotelemetry: capturing snakes, surgically implanting radio transmitters, and then tracking their movements in the field.

Agnes clicked open the e-mail to see a photograph of the familiar reptilian face. It looked ancient, leathery, and was covered with little bulbous pouches. Its mouth was set in a deep scowl, and its eyes stared out coldly. There was nothing soft and cuddly about *Crotalus horridus.* It would be no one's pet. Agnes stared back at the picture and wondered what it reminded her of. After a minute she had it: old lady gamblers in Atlantic City.

Chapter Three

Moving was like a war, Heather decided—a strategic enterprise that required constant viligance, courage, and action. If you didn't pay careful attention, you could be blindsided at any time. By a title inspector, for instance, who wrote down the wrong block and lot number. Or a mortgage company trying to stick you, at the last moment, with two hundred dollars in photocopying fees. Heather was alert to people taking advantage of her. Her father, rest his soul, had always let people walk all over him. That was why she grew up in such a small house, why she never had all the things the girls on the rich side of town took for granted.

Heather didn't have a giant war map or a situation room. But she did have a PalmPilot, and—for moving boxes and other chores that required heavy lifting or the ability to reach tall places—she had Kevin.

Operation Galapagos Estates started the minute they signed the contract on 63 Giant Tortoise Drive. On the way home, while Kevin nattered on about some woman with geese and cats, Heather had managed to call five banks, maneuver through their idiotic phone menus, find actual human beings to talk to, and lock in a very favorable rate. Not that Kevin was any help. He kept talking about leaving Connor with his parents so the two of them could go home, open some wine, and celebrate the new house. Celebrate? Heather knew what *that* meant. Sex!

Like she had time. She had to get boxes, call movers, take care of a million details. What the hell was he thinking?

Thank God she didn't work. For that, at least, she could be grateful. BC—before Connor, that is—she'd been the regional manager for a chain of women's clothing stores, a job that didn't pay much but at least afforded her a lot of cute clothes at a steep employee discount. But AC Heather was just as happy to throw herself into motherhood and support Kevin's bid to become a partner at Brockman, Brockman & Liebowitz. Frankly, she couldn't imagine how she'd manage everything now if she also had to go to work. It was a full-time job to run a household, more than a full-time job to move one. People might think she was a control freak, but she knew: as much time as it took to be organized, it took even more time if you weren't. Things would fall apart. Trust but verify, that was her motto.

Heather's pièce de résistance, the centerpiece of the entire move, was her scheme for color-coding the boxes. She'd gone to Kinko's, copied a blueprint of the new house, then taken each room, colored it with marker, and used the same marker on the packing labels of all the boxes. It was an enormous undertaking—not helped by Connor grabbing the markers every time she turned her back—but it would keep the spatulas from winding up in the guest bedroom and the guest linens from turning up in the pantry. Chaos, Heather thought. That was the enemy. It was a fierce, relentless foe that could shred your plans into confetti. If you didn't overtake it, it would overtake you. Well, she was Heather Peters, and she had no plans to let chaos defeat her. She would outsmart the hydra-headed forces of disorganization. She had lists, goddamn it, and Kinko's and colored markers on her side.

Still, organized as Heather was, shit happened.

First there was the matter of the interest rate. See? She knew the banks would try to screw her. Rates had risen slightly since Heather had locked in their mortgage—or, more to the point, they had risen since she thought she'd locked it in. Turned out there was some small loophole involving signatures and the post office, and the loan officers at the bank were slithering right through it. Well, they would pay, that was all. There were principles involved. And think of all the suckers who weren't as smart as she was, who'd just let the bank walk all over them.

She was fighting for them too! She would call the Problem Solvers on the Channel 5 News and have them tell the whole world what conniving, cheating, lying bastards—what snakes!—those bankers were. That would teach them. She also had calls in to the New Jersey Department of Banking and Insurance and the state attorney general. Really, jail would be too good for them.

The thing was, reaching the Problem Solvers on the Channel 5 News wasn't so easy. Heather had been on hold for ten minutes, and though she was maximizing her time by wrapping wineglasses in tissue while she waited, it was taking annoyingly long. Who, she wondered, could she report the Problem Solvers to? Didn't they know that people with problems were, by definition, busy?

Then call waiting clicked through, presenting a difficult split-second choice. Heather sucked in her breath, reluctant to leave her place in the phone queue but equally reluctant to miss the call, in case it was the state attorney general. She hit the flash button.

"Mrs. Peters?" came the voice. "I'm from International Famine Relief. First, I'd like to thank you for your support in the past and your generous contributions to the Ethiopia famine campaign. But the reason I'm calling today is to tell you about a drought that has gripped Mauritania—"

"You know," Heather said, "people in Africa aren't the only ones with problems."

Okay, maybe that wasn't too nice, but really. She'd just given last spring. And to the Red Cross too. Was she responsible for saving the whole world?

She hit the flash button. Too late. The Problem Solvers had not waited. She slammed the phone down.

A second later the phone rang, and for one hopeful moment Heather thought it might be the Problem Solvers calling back. It was just Kevin, though, calling from work to say he'd be a bit late.

"There, there," he said, when she told him about the mortgage. "It's really only a matter of half a point."

"Half a point! Do you know that over the life of the loan"—Heather punched some numbers into her calculator—"that comes to"—she hit the equals button—"thirty-eight thousand four hundred and sixty-two dollars."

"Heather."

"And eighty-six cents!"

Then there was the thing about the muslin Roman shades Heather had ordered for the sunroom. Those shades, what could she say? They might possibly have been the most gorgeous thing she had ordered from a catalogue—ever. And how she'd agonized over them! Should she pick the "parchment" or the "sunrise"? Should she get the lining, or go for the sheer look? Finally she chose: parchment and sheer. Anyway, they were a classic. An absolute classic.

The UPS man walked up with the boxes on a Saturday, and Heather was so euphoric, and impatient to see how they'd look in their actual "space," that she talked Kevin into driving her all the way down to Galapagos Estates. It was ridiculous, she knew that. But really, she was working so hard. And she deserved it, didn't she? Besides, it would be such a nice drive. And they'd get fresh air! Maybe Kevin and Connor could even throw a ball around. But when they got to the new house, took the shades out of the box, and Kevin held them up to the windows, it turned out they were five eighths of an inch too wide. Her new muslin shades—fourteen hundred dollars!—and utterly worthless. They could never be recut. It was a disaster.

After a thorough investigation, Heather discovered what went wrong. The measurements she had used, printed in a Galapagos Estates spec sheet, were five eighths of an inch off.

"And whose fault do you think that is?" Heather asked Kevin. "Ours? I don't think so. I have half a mind to send the bill right to Galapagos Estates." She did too. They didn't admit wrongdoing, or pay for the shades, but they did offer a nice upgrade on the back patio, giving her the better variety of flagstone and agreeing to extend it another ten feet. Heather suspected that they simply had a surplus of flagstone, but a quick calculation told her she'd more than made out.

But the most serious setback was the thing about Connor's school. In the midst of all the packing, the measuring, the mortgage negotiating, Heather found the time to get the names of some local moms from Maryanne so she could find out what teacher Connor should get. Due diligence, that was all. Heather strapped her cordless headset on, culled sock orphans and torn underwear from Kevin's dresser, and kept an eye to the clock while she worked the phone. There was one golden hour of telephone time on weekday evenings—between eight and nine o'clock, late enough not to interfere with dinner, early enough not to interfere with bed—and Heather was intent on exploiting it.

Finally, after three evenings of cold calling, Heather walked into the living room and announced the result of her research. "Mrs. Gately!" she said.

"Mrs. Gately?" said Kevin.

"Mrs. Gately is the best third-grade teacher at Pine Hills Elementary School. Firm but not too strict. Caring but not a pushover. Everybody says so. Tomorrow I'll call the school and insist that Connor get Mrs. Gately. After all, he will have all the trauma of the move. And he doesn't know a single soul."

In the middle of her speech, Heather noticed that Kevin was wearing what he considered his poker face, an expression that she knew was supposed to convey complete neutrality. But of course she'd been married long enough to know that neutrality on Kevin's part actually meant disapproval. After all, if he agreed, he'd be nodding.

"Really, he needs this, Kevin," Heather said. She was only thinking of poor Connor, with all his little social issues, adjusting to a new school, new peers, a new house, a new neighborhood. Connor, who over this short lifetime had generated more than his share of phone calls from teachers, complaints from other parents, and referrals to behavior experts and learning consultants. It went without saying that he deserved—no, *needed*—the best the school district had to offer.

Kevin nodded ever so slightly.

"You, of all people, know that," she said.

He nodded again.

Not exactly a ringing endorsement, Heather had to admit. But what did men know about schools?

Kevin knew better than to start an argument. Still, he had a feeling this wouldn't go well. Heather's campaigns to find the perfect teacher never did. Every spring since Connor was four, Heather had conducted extensive market research with mothers whose children were a year ahead to find out the best teacher for the coming grade. Then she tried to strong-arm the school into assigning that teacher to Connor. What Heather never seemed to notice was that this strategy didn't work.

He couldn't fault his wife for wanting the best for their child. And he certainly had to commend her for her diligence and persistence. It was just that she wasn't picking up on the overall pattern. No matter whom she requested, the schools would give Connor someone else. And not just any someone else. Connor always got the worst teacher in his grade, the one who couldn't stand boys, or who punished the whole class when it was just one kid who acted up, or who assigned elaborate diorama projects over Thanksgiving break. It was like a law of physics. The harder Heather pushed, the more wretched the teacher Connor would wind up with. Yet each year, Heather pushed harder.

"Do you think, maybe, we should—"

"Just wait and see?" Heather said. "Leave it to chance? No way." He might have been suggesting that Connor traipse off by himself to New York City, leaving a trail of bread crumbs to find his way back.

When Kevin came home from work at seven-thirty the next evening, exhausted and ready for his evening beer, he found Heather more worked up than she'd been in a long time. He tried walking to the bedroom so he could take off his jacket and shoes, but Heather blocked his path like an all-star defensive guard.

"Do you know what our taxes will be at Galapagos Estates?" she asked, before he could even put his briefcase down.

Kevin knew witness badgering when he heard it.

"Tell me, Heather, what will our taxes be at Galapagos Estates?"

"Eight thousand seven hundred dollars." She folded her arms, as if she had just won a major argument.

"So stipulated," he said. "Your point?"

"Don't you think that would entitle us to a little say in our son's education?"

"He didn't get Mrs. Gately," Kevin guessed.

"No, he did not."

"A shame," Kevin said. He loosened his tie. "Heather, can I get a beer? First? Before we discuss this?" He walked in the direction of the kitchen. Heather blocked him again.

"Not only did Connor not get Mrs. Gately, he's going to get Miss Kindermack."

"Miss Kindermack?"

"Miss Kindermack. One year out of ed school. Her first year teaching third grade. Last year she taught fifth grade. And I heard that she really trained to be a gym teacher. A seventh-grade gym teacher. But she changed her mind halfway through ed school and went into elementary education. Kevin, do you know what that means?"

"It means . . . um . . . she's not going to be a gym teacher?"

"It means she's tough. She'll be barking orders, making the kids scramble up ropes, that sort of thing. And Connor, poor Connor. He's so sensitive, you know."

Ah, yes, poor, poor sensitive Connor. Like when he was a toddler and a confirmed hair puller. Kevin remembered those Saturdays at Gymboree and his dread every time they played the parachute game. The grown-ups would all hold the sides of the parachute, and the children would disappear underneath, and then at the command of the teacher, the multicolored fabric would float up like a butterfly to reveal a group of delighted giggling kids. In theory, at any rate. Only when Connor played, something would happen underneath the parachute, and when the silk came up, there would be some poor innocent child screaming and pointing hysterically at Connor. Connor, who was always "accidentally" sticking out his leg and tripping the other kids in class. Connor, who squeezed puppies in the park just a little too hard. But Kevin knew, after ten years of marriage, that there was only one thing he could say.

"That's terrible," he said.

"Outrageous!"

"Where is Connor, by the way?" Kevin asked, thinking that it might not be such a great idea to be discussing the horrors of Miss Kindermack within earshot of his son, in the altogether likely event that she would, indeed, become Connor's teacher.

"Oh, back in his room," Heather said. "Packing. I gave him a great big garbage bag and said he had to purge his room, get rid of those stupid Happy Meal toys and action figures from the Truman administration. Like Aladdin. I mean, who cares about Aladdin? That was, like, eight Disney movies ago. He sulked a little, but I promised him that he'd get all kinds of new toys when we moved, and he could keep them all neat and clean and organized in his new bedroom."

She would do it too. If there's one thing his wife would make good on, it was a promise to get her son the best, the newest, the most enviable possessions. Connor had had a leather bomber jacket at age two. He'd had his own TV, with video-game controls, from the time he was five. Kevin pictured large bags from Toys "R" Us, with multicolored plastic toys spilling out. He imagined his slightly overweight son, glossy-eyed in the middle of his new room in Galapagos Estates, in a veritable toy stupor, not knowing which of his many treasures to play with first.

There were more calls, to the superintendent of schools, the president of the school board, to Maryanne at Galapagos Estates. But of course Connor's teacher remained Miss Kindermack. Mrs. Gately's class already had two kids too many, the principal, the superintendent, and the school board president all said. Their hands were tied. There was nothing they could do. And there was a firm policy against letting parents interfere with student placement.

Thus started the period, a week before the move, when Kevin would come home and find his wife surrounded by boxes, staring morosely at the TV. She wouldn't talk except to repeat, in a flat monotone, the latest platitudes of Dr. Phil. Kevin was beginning to worry. He'd seen Heather in moods like this for an hour, maybe two. But never for days at a time. She really seemed depressed, maybe even clinically so.

For almost a week, with Heather sitting in zombielike defeat, Kevin actually had to think about the details of the move himself. "What about the wardrobe boxes?" he said. "I thought the movers were bringing wardrobe boxes."

"Tomorrow," Heather said dully.

"And the insurance?"

"Taken care of."

"Well," said Kevin. "Did you find someone to clean this place the day we move out?"

Heather looked temporarily stunned. A detail had gotten past her.

"Oh God," she said. "I forgot. What's wrong with me?" She grabbed the phone, pressed speed dial, then spoke to somebody in rapid-fire Spanish.

"Done," she said, sounding as if she had woken from a sound sleep.

The funny thing was, one of the moving guys was color-blind. Just one. But that was enough to screw up Heather's plan. Three of the four guys could follow her color-coding schematics just fine. It was just that a quarter of the boxes wound up in the wrong place.

It hadn't even occurred to Heather that something could go wrong with the boxes. But after they'd tipped the movers fifty dollars apiece, picked Connor up from Kevin's parents', settled him into his brand-new bunk bed, and were ready, exhausted, to sink into bed themselves, Heather looked for the box that she had clearly labeled "master bedroom sheets."

She walked into the master-bedroom linen closet and began reading box labels. "Hand towels," she said. "Bathroom cleaning supplies. Canned food. Canned food?"

"Just lie down," Kevin said.

Half an hour later he found the master-bedroom sheets, clearly labeled with their green-blue tag, underneath a box of kitchen utensils that, somehow, had wound up in the garage.

Despite everything, the mortgage, the Roman shades, Miss Kindermack, the boxes, they were settling in. Yes, Heather did sigh heavily whenever she had to go looking for a box in the nether reaches of the house—it was amazing how large a model called the Walden could be—but the place was starting to look and feel like a home. Heather didn't have window treatments for the living room yet, but she'd found the name of a seamstress nearby—an old lady—who sewed for practically nothing.

The builder, Jack Barstad, had made good on the flagstone patio, and in the late afternoon, after the patio men had gone home, Heather could look out her new Pella windows at the pond, with its tall, waving grass set against a sky just beginning to turn pink, and feel that she'd finally found an earthly heaven. It was true that there didn't seem to be many children playing outside, that it was a little buggy, that none of the neighbors had come over to introduce themselves, that Connor spent all his time hooked up to his new PlayStation, and that Kevin's commute was forty-five minutes longer each way than it had been before. Still, Heather had to count her blessings. Like the fact that she'd upgraded to Pella windows.

It was time, she decided, to have her mom and Kevin's parents over for a Sunday barbecue. After all, what was the point of moving up in the world if nobody saw it?

When Sunday arrived, it seemed that finally one event in the life of Heather Peters would come off without some idiot or idiocy getting in her way. The day had dawned sunny. The temperature hovered in the low seventies, perfect September weather. Kevin had volunteered to take care of marinating the steaks and operating the grill, so Heather merely had to make her trademark German potato salad and pick up a dessert.

"Aren't I calm?" she said, strutting through the kitchen, polishing and repolishing the countertops as if they were made of solid gold rather than granite. "Aren't you proud of how calm I am?"

"Very calm," Kevin said, patting Heather's hand.

The doorbell rang. Heather's mother had brought a bouquet of flowers, but as was typical of gifts from Heather's mother, they were utterly pedestrian, looking like they came from a gas station rather than a florist. "How lovely," Heather lied. She'd dump the flowers as soon as her mother left. But until then, she'd dutifully pretend it was the loveliest arrangement she'd ever seen. Then Heather's mother reached into a plastic bag and pulled out something truly hideous, a patchwork doll made from scraps of calico, with a pointy hat and—was it? Yes—a broom.

Heather's mom took the doll and, without even consulting Heather, installed it on the windowsill behind Heather's stove. "A kitchen witch," she said. "For good luck. Handmade. I picked it up at the general store."

"How, um, thoughtful of you," Heather said. "Good luck? Well, I certainly can use that!" The kitchen witch she'd definitely ditch, even before she chucked the flowers. She smiled uncertainly. Or would she? Her mother was awfully superstitious about good-luck charms and would look for it every time she visited. And though she hated to admit it, Heather was a touch superstitious herself. Might it be unlucky to throw away a good-luck housewarming gift from one's own mother? It just might.

A picture came to mind of the old house in Nutley, all cluttered with doilies and little Hummel figurines and, worst of all, furniture covered in plastic. All of these things had seemed normal and natural to her until one day a new friend, who'd moved to New Jersey from California, came over and actually laughed at the plastic-covered sofa. It was like a slap, like a wave of consciousness, a revelation. Her mother had terrible taste! Heather had felt the heat go to her cheeks as she blushed in horrified embarrassment. From that moment on she'd seen the world a different way. There was good taste and there was bad taste, and like Scarlett, who'd never be hungry again, Heather had vowed, at the age of twelve, that she would never be humiliated again for such a lapse. She threw out her old college textbooks a year after she'd graduated. Beach novels and self-help books were read, then passed to a girlfriend or donated to the local library. But old *Architectural Digests* she would never part with. She kept them stored, in chronological order, in rattan organizers from Hold Everything. And she'd never seen a kitchen witch in one of those.

A few minutes later, Kevin's parents pulled up. Kevin's parents who, though not much wealthier than Heather's, had infinitely better taste. Although they had their own issues. Lateness, for example. But today, for once, they weren't going to arrive hours late, leaving everyone to worry about car accidents or when to put the steaks on. There were kisses, greetings, oohs and aahs about the house, when finally the grandparents realized that their beloved grandson was missing.

"Connor!" Heather called. "Connor!"

"I bet he's out back," Kevin said. "Let me show you the patio. It's almost done. Heather got them to expand it because of the snafu with the window treatments."

"That Heather," Kevin's mother said. "So resourceful."

Heather beamed.

They walked out back and found Connor playing at the edge of the pond. That was strange. He'd never expressed any interest in nature before. Oh no, for goodness' sake, he was *in* the pond. "Connor, get out!" Heather yelled. "Come say hi to your grandparents."

The freckle-faced redhead ran toward them, his khakis dark with water below his knees. He approached his mother with a playful smile. "Boys," Heather said with an affectionate shrug. "Those pants were twenty-four dollars at the Gap. I should shop at Goodwill, the way he treats them." Nobody seemed to notice, until he was right upon them, that Connor was hiding something.

"Surprise!" he said, bringing his hands close to Heather's face.

Something squirted out, flying like quicksilver up to Heather's neck. And in the instant before it landed, wet and squishy, right inside her collar, Heather's mouth contorted into a frozen scream. Because the thing that had flown out of Connor's hands was . . . no, it couldn't be . . . yes it was . . .

A frog.

Heather tried to flick it off, but it fell down her shirt.

The scream that had been caught in Heather's throat let loose then and, with the others that followed, roused the entire neighborhood, which was rare in Galapagos Estates. It was probably just because of the temperature outside. The air-conditioning units were off, which had rendered the development—until that moment—exceptionally quiet.

Chapter Four

Jack Barstad had needed a night away. It had been nothing but work, work, work, finagle, finagle, finagle, for weeks on end. The first phase of Galapagos Estates had gone well—all but one of the houses had been sold, he'd heard from Maryanne—and now it was time to embark on Phase 2. It was just September, but if he was to begin building by spring, he'd have to get busy. For one thing, he'd have to break the news about his plans to build two hundred more houses to the Galapagos Estates Homeowners Committee. He wasn't too worried; he'd handpicked the committee himself and bought their loyalty with extra amenities and perks. Every time any of them took a leak in their powder room, they'd notice the marble-and-brass upgrades he'd given them, no charge. And after that July Fourth banquet on his yacht, with the Macy's fireworks erupting above, how could they deny Jack Barstad a right to earn a living?

But the Homeowners Committee might get a hard time from some of the other denizens of Galapagos Estates. Barstad knew his buyers. They loved the country. They were drawn by the quaintness, the open fields, the farm stands, and the pines. But they also felt entitled to a certain type of house, a house they felt they'd earned, the kind of house that Jack built, a sixty-five-hundred-square-foot luxury estate. The thing was that all of them, every single one, wanted to be the last one in. The fact that bulldozers had cleared the land for their suburban castles didn't ruffle their sensitivities. But when the big bad machines came to clear land for someone new, their acquisitive little souls suddenly turned sensitive. They were hypocrites, babies, whiners, the kind of people who could order Chateaubriand at Smith & Wollensky but weep if they happened to see a news show about slaughterhouses. They wanted, in other words, to have their steak and eat it too.

"Jack, baby, when are we going to go down to eat?"

He looked over at the brunette in bed beside him, Dana, a bright girl, fresh out of college, who had come to his office a few months ago in search of a career in real estate. When she'd made the appointment, he thought he might put her in the Galapagos sales office with Maryanne. That was at the beginning of the summer, when there were still thirty houses left. But after meeting Dana, Barstad realized she was destined for bigger things. She was a looker, five feet eleven, svelte, with lips as juicy and delicious as summer fruit, and a voice that was a deep purr. Her hair was cut in a severe bob, and her dark eyes flashed intelligence.

Barstad's wife, Barbara, on the other hand, was a gray-haired frump who cared only about acquiring new furniture and throwing successful parties. She had lost her youthful glow after their first child, her waistline after their second, and her sense of humor after their third. Barstad didn't seem to notice a similar deterioration in his own looks. So what if he had a comb-over, or was carrying thirty more pounds than he had in college? Maybe he was just a little puffy under his eyes. It didn't seem to matter to any of the sweet young things who climbed into his Jaguar. But Dana was different from any of the mistresses he'd had before. She was special. She wasn't just a bimbo. Jack had made her his director of development and begun taking her on "planning retreats" to Atlantic City.

"I thought we'd have room service," he said. "I've got some calls to make."

Last night's planning retreat had gone particularly well. They'd arrived at the hotel at nine, in time for a late dinner, and then gone down to play poker and blackjack. Dana looked stunning in tight jeans and a sheer beige camisole, her nipples grazing against the silk and driving the poor dealers mad. This alone would have increased Jack's odds against the house, but Dana was more than just a looker. She was smart. She kept an eye on all the players and could signal an observation to Barstad just by touching his knee. Barstad had bagged five grand, not bad for a night's work, and then he and Dana had gone back to their high-roller suite and tried some new positions from the portable *Kama-sutra* that Dana kept in her purse.

Then, from 3 to 4 A.M., they'd discussed some of the trickier aspects of developing Phase 2.

The biggest problem, besides how to tell the neighbors, was getting the rights to the land. Barstad had managed to secure six of the seven parcels he needed, but one landowner was holding out, a guy named Harlan White, and his property was smack in the middle. Actually, Barstad didn't know for a fact that Harlan White was refusing to sell. That is, Harlan White hadn't said no directly. But White hadn't responded to a single one of Barstad's letters either, despite the fact that each had contained a generous offer, and that the offers kept getting bigger. And when Jack tried to pump the other farmers about White, after their closings, they didn't give him anything to work with.

"Quiet guy," one had said.

"Old-fashioned," said a second.

"Stuck in his ways," remarked a third.

"Oh, Harlan?" said the wife of the fourth. She slapped her knee and laughed. "He'll never sell."

Jack Barstad didn't know how to deal with men like that. He didn't understand those quiet types. Sure, down on the casino floor he could be tight-lipped himself. But even there it was hard to repress his natural instincts, to work a room with a friendly, backslapping old-boy charm.

It was funny how often people asked if he was from Texas. He was tall, of course, with a bit of a drawl. But no, just South Jersey by way of North Carolina, he'd tell them. It must have been those first ten years in Carolina, or maybe the summers he went back as a teenager, staying with his grandparents and working as a caddy at the Marlboro Country Club, that made people think he was a Texan. It was also the foundation of his business education, observing rich southern men on the golf course and off. He'd watched them negotiate million-dollar business deals over a pork sandwich, without ever producing paper or pen, and competing the whole time to see who could get the waitress to laugh.

These were men who made work look like play. They lived life large. They didn't carry briefcases. Everything they needed for business they kept right in their little old heads. And they'd done it all without the benefit of cell phones.

The biggest lesson he'd learned from these men—and he'd learned a lot, on subjects ranging from golf to women—was not to be tight with money. Money was what oiled the machinery of small-town life. Hell, it oiled the machinery of the biggest cities too; you just needed more. But in places like North Carolina and South Jersey, it was simple. Tips at the dinner, flowers for the secretaries, contributions to all the politicians, Dems and Republicans alike. You put your name on the T-shirt of every Little League team you could and bought ads in the programs of every high school play and underwrote a barbecue every spring for the Kiwanis and every fall for the Rotarians. You gave lavish baby presents and communion presents and graduation presents and wedding presents to the children of your friends and business associates and clients. And in the end, all that money built a shimmering web of relationships. There was almost nobody you couldn't pull in.

Except. He'd noticed, even back then, as a boy, there were a few men who seemed to stand outside the web, men who kept aloof, who were immune to charm. Tobacco farmers who would shift their weight in their chairs and assume blank expressions whenever Barstad's grandpappy entered the diner. Barbers who refused to banter. The planning-board members who took laws and regulations and their own authority too seriously. Quiet, closed-up, suspicious men.

Well, Barstad thought, it was like dogs. There were the friendly dogs, the Labs and the retrievers, dogs who were built to love and run and play, and with them you'd just bend down on one knee, fluff their fur, call them "boy" or "girl," and toss the occasional bone.

And then there were the mean dogs.

The mean dogs you had to show who was boss. You had to look them in the eye and command them with authority. This Harlan White, he'd told Dana last night, was one of those mean dogs. And if Barstad couldn't entice him to sell his property with a friendly offer, he'd just have to go about it differently. Barstad preferred to get what he wanted by giving people what they wanted. It was his method of choice. But when a person wouldn't play—like those mean dogs—you had to show him who was boss.

"I love when you talk doggy to me," Dana had said last night, assuming the doggy position and panting suggestively. God, he loved that girl!

But now in the cold glare of morning, Barstad was worried. Exactly how would he show Harlan White that he, Jack Barstad, was boss? He could, of course, go ahead with Phase 2, and put up 160 houses rather than the full 200, arranging them in a nice even perimeter around White's property. Mr. White would have the pleasure of waking up every morning to the sound of trucks, hammers, saws, bulldozers. Hell, Barstad could order his crews out extra early, to beat the roosters, so White could hear trucks rumbling by from the comfort of his very own bed. White would have the pleasure of looking at mud for months. And finally, when it was all done, he could enjoy hearing the bounce, bounce, bounce of kids playing basketball from his very own front porch.

Then, totally surrounded by suburbia, Harlan White would finally surrender. He'd put a call through to Jack Barstad and beg to sell. But Jack Barstad wouldn't take that call. He'd make Harlan White call back, once, twice, maybe three times. And when Barstad finally did pick up, Mr. White would discover that the price he would get for his land now was just half, maybe a third, of what Barstad had offered way back when he was playing nice.

Barstad frowned. Plausible, but he wasn't sure he wanted a stinking run-down chicken farm as the centerpiece of his development.

Then there was the matter of dealing with all the bureaucrats, who would demand all the usual studies of traffic and drainage and environmental impact, and the crooked local politicians, whose hands would be out for bribes. And people thought it was easy making money in America.

"Eggs," Dana said.

"Fine," Barstad said. "Anything you want. Eggs, steak. Just call room service."

"No," she said. "That Harlan White fellow. He sells eggs."

"So?"

"Organic eggs. He delivers them all over the county. People want nice, fresh, organic eggs."

"Well, that's very nice, but—" Barstad stopped. "Ohhhh. I see."

"Maybe the eggs aren't really organic," Dana said. "Or maybe he's supposed to have some kind of USDA permit to sell them. Or maybe he just paints them brown. Or maybe they sit around too long on people's porches. Maybe the eggs have—"

"Salmonella!" Barstad said.

"And it wouldn't even matter if the story we circulated was exactly true," she said. "I mean, of course, we'd aim for the truth, but if we happened, accidentally say, to fall a little short, well, it would take a little while for things to straighten themselves out." Dana put her hands together primly, assuming the expression of a Catholic schoolgirl.

"Baby, I love how you think," Barstad said.

He looked out the window at the city Trump built. Someday, Barstad thought, he would build houses on this side of the Monopoly board. Park Place, maybe even Boardwalk. What did Trump have that he didn't have, besides a few billion dollars and a penchant for blondes? He glanced at Dana, who had unpeeled her nightgown.

Nah, Barstad thought, the Donald didn't have anything on him. He didn't know the first thing. Brunettes were smarter.

Chapter Five

Harlan found blood splattered all over the henhouse, and dozens of eggs smashed, their yolks oozing all over the floor. It was hard to count the number of hens that were missing, because Harlan let his chickens wander the henhouse "free-range." That's what you had to do when you promised people organic eggs: let them run free, feed them natural grain, and use no antibiotics. Some farmers actually let their hens wander around a barnyard like cows, without any enclosures at all, but Harlan had grown up in an egg family and thought that chickens belonged inside some kind of a henhouse.

When he decided to go organic, though, he threw away the cages. Not that he saw much difference. It wasn't like free-range chickens were going to go to college or be painting masterpieces or anything. Not much they could do in a yard, a henhouse, or a cage. But if that's what the people wanted, he'd sell it to them.

Harlan shook his head. By the looks of it, twenty or thirty hens were missing, undoubtedly dead and dragged away. Dogs, he thought. Or foxes, raccoons. It could be just about anything. A satanic cult? Kids out for some fun?

He had to admit that he'd done some fool things in his time, growing up. Like the time that he and Otis Bagwell painted spots on some Guernseys to turn them into Holsteins. But it was September: too late for graduation pranks and too early for Halloween, and besides, the mess of blood, feathers, and broken eggs suggested the work of animals. If it was humans, it had to someone with a real evil streak. Not kids.

The Jersey Devil? People from these parts used to talk about the Jersey Devil all the time. Used to be that every time there was trouble in a henhouse, people blamed the Jersey Devil. No such thing, as everybody knew. Just an old schoolboy legend, something about a woman putting a curse on her unborn kid.

Well, he'd have to clean this up good, and shore up the chicken wire, and check to see if there were any loose or missing planks where a predator could have gotten in. And with his aching knees. It pained him to even think about it.

Damn. What a shitty day.

There'd been another letter from the bastard, Jack Barstad, giving him one more "final offer" to sell his land. This letter was supposed to intimidate him. It was sent registered mail, requiring his signature, and filled with all kinds of legal mumbo jumbo. Harlan knew that all his neighbors on Route 381 had all folded like bad poker hands, selling away family ties to the land that went back fifty, a hundred years—some even longer. Or maybe a poker hand wasn't the right thing to compare it to, because his neighbors didn't feel like they were giving up or losing, throwing in their cards. They were greedy, that's all. Or maybe Barstad was the Jersey Devil, an evil monster with a talent for exploiting the weaknesses of good men.

Harlan had run into some of the farmers who'd sold out at the general store, and a couple had called offering to sell him some old John Deeres. They'd all looked down at their feet when they ran into him, explaining how they had kids and grandkids who needed inheritances. And farming just wasn't what it used to be.

No, it wasn't. And it's true that Harlan didn't have to worry about inheritances. He'd never married, and had been an only child too, so he didn't even have nieces or nephews to think of. But he wouldn't let his neighbors off the hook, not easily anyway. He'd just kind of nod and walk off when they tried to apologize, leaving them tongue-tied and sputtering. Why give comfort to the devil's consorts?

Harlan had inherited his land, so he didn't have a mortgage to worry about, although there was the matter of some credit-card debt he'd taken on to solve short-term financial crises. But his material needs were small. He didn't go to restaurants or have a need for fancy clothes or cars. As long as he made enough to pay his taxes and buy his groceries, he was satisfied. He just wanted to sleep in the house he'd slept in his whole life, and sit out on his front porch in the summers and watch the sunset and then come inside and watch his shows on TV. And he wanted to do this in peace and quiet, which was getting even harder to come by these days than land.

This Barstad fellow was getting on his nerves. Harlan might even have to consult Bob Werble, the old country lawyer who'd handled wills and divorces around these parts for years—although he had his doubts whether a bumpkin like Bob could take on the fleets of lawyers Barstad must have.

And then there was this Heather lady, from Galapagos Estates, who kept pestering him morning, noon, and night with all her handyman jobs. Yes, he had his little sign on the bulletin board in the country store, offering his services as a handyman. He helped all those damn fools who couldn't hang their own pictures or figure out what to do if the pilot went out on their hot-water heater. But most of them seemed to understand that he liked to do it on his schedule. Wait until you've got a whole day's work, he told them. Most were so grateful for a good handyman they didn't call until they had a list of at least ten chores. But not Heather Peters, who never seemed to recognize him from the time he'd given her his little welcome at the general store. She called constantly. Sometimes she called right after he'd gotten home from her house. What kind of man was she married to, anyway? Couldn't he do anything? Did he even own a hammer? Mr. Peters was probably a briefcase-carrying sissy who didn't know a pliers from a wrench. Still, Harlan had to feel sorry for him. Anybody who could live with that lulu deserved a medal.

Mrs. Peters had already called him twice that morning. Something about a hornet's nest, and some ladies coming over for "high tea," whatever that was. Maybe they got high on pot and drank herbal tea. And the door to her closet wouldn't close over some new carpet. And she needed some cleaning up done outside.

Harlan took one last look at the bloody henhouse and vowed to scrub it clean when he got back from Galapagos Estates. Then he smiled. He hadn't thought of it before, but the comparison was perfect. Running around like a chicken with its head cut off. That was Mrs. Peters, all right.

The front of the Peterses' house was made of stone, but the sides and back were sided with vinyl. The week before, when the lawn men were watering, they'd managed to splash some cedar mulch and grass trimmings onto the siding. Of course, Heather told Harlan, she would have had the lawn men take care of it, but she was on the phone when they left. She'd been on hold with the moving company, those bastards! They'd broken a mirror the day of the move, and still hadn't lifted a finger to replace it. "Just what I need," Heather said. "Five years of bad luck."

"Actually, seven, ma'am," said Harlan, moving toward the hose. If he stood there another minute, and had to hear about the color-blind moving man again, and everything else that had gone wrong in Heather Peters's life, he just might have to kill her.

Harlan looked at the siding with its slight spattering of mulch and grass and wondered why Mrs. Peters couldn't take a hose and spray it down herself. She was following him anyway, blabbing nonstop about all the fools and crooks she'd suffered: the lawn men, the moving men, the decorator, the builder. That's who she was most burned at—the builder, Jack Barstad. All the corners he'd cut, the cheap bastard, the things he'd promised but never delivered.

Harlan turned around. "Barstad?" he asked.

"Yes, Jack Barstad," she said. "The builder."

"Oh," Harlan said. Of course. The same jerk who'd been sending the letters. Somehow he'd never made the connection.

"Why?" Heather said. "You know him?"

"Not really. He's just been trying to buy my farm."

"That's interesting," Heather said. But he could tell she wasn't interested. She'd said it the way you talk to a child when you're not really listening. "And then as long as you have the hose out, would you mind taking some of the extra lawn furniture out of the basement? Because, as you see, I'm having this tea, and we just have this little bistro table out back, and anyway, the stuff in the basement is all covered in mildew. It's actually green in some places, and I'm sure some of the women will be wearing white, even if it is after Labor Day. I'll bring you some cleanser. Okay?"

Again, Harlan thought, something she could manage perfectly well herself. But he charged Mrs. Peters forty-five dollars an hour, and if she wanted to throw away her money, that was her choice. Still, as he unrolled the hose, he recalled the scene in his henhouse, which really did need cleaning up. And that got him agitated again, wondering what had preyed on his hens.

Harlan was balancing two lawn chairs and just about to climb the narrow cement steps that led from the basement when he heard the scream. It was piercing, like the kind of scream perfected by cheap starlets in horror movies. Of course it came from Heather Peters. It sounded like she was being murdered. Nah, he couldn't be that lucky. Probably just broke a fingernail. She kept screaming.

Harlan set down the chairs and followed the screams to the patio, where he found Mrs. Peters standing on a chair. When she saw him she stopped screaming, but her face was ashen and she pointed a shaky finger toward the ground. Whatever had incited her hysteria was down there, but she was so frightened or repelled she couldn't even look at it.

Harlan looked. At first all he noticed on the flagstone patio was an overturned tray surrounded by pieces of broken teacups. That might explain the scream, he thought, but not the horrified finger pointing. And that's when he saw it.

A timber rattler.

"A snake!" Heather said.

Harlan narrowed his eyes and shot Mrs. Peters a hard stare. "It's not just a snake," he hissed. "It's a rattler. Don't scare it."

Heather arched her eyebrows in an expression of incredulity. "Scare *it*?"

Harlan knew rattlers. You grew up around here, you knew rattlers. If you fished, if you hunted, you knew rattlers. Rattlers were common in this neighborhood. They lived in dens under rock outcroppings. They slipped through the marshy grasses on the edge of ponds. In the spring and the fall, when it was cold at night, they'd go out during the day and look for warm places to collect heat. They'd bask on rocks and ledges, and sometimes asphalt roads, anything hard that could absorb the sun. Well, this was a flagstone patio, and it was mid-September. The temperature had been dipping into the forties some nights, but it warmed up nicely during the day. From the snake's point of view, Heather Peters's new patio was Palm Springs.

If you could ignore its cold reptilian eyes, Harlan thought, the rattlesnake on Mrs. Peters's patio was actually kind of elegant. That is, he could imagine Mrs. Peters wearing a belt or shoes or a bag made out of it. Its scales formed a perfect chevron pattern, and its color alternated black and tan for a length of about five feet. It was coiled and watchful and, like the hero in a kung fu movie, seemed to have things covered: one eye on Mrs. Peters and the other on him.

Rattlers, Harlan knew, didn't go looking for trouble. If you left them alone, you didn't have much to fear from them—unless, of course, you were a mouse, a mole, or a duckling. If you didn't threaten a rattlesnake, or accidentally step on it, or lunge toward its young, it would eventually glide away. But rattlesnakes would accept trouble. Oh yes, sadly, he knew that all too well. And the hysterical Mrs. Peters, though a good ten feet from the rattler, was trouble. Harlan looked carefully at the snake, considering the effects of her screams.

And he listened. This wasn't a skill in much use these days, with most people just yapping all the time. People often felt uncomfortable around Harlan because he wasn't a talker. But a listener he was. And what he heard now scared him.

It sounded like something you'd find in a toy store, or one of those blowers that you gave kids at birthday parties. Only louder. It was the sound of a child's percussion instrument, of something unraveling and then pulling itself back into a coil, a tinkling sound, hollow and tinny. But none of these descriptions did it justice, because there was malice behind the sound, not amusement. Harlan had heard this sound exactly once, and when he recognized it, he felt like a piece of ice had just stabbed his heart. It was, of course, the sound of a snake's rattle.

"Be perfectly still," Harlan said. "It's nervous."

Of course that was like telling someone not to think of an elephant.

Mrs. Peters was not one to take orders—not from him, and not from a snake. She gave orders. If Mrs. Peters had a rattle, it would be clattering too. He could practically smell her fear.

Harlan knew what was coming next, almost as if he were watching an old John Wayne movie, with a standoff, and everybody pointing guns at one another. Somebody would move, and then the guns would all go off and there'd be a heap of bodies on the ground. And it was always the most fearful person who made that sudden move and got everyone killed.

Heather's order was loud, shrill, and penetrating: "Kill it!"

And with that, the snake's rattle started shaking like Ricky Ricardo's maracas.

Harlan hadn't planned to kill the snake, but the rattler was freaked out, ready to pounce. He didn't, of course, have his shotgun. He looked around for something with decent heft that he could throw at the snake. He would have liked a big stone, but he couldn't find one, so he picked up the first thing he spotted, a blue-and-white ceramic vase, about three feet tall, sitting next to the patio door.

Luckily, the vase was heavier than it looked. Harlan sensed it could actually do some damage. But his reaching for the vase caused the rattler to lunge forward, and the snake's lunge, in turn, drew a new scream from Mrs. Peters. The distance between Harlan and the snake was now just a few feet, and he had mere seconds before the snake would pierce his skin with its fangs and release its deadly venom. But he could barely think for the sounds of the hysterical woman above him.

Harlan heaved the vase.

It smashed, instantly, into thousands of tiny shards. It appeared to have hit the snake square in its neck, right below the head, and drawn blood. That was a good sign. Still, the snake was moving. Whatever damage Harlan had inflicted, he'd failed to kill it.

While Mrs. Peters screamed like a ninny, Harlan looked for a rake or a shovel to finish the job. But of course people like the Peterses didn't have rakes. They had lawn crews, and the lawn crews had leaf blowers. So he did the only thing he could think of. He lifted his foot and brought it down hard on the snake. Luckily his work boots were heavy, and the snake's neck, already bloody from the vase, squished beneath his heel.

When he stepped back, the snake seemed to let out a final, primordial shudder. But was it really dead? That's when Harlan finally noticed, on the other side of Mrs. Peters, a croquet set.

"Grab me a mallet," he said.

"But—"

"Now!"

Mrs. Peters leaned down and took the red mallet out of its rack. Harlan grabbed it.

One sharp whack and the snake was safely dispatched to rattler heaven.

Harlan looked at Mrs. Peters. He didn't expect gratitude, exactly, but he thought she might at least show relief. What he saw, however, was 110 pounds of blond fury, all focused directly on him.

"That vase was a Ming!" she screamed. "I got it on eBay! I followed that auction every minute for a whole week. Do you know what that's worth?" She was still standing on the chair, but now that she was out of danger, it had become a throne.

"It was worth a thousand dollars," she said, answering her own question. "Even if I only paid a hundred fifty. And that croquet set was from Restoration Hardware."

Restoration Hardware? She acted like it came from the British Museum. She folded her arms, as if awaiting an apology.

"Furthermore," Heather said, "I will not get down until all that disgusting snake blood is cleaned up."

Who did she think he was, her husband? Harlan had half a mind to leave her standing on the chair. Shit, he wanted to spank her.

"Well," she said. "Aren't you going to do something?"

Harlan looked hard at her, and as he did, he felt his brain begin to whir. He could almost picture it, working inside his head, spinning out data like a calculator. Harlan wasn't much of a businessman, but even he sensed that he'd gained some advantage over the past few minutes. Heather Peters might still be on her high horse. But, whether she knew it or not, he'd saved her life. And that was worth something.

"My price just went up, lady," Harlan said. "Killing rattlesnakes ain't in my normal line."

Heather looked as if she'd just been slapped.

"Now, where are the lawn bags?" Harlan said. "We got to get this cleaned up before anyone sees."

"Oh my God," Heather said. "My tea!"

Stupid woman, Harlan thought. Stupid, vain, idiot woman. He took some pleasure in delivering the news. "Mrs. Peters," he said, "your little tea party is the least of your worries. Didn't you know? Killing rattlesnakes is illegal in the state of New Jersey. They're endangered."

Chapter Six

The telephone cord coiled around Heather as she marched around the kitchen. "Endangered!" she said. "Can you believe it? Poisonous rattlesnakes, endangered! Next thing you know they'll be saying that people on death row are endangered. Let them order filet mignon before they go to the electric chair."

She pulled a cookie tray out from under the oven. "Oh, they do? Really? What's the world coming to?"

Heather was baking cookies for Back to School Night at Pine Hills Elementary. Naturally, she'd volunteered to be a class mom—Connor being new to the school district and all. God knew, it was like signing up to be an indentured servant, but if Connor was to have any chance of clawing through the vinelike social cliques of his classmates, who'd been together since pre-K, she'd have to do some serious networking. And being class mom would also let her keep an eye on Miss Kindermack.

It wasn't as easy as you'd think, though, to indenture yourself into slavery to the public schools. Heather actually had to elbow out the competition. Imagine, more than one person willing to wake up at five-thirty in the morning on snow days and make twenty-two calls? More than one person willing to go to Costco and buy twenty-five-pound packages of paper plates for all the class parties? But two other moms had also volunteered for the position. Miss Kindermack suggested letting all three mothers share the job. Luckily for Heather, though, the teacher had called her first.

Heather thought fast. Yes, it would be nice to have help with the phone chain on snow days. True, she'd never really had a talent for baking cupcakes. But Heather was thinking of Connor, she really was, and being just one of three class moms would dilute the value of the position. Besides, it seemed likely that the other two moms, who undoubtedly already had each other's numbers on their speed dials, would wind up leaving Heather out of the loop. When it came to females, threes never worked. That was a fact.

And just like that, it came to her.

"Amazing," she told Miss Kindermack. "Janet Parsons just got promoted to head of mergers for her law firm, and she's volunteering for class mom! My goodness, what spirit. I guess she'll be icing cupcakes at three in the morning." She finished off Jean Kobel's chances by mentioning a juicy item she'd heard through the grapevine, that Mrs. Kobel had actually put walnuts in the brownies she'd baked for last year's second-grade graduation. "It's up to you, Miss Kindermack, of course," she said. "I mean, I'm sure teachers don't have to worry about liability personally. I'm just surprised that Pine Hills Elementary might take the risk of having a class mom so oblivious to the issue of nut allergies in children."

Heather took a few rolls of slice-and-bake cookies out of her refrigerator. It was cheating, of course, but really, who would know? "Oh, Mom, you should have seen it," she said into the phone. "Of course, you're lucky you didn't. It had these creepy, snaky eyes, staring at me, and it was just so slithery and gross, and, I don't know, I can't get it out of my head. And there's all kinds of other beasts out here. You should have seen the huge hornet's nest I had my handyman get rid of the other day."

She punched the digital timer on her oven. It emitted a series of ten beeps. "Drat," she said. "I did this wrong. Mom, sorry. The oven is giving me a quiz. Gotta go. Yes, a shopping day. Very soon."

Heather placed the cookie tray in the oven, squinted, and gave full attention to the timing apparatus. The thing was so damn complicated. You'd think she was programming the space shuttle.

Ten beeps again.

She took a deep breath. Relax, she told herself. Take some deep yoga breaths. It was, after all, only the timer. The oven itself was working. The cookies would bake. She would just have to keep an eye on her watch.

Heather looked down at her wrist. It was five. Just enough time to take a quick shower, refresh her makeup, bake a second batch of cookies, and make some macaroni and cheese for Connor. "Connor!" she screamed. "Have you finished your homework?"

Without waiting for an answer, she dashed off to the bathroom.

Professor Richard Artemus had been tracking rattlesnakes all day. It was painstaking, unglamorous work, and although it allowed him to be outdoors, in the pine forest, there wasn't anything natural or transcendent about it. It was like a cross between looking for coins with a metal detector and filing your taxes. Over the past year, he had captured thirteen timber rattlers in this neck of the woods, surgically implanted radio transmitters and antennas into them, and then released them back into the wild, exactly where he'd found them. Now, using a special radio receiver, he was plotting the snakes' movements on a map.

This was a critical time of year because new snakes were born in August, and there was a narrow window for studying the maternal patterns of the timber rattler. For now, with the weather cold at night but still warm during the day, the snakes were moving a lot. They'd leave their dens in the morning in search of any hard surface that held the heat. But by early November, they'd all be in hibernation and Artemus wouldn't be able to collect any more data until spring.

Somehow, nobody had bothered to do a thorough timber-rattler study before Galapagos Estates had erupted from the pinelands like a naturalist's bad dream. In fact, the developer had maintained there weren't any endangered snakes on the property. Well, he couldn't have been looking very hard, Artemus thought, because this habitat was literally crawling with them. Or had been. Three of the snakes he'd outfitted with transmitters last spring had already become roadkill.

As an assistant, Artemus had brought along Agnes Sebastian, leader of the local Friends of the Fauna group and director of the Rolling Hills Nature Center. It was her job to carry the radio receiver, snake hook, cage, and antivenom kit, and to monitor the strength of the radio signal while Artemus took notes. Agnes was also there, frankly, in case they got too close to the subject of their investigation. When tracking rattlesnakes, Artemus had found, the buddy system was always a good idea.

Of course, he used the term "buddy" loosely. Although Agnes was fairly agile for a woman of her age and had no problem keeping up, even when the terrain was steep or rocky, she was an odd duck, and not much of a conversationalist. Probably didn't get much practice, living in the woods with a houseful of animals. But then most of the people who had an interest in rattlesnakes were a bit odd, he had to admit. It wasn't just anyone who volunteered to go out into the field to track poisonous reptiles. The others, though, tended to be young men with bulging muscles who'd spent significant chunks of time out west, doing major hiking and mountain climbing. It was rare to find a woman willing to handle snakes.

And then there was the puzzling rumor, unconfirmed, that Agnes had a brother who'd died of a rattlesnake bite.

It was getting late, and they'd spent the past hour following the signal of a female snake known simply as number twelve. She was easy to track. The signal didn't seem to vary; it just got stronger as Artemus and Agnes moved toward it. That was unusual. A moving snake could be hard to follow. But this one seemed to be staying put, and it was leading them right toward Walden Pond in the Galapagos Estates.

"Think it's asleep?" Agnes asked.

"I hope so," said Artemus.

"You don't think it's—"

"Dead?" Artemus said. "Could be. Some lawn crew could have hacked it up. Or it could have been run over by an SUV."

As they started walking through some of development's backyards, it struck Artemus, as it always did, how Galapagos Estates and the other new developments seemed like ghost towns. Most of the backyards had those high-priced wooden swing sets—but you never saw a little kid on them. Nor did you ever see anybody enjoying the patios or decks. In fact, the landscape—stripped of every single indigenous pine tree—seemed positively lunar. Or would have, but for the unnaturally green, chemically assisted lawns. The only movement you ever saw, Artemus thought, was that of the big, lumbering sport utility vehicles, occasionally stopping to release some human cargo after soccer practice or ballet lessons. As if to prove his point, a red Jeep pulled into a driveway to discharge a tiny ballerina. Which is when it hit him. Savannah! He'd forgotten all about her. "Shit!" he said. "What time is it?"

Agnes looked at her watch. "Almost five-thirty. Why?"

"Shit, shit, shit."

It was Tuesday. He'd promised Lisa he'd pick Savannah up from day care. Lisa had reminded him twice; she had a meeting with her thesis adviser. And of course he'd forgotten. Artemus punched his blue jeans with his fist. He pictured traffic on Route 70. It could be awful this time of day, and if he didn't get to the center by six, they'd charge him an extra twenty-five dollars. After six-thirty, the late fee went up to fifty. And he'd never hear the end of it from Lisa.

"Look, Agnes, I hate to do this, but I've got to run," he said. "Savannah. My kid. Day care."

"Sure," she said.

"Look. Just find out what's going on with number twelve. Okay? You've got my cell. Call me. I'll get the equipment tomorrow."

Luckily, they'd taken separate cars. Artemus fled Galapagos Estates like a convict breaking out of prison. He crossed the sandy field they'd covered earlier, leaped over a narrow creek, jumped into his car, and—offering a silent prayer to the traffic gods—sped off in the direction of the Jolly Beanstalk Day Care Center.

It was nearly impossible to find a sitter in Galapagos Estates. There were practically no teenagers in the development, as the families skewed toward the later years of the baby boom generation and into Gen X, or whichever generation it was that came next. Judging by the prevalence of those horrid yellow-and-orange Cozy Coupes in the yards, the average age in the community was about four. And the few teenagers who did live around there didn't need babysitting wages, like Heather had when she was growing up. They had daddies, big, powerful, wealthy daddies who were as generous with their wallets as they were chintzy with their time. These girls had all the accoutrements—cell phones, credit cards, and Prada bags—and they strutted the earth like trophy wives, only younger and skinnier. Luckily, though, the seamstress that Heather was using for her cushions and window treatments, Sally Jo, did a little nighttime and weekend babysitting. She had agreed to watch Connor on Back to School Night.

Heather was her usual vortex of motion—covering the second batch of slice-and-bake cookies with tinfoil, putting the back on one of her earrings, opening windows and turning on fans to try to rid the kitchen of a billowing cloud of smoke. How the first batch of cookies had burned, she couldn't understand. Her shower couldn't have been any longer than ten minutes.

Kevin was going to Connor's school straight from work, so Heather had to manage on her own. She had only two hands, of course, but she used her wrists, elbows, and teeth to great effect, all while giving last-minute instructions to Sally Jo. "No PlayStation until all his homework is done," she said. "And if you wouldn't mind cleaning up the kitchen. I'm sorry. I was in such a rush. And, um, well, there's some Sara Lee banana cake for you, but only one slice for Connor, or he'll be just a beast at bedtime. And make sure he brushes his teeth."

Sally Jo didn't seem particularly swift. Heather figured she had gotten about half of it. Inbreeding?

The babysitter smiled, exposing teeth that looked like one of those "before" pictures in an orthodontist's office. "A kitchen witch," she said, pointing at the calico doll on the windowsill.

Now Heather wondered if Sally Jo had registered a single one of her instructions. "Yes," Heather said. "A gift from my mother." Every time she'd picked it up to throw it out, her hand started shaking. Was it because her mom said it was good luck? Or was she just afraid that her mother would notice if it wasn't on the windowsill next time she visited?

"I made it," Sally Jo said, beaming.

"Isn't that nice?" Heather glanced at the clock and picked up her cookies. "Our cell numbers are on the bulletin board." Then, rushing toward the front door, she yelled in the general direction of the TV. "Bye, Connor! Be good!"

Heather almost collided with the woman standing on her front steps.

The woman wore her white hair in a long braid, which made her look something like a Native American medicine woman. Her skin was bronzed and toughened by the sun, and she was wearing blue jeans and cowboy boots and carried a leather knapsack on her back. She was holding a little machine that looked something like a portable radio, which was beeping madly. The woman planted herself directly in front of Heather—to prevent her from leaving—and then peered into the house, staring at its sleek possessions and circular stairway as if catching a rare glimpse at the inside of an Egyptian sarcophagus.

"My name is Agnes Sebastian," she said. "And I'm here on a matter concerning wildlife in the state of New Jersey."

Sally Jo walked up behind Heather, drying her hands on her skirt. "Hi, Agnes," she said.

"Hi, Sally Jo," said Agnes.

Connor appeared behind Sally Jo. "Hey, what's that cool machine? Is it some kind of PlayStation?"

Heather took a deep, impatient breath. Even if she got into the Land Rover this very minute and hit no traffic whatsoever, she'd be five minutes late. "Well, that's really very interesting," Heather said. "And I'm happy to send you a check. But right now, I have to go to my son's school—"

Agnes didn't budge. "Let me get right to the point," she said. "Have you injured or killed a rattlesnake in the past forty-eight hours?"

Heather looked at Connor. She hadn't wanted to tell him about the rattlesnake, didn't want him having nightmares. In fact, she'd barely discussed it with Kevin. Then she remembered what Harlan had said, about rattlesnakes being endangered. This, she suddenly realized, could be trouble. What would Kevin do? Well, he was a lawyer. She knew exactly what he'd do in her position. Admit nothing.

"I don't think I have to answer that," Heather said.

"Oh, yes, you do," Agnes said. She reached into her pocket and produced a small man's wallet, which she flipped open to show an official ID that identified her as a member of the Wildlife Conservation Corps. "I happen to represent the State of New Jersey, Division of Fish and Wildlife. And I'm afraid that harming, harassing, or collecting a timber rattlesnake is illegal, punishable by a fine of up to three thousand dollars."

"Harassing a rattlesnake?" Heather said, her lips curling.

"Oh, yes," Agnes said. "I'd like you now to open your garage, so that I can examine said specimen. Then we can do the paperwork."

"And if I refuse?"

"Interfering with a conservation officer," Agnes said. "Punishable by a jail sentence of up to thirty days."

Heather squinted hard at Agnes, sizing her up, and decided she had nothing to fear. She was just a weird little old lady, after all. Heather had, in self-defense, killed a rattlesnake. Or at least her handyman had. So? This was still America, wasn't it?

"I'd love to chat," Heather said, sidestepping Agnes. "But I have responsibilities that require my presence elsewhere."

She ran past Agnes and hopped into the Land Rover, pulling out of the driveway so fast she almost flattened some hostas in the process.

Chapter Seven

Heather hurried down the shiny hallway, her Italian heels clicking in staccato, as if she were stepping on small firecrackers. Not the right shoes for showing up late and trying to slip in unnoticed—and of course Heather *was* late, all because of that dreadful lady on her front steps. Many of the doors on the second floor of Pine Hills Elementary were already shut, reminding Heather of that awful high school feeling of being caught between classes without a hall pass. But the open doors were even worse. Necks craned in her direction. Eyebrows arched. At least it seemed that way. One teacher closed the door as Heather clattered by, a gesture that seemed sharp, accusatory, like something from Connor's report card. *Doesn't play well with others. Doesn't respect school rules.*

The teachers—some gray-haired and matronly, some looking like they were still in high school themselves—were all explaining their class rules and curriculum for the coming year. Heather picked up snatches of the current educational jargon: "integrated reading," "inside voices," "experiential learning," "parental involvement," "speaker power." It all sounded rather forward-thinking, although Heather sometimes wondered about the old standbys, "Reading, 'Riting, and 'Rithmetic" and "Obey the Golden Rule." The bulletin boards, at any rate, appeared relatively normal. Brightly colored drawings, things made out of construction paper.

Heather was hoping that the door to room 201 would be open, and that she could slip in quietly. But as luck would have it, it was closed. She inhaled deeply and, before turning the doorknob, tried to assume the dignified but cheerful bearing of a class mom. Unfortunately, as she stepped into the room, she bumped into a mobile the children had made the first week of school using soda cans and bright-colored yarn. Each of the cans was wrapped in construction paper and colored with words that represented feelings—"happy," "sad," "angry," and so forth. An orange can labeled "embarrassed" clanged to the floor.

"Please, forgive me," Heather said. She picked up the orange can, wincing at how loudly it had announced her arrival. "I had an unavoidable delay."

Miss Kindermack was a solidly built brunette with a doughy face and small, suspicious eyes, making Heather think immediately of a pit bull. When she'd talked to her on the phone, Heather had imagined Connor's teacher to be lithe and willowy, a tennis player. She now revised her opinion. Miss Kindermack most certainly had some rugby experience on her résumé.

"This must be our class mom, Heather Peters," Miss Kindermack said. Was there sarcasm in her voice? Reprimand? "Please take a seat anywhere. We were discussing classroom rules."

Easier said than done. The only chairs around, first of all, were made for the tiny behinds of third-graders, small even for a size 6 like Heather. And they were all occupied. Covering each chair was a T-shirt supplied by the child who sat there, and sticking out the neck hole was a cardboard head, on which the children had drawn renditions of their own face. Heather frantically scanned the room for Connor's shirt, thinking that if she found it, a vacancy might miraculously appear. Before she could spot it, however, a father sitting in a chair that clearly belonged to a little girl with brunette ringlets stood up to offer his spot.

"I was saying," Miss Kindermack said to Heather, "we are having a little trouble so far this year with pushing and line-cutting. And also tardiness."

Heather wondered if Miss Kindermack was chiding her for being late, signaling that Connor had a problem with the pushing and line-cutting, or just catching her up. Line-cutting had been a bit of an issue in Connor's last school, and it had taken an elaborate system of candy-bar bribes, scrupulously administered, to break him of the habit.

"On each of your desks, you'll find our Classroom Rules Contract, which you and your child will be expected to sign." Heather looked across the room to find Kevin, who must have shown up on time. She saw him roll his eyes. As a lawyer, certain issues rubbed him the wrong way. Required contracts for minors was, apparently, one of these issues. Heather shot him a dirty look and hoped none of the other parents noticed.

"And then there is the matter of our spring camping trip," Miss Kindermack continued. "Which Mrs. Peters will be instrumental in coordinating. It's a two-night trip that the third grade takes every year, a longtime Pine Hills tradition, and they all look forward to it."

Camping trip? When had she signed on for that, Heather wondered. And how could she get out of it?

Camping. She'd been a Girl Scout and had successfully repressed memories of that era for more than two decades. But when Miss Kindermack said the words "camping trip," quickly followed by Heather's name, those unpleasant memories all came flooding back. Drinking Kool-Aid out of collapsible tin cups that always picked the worst times to collapse. Foraging in the woods for kindling and finding out a few days later that she'd foraged right through poison ivy. The mean tricks that groups of girls played on one another at night, like the time they'd filled a cup with warm water and, stifling their giggles, dunked the hand of a sleeping Linda Hatcher into it, causing Linda to pee in her sleep and wake up in a drenched sleeping bag, mortified.

And finally—the worst indignity of all—the latrines. With the smell of crap, pure unadulterated crap, crap going back perhaps for generations of Girl Scouts—as bad as it smelled—to the beginning of time. The smell had made Heather gag, made her want to vomit, introducing the even more horrible prospect of having to kneel down and bring her face even closer to the putrid source.

So Heather, as a little Girl Scout, would hold her bladder and her bowels, for fear of having to visit the latrine, and fight valiantly against sleep, not wanting to become the victim of a practical joke, and hold tightly in her mind the sweet picture of her bed at home, with its cool, tight sheets, and the bathroom down the hall with its shiny white germ-free surfaces. Despite her determination, though, there would always come a time when she knew the battle was lost, and reluctantly, as if she were being asked to walk the plank, she would pick up her flashlight and tiptoe out of the tent to face her fate. There, squatting, careful to never ever set her butt down on the rotten wooden seat, trying to ignore the flies, Heather would try to relax until finally the hot water could flow. Release, sweet, sweet release. And now it came back to her. Sitting in the little chair in Connor's classroom, while Miss Kindermack talked about God knows what: the horrifying thought that would always come to her as the water left her body with the force of a fire hose, a force she could not stop. What if there was a rat down there on the floor? Or, equally awful, a snake?

Heather had been in such a hurry to leave Giant Tortoise Drive that she altogether forgot about Connor and Sally Jo. If she hadn't been so furious, and in such a hurry, she undoubtedly would have ordered them inside the house, and given Sally Jo additional instructions involving strangers knocking on doors. Drama and pragmatism occasionally warred in Heather's brain. Though Heather considered herself a practical person, sometimes a dramatic exit was necessary. Which left Connor, Sally Jo, and Agnes standing on the steps, watching together as the Land Rover squealed off.

It was Connor who spoke first. "A rattlesnake!" he exclaimed, in a tone usually saved for birthday parties or unexpected offers of Phillies tickets. "Cool! Can I see it?"

Agnes and Sally Jo looked hard at each other, as if trying to solve a riddle. They'd known each other a long time, from way back in school when Sally Jo had been pretty and popular and Agnes quiet and tormented. It was hard to imagine now, but there was a time when Sally Jo had walked the halls of Hebron High School like a regal she-cat, alternately purring and hissing, exalting or condemning the peons in her path. Sally Jo's good looks, however, had gone the way of saddle shoes, and so her reign of terror was short-lived. Moreover, Bob Meehan, the star high school running back whom Sally Jo had married at nineteen, knocked up of course, had turned out to be a lout and a pussy-chaser. He'd stranded her at age twenty-four, with no money and three little kids. Over the years, Sally Jo had gone fat and soft and stupid—as girls who peak in high school often do—while Agnes had gone lean and hard and smart.

Sally Jo, in other words, didn't have a chance.

"Why, yes," Agnes said, smiling. "A good healthy interest in nature. Nice to see in a young man these days." She put her arm around Connor and led him toward the garage. She wanted to get the goods on this uppity bitch, but even though she was given the powers of a state game officer on these missions, she didn't have a warrant. She really had no right to rummage through the lady's garbage bins. But if the lad wanted to learn something about nature . . . if he had a healthy interest in the reptile cohabitants of his neighborhood . . . well, as a nature educator, did she really have any choice but to assist in his enlightenment?

Sally Jo's mouth formed an *o*—making her look like a particularly stupid fish. She searched her brain for the right response. Mrs. Peters hadn't specifically said anything about the garage or seeing snakes. She was pretty sure of that. She'd said something about PlayStation. She'd said something about banana cake. She'd said something about teeth brushing, about cleaning up the kitchen. But no, nothing in particular about this set of circumstances. Still, knowing Mrs. Peters, Sally Jo was fairly certain that she would disapprove. There was something about her that was quite disapproving. In fact, the more she thought about it, the more Sally Jo was sure that Mrs. Peters would not only disapprove, but she'd be furious if she knew Agnes was now leading her son in the direction of the garage. Unfortunately, by the time all these thoughts had formulated themselves into a word—"Wait!"—Agnes and Connor had already disappeared.

As Connor led the way, the beeping noise on Agnes's machine grew more urgent. In the garage, they found three new pale green plastic garbage pails. Agnes put her machine down and began lifting off lids. Two of the cans were filled with white plastic bags, the kind used for kitchen garbage, but the third can contained just one thick black bag, the kind used for lawn waste. Agnes took the bag out. Yes, it had exactly the heft she had expected, about twenty pounds. She looked around quickly, spotted the recycling, snatched the real estate section from the top of a newspaper, and spread it on the floor. Then she dumped out the lawn bag.

It was the rattlesnake, bludgeoned and matted with blood, hacked into two pieces with some kind of blunt instrument. "Cool!" Connor said again, bending down to inspect.

Agnes grimaced. To her it looked like a corpse, a murder victim.

"No," she said. "It's actually sad. The rattlesnakes lived here first, you know. This is their yard as much as it is yours."

"But aren't they poisonous?"

Agnes stared at the boy but looked as if she were seeing someone else entirely. "Yeah," she said slowly. "But they rarely bite—if you leave them alone."

Sally Jo, breathing heavily, appeared at the kitchen entrance to the garage. She held a plate in the air and kept her gaze high, to avoid seeing whatever was on the floor. "Connor," she trilled. "Banana cake."

Connor turned toward Sally Jo. He saw the cake. He looked back down at the snake, then again at Sally Jo. Cake, snake; snake, cake. The poor boy looked like a laboratory rat trying to decide which way to turn.

Agnes, meanwhile, had pulled out her cell phone and dialed a number. "Artemus," she said. "It's me. Worse than I thought. The poor thing was hacked to death. And the home owner completely refused to cooperate. Went running off in a huff . . . some meeting, I don't know . . . Uh-huh. Uh-huh . . . Yes, I warned her . . . Absolutely, endangered species, fine, jail . . . Yes, I showed my badge . . . After they left? I found it in the garage, in a lawn bag . . . Their little boy showed me in . . . Totally voluntarily. He asked me. Damn it, Artemus. Do you want to see the snake or not?"

She held the phone away from her head and pointed it down at the garage floor, like a camera, and clicked. She aimed it several more times, to get different angles, before returning the headset to her ear. "Did you get that? Yeah, pretty fancy. But it gets the job done . . . I agree . . . Definitely . . . Uh-huh . . . Where? She said something about her son's school."

"Back to School Night," Connor volunteered.

"He says Back to School Night. That would be, I think, Pine Hills Elementary." Connor nodded. "Yes, Artemus. Have them send someone over. We've got the proof."

"Send someone over?" said Sally Jo. "Where?" She took a few steps closer. "Proof of what?" She was coming to get Connor, still holding the cake high. She was in charge. At least she was supposed to be.

Then Sally Jo made the mistake of looking down. There was the timber rattler, its body thick, reptilian, and disturbingly phallic. Even perfectly still, it embodied the essence of things that slithered—creepy, awful, nightmarish things. Even hacked up and covered with blood, it was full of menace. Sally Jo screamed, dropping the cake on the garage floor, right on the dead snake, and then she swooned, falling to the floor herself.

Heather surveyed the table, evaluating her class mom debut. Paper plates, napkins, and cups—standard-issue, nothing special, but at least not some cloying trying-too-hard-to-be-cutesy design either. Her slice-and-bake cookies had a nice uniform shape, but they did seem a bit, well, generic next to Jean Kobel's raspberry streusel bars. Well, she told herself, Jean Kobel didn't have a house filled with boxes to dig out from, like she did. Nor, Heather would bet, had Jean Kobel had to fend off life-threatening rattlesnakes. She probably had nothing to do, once her kids went to school, but experiment with cookie recipes. Anyway, it was just Back to School Night. There would be plenty of other opportunities for Heather to shine.

A mousy woman in a bulky cardigan, which she clearly wore to cover up overly generous breasts, reached past Heather to grab two streusel bars. She crammed one into her mouth and then faced Heather. "Heather Peters?" she asked.

"Yes?"

"You're Connor's mom, right?"

"Why, yes." Heather hoped this might be a prelude to a playdate. Connor had been spending quite a lot of time with his PlayStation lately, and though his proficiency at inflicting grave bodily harm to animated creatures was clearly improving, his social skills, never much to start with, were languishing. Heather collected potential playmates for Connor like a yenta keeping a steady lookout for unattached dentists or a spider keeping an eye out for flies. "Do you have a little son?" Heather asked brightly.

"No, a daughter," the woman said. "Chloe."

"Chloe?"

"Connor hasn't spoken of Chloe?"

"I'm afraid not. Well, that is . . . I don't think so."

"That's funny," Chloe's mother said. "Because Chloe certainly does talk a lot about Connor."

Heather smiled. Well, then, Connor had been making an impression. Perhaps she was wrong to always underestimate her son. Why, of course. He was quite handsome. Of course the girls would be attracted to him. Maybe that was Connor's problem all along. The other boys were jealous.

"And what does she say?" Heather said.

"Well, he's been running up and hugging her on the playground," the woman said.

"Oh, isn't that cute?"

"Well, actually," the woman said, "she really doesn't like it. He hugs quite hard."

"Oh."

"And then there's the thing about the swings."

"The swings?"

"Well, apparently he looks up the girls' skirts when they're on the swings, so he can see their underpants. Lately, I've been making Chloe wear pants to school every day."

A brunette dressed very smartly in a taupe pants suit walked up. "You must be talking about Connor," she said.

"Yes?" said Heather, smiling and cringing simultaneously.

"The one with the scissors?" said a third mom, joining them.

"Yes!" the first two mothers chorused.

Scissors?

Heather glanced around the room looking for Kevin, but his back was turned to her, and he was engaged in a conversation with several men. They were all laughing easily. Men were so damn lucky. Their reputations weren't tethered to those of their offspring. All they had to do was keep up with sports.

"It's very dangerous, Mrs. Peters," the third woman said, her voice grave.

The sudden, mechanical chimes of "La Cucaracha" ended the conversation. Heather was never so happy for a conversation to be interrupted—until she realized that the music was coming from her purse. That damn Connor, always changing the ring on her cell phone. She never knew whether she was going to be summoned to the phone by way of the William Tell Overture or the Barney theme, but whatever tune he selected always seemed the most embarrassing. Heather fished in her bag, through strata of receipts, flyers, tampons, and used tissue, until she finally found it.

"Yes?" she said into the phone, throwing a sheepish glance at the other women.

"Mom," came the voice. "It's me. Connor."

"I know who it is," Heather said. The Marquis de Sade of the third grade.

"Mom, the babysitter fainted."

"Oh my God!" Heather shouted. "Oh my God! What happened?"

The three moms, who'd just been pressing in on Heather like a horde of angry water buffalo, now leaned in with expressions of concern. Heather noted the change on their faces and began to relax. A crisis. Okay. She was good in a crisis. Meanwhile, she would milk it.

"The babysitter," she mouthed.

Heather might have played the crisis card to even greater advantage, had it not been that very moment when two uniformed policemen appeared at the door of the classroom, their walkie-talkies squawking.

"We're looking for Heather Peters," the taller one said. Two dozen index fingers pointed in her direction.

It was the shorter one who cuffed her. "Sorry, ma'am," he said, removing her cell phone and handing it to his partner. The room was utterly silent except for the sound of Connor, shouting through the instrument, "Mom! Mom!" The partner pressed the end button on the cell and started moving Heather toward the door. "You have the right to remain silent," he began.

Kevin untangled himself from the knot of sports-loving dads and ran toward Heather and the cops. Heather had not chosen to remain silent. The rest of the parents, however, had. Some just stared, but others turned toward one another with sly smiles and raised eyebrows. This had turned out to be more interesting than the typical Back to School Night.

Once the Peterses and the policemen were well down the hall, the classroom began to buzz back to life. Jean Kobel leaned in to Janet Parsons. "I didn't know you could be arrested for trying to pass off slice-and-bake cookies as homemade," she whispered.

Chapter Eight

Heather huddled in her cell in the county jail, rubbing her arms furiously to generate some heat. She was disgusted by the blood- and urine-stained bed provided by the county and had taken the precaution of removing her blazer and laying it on top of the mattress before sitting down. Two wool blankets, folded neatly, had been left at the end of her bed. But since they were no doubt teeming with vermin, she'd kicked them into the corner of the room. She would never let a blanket touch her skin directly, even in a four-star hotel, and she wasn't about to abandon those principles now, in a county jail. She would just as soon have wiped herself with toilet paper from the floor of a public bathroom. But the cell was cold and damp, and she was shivering.

In the corner of the cell stood a stainless-steel toilet—if you could call it that. It had no seat. She was supposed to squat on the apparatus, which looked like it hadn't been cleaned in weeks, to do her business. And it was in full view of the front of the cell! Anybody could walk by and look through the bars while she was making. It was horrid. Horrid! Naturally, Heather refused to avail herself of that too. So in addition to shivering, and refusing to lay her head down on the dreadful pillow, also stained—and bulging with suspicious lumps—Heather was burdened by a full bladder. Where was Kevin? If he didn't get here soon to bail her out, she was certain to come down with a urinary tract infection from holding her bladder so long.

Her throat, also, was quite sore. She'd asked the guard for a cough drop or a throat lozenge—a perfectly reasonable request—but he'd just laughed. Well, they would hear about that when she got out, and about the urinary tract infection if she came down with one. It was torture was what it was: withholding medical attention. She was pretty sure there was something in the Geneva Convention about that. Or was it the Helsinki Conference? The Bill of Rights? Well, something.

Heather's throat was inflamed, she supposed, because she'd stood up for her rights after being arrested. Well, anyone would have. Who could blame her? So what if a profanity or two had escaped her lips? And maybe she had tried to bite one of the policemen, like they kept saying. It was hard to say. She really didn't remember. It was all such a blur, being snatched away from Back to School Night, having just received that call from Connor about the babysitter and, before that, being confronted by those awful mothers. What political prisoner wouldn't kick and scream a little—resisting arrest, as they chose to call it—under such circumstances?

Because she was a political prisoner. Of that Heather was certain. She didn't know what they had done with all her jewelry, or how Connor was, or why Sally Jo had fainted, or who that loathsome woman snoring loudly in the cell across from her was. But she knew she was the victim of an outrageous government scheme to set the rights of rattlesnakes above the rights of taxpaying citizens. Endangered species: she remembered hearing those words from Harlan. And come to think of it, why was *she* in all this trouble? It was Harlan who had actually killed the snake. Although he was under her employ at the time, which would, she supposed, make him some kind of contract killer. But endangered? Rattlesnakes? Didn't they have more than enough venom at their disposal, without needing protection from the State of New Jersey? And what about *her* rights? What about the safety of her family? They were the ones who were endangered.

Heather looked down at her watch. Well, her wrist. They'd taken her watch when they took the rest of her jewelry, the bastards. Where was Kevin? It was discouraging how poorly he seemed to be coping with this crisis. True, he hadn't known what was going on. He hadn't been there, after all, when that awful woman had shown up on the front steps with that beeping machine and demanded to see the rattlesnake. She knew she'd told him about the rattlesnake, of course, but had she mentioned to him that it was endangered? And even if she had told him, had he been listening? Moreover, Kevin wasn't the one who'd gotten the phone call from Connor about the babysitter fainting. All he knew was the same thing that every other parent at Back to School Night knew: that Heather Peters had been led away in handcuffs.

The one thing she was sure she'd managed to communicate, just as they shoved her into the backseat of the patrol car, was that the babysitter had fainted, and Kevin had to go home and check on Connor.

But had he heard what she'd said next, to come back to the police station? Sitting in the cold dingy cell, replaying her arrest, Heather wasn't sure Kevin had heard that second part. Maybe he thought he was just supposed to go home and check on Connor. And, come to think of it, why was she in a jail cell in the first place? He was a lawyer, for God's sake, and he'd been there when she was arrested. If he had any kind of talent or pull, he would have had this whole thing straightened out before they even were out of Miss Kindermack's class. Who knows? Maybe he wouldn't remember to bail her out unless she specifically reminded him.

But that was ridiculous. Even if Kevin hadn't heard her instructions, he would know what he was supposed to do, wouldn't he? He was a lawyer. His wife was in handcuffs. He'd go to the police station. But what if . . . what if something really awful had happened that had caused Sally Jo to faint? What if there'd been a break-in, some kind of bad guy? What if there'd been . . . another . . . snake? What if there'd been blood? If she didn't get home soon and take care of it, the blood would set.

Her mind raced. Right now, Connor could be lying dead on the floor. Maybe Kevin too. Maybe the bad guy—or the snake—had hidden by Connor's dead body and gotten Kevin as soon as he walked in the door. She was a widow! A childless widow!

It came to Heather like a bolt of truth. Her family was dead. Everything she loved in the world gone, everything that mattered. Her dear, devoted, hardworking husband. Her sweet, sweet, innocent son. Dead! In their brand-new house. And the house! All that planning, all that effort, the mortgages, the boxes, everything—Barstad's agreement to extend the back patio by ten feet—all that she'd worked so hard for since the beginning of August. She could never move back. And resale, after a double murder? Impossible!

"Jailer!" she shouted, grabbing the bars and trying to shake them. "Jailer!" She sounded as if she were hailing a taxi.

A voice came from the cell across from hers. "They don't like it when you yell," it said. The woman had been sleeping when Heather came in.

"Mind your own business," Heather replied. "Jailer!"

The jailer, who had a Santa-like gut and thinning black hair, ambled down the hall, a large set of keys jangling with each step. He seemed to be making a point of walking slowly. When he got to Heather's cell, he stopped and folded his arms. "Yeah?"

"Have you heard from my husband yet?" Heather asked.

"Your husband?"

"Yeah, have you heard from him?"

"Nope. Haven't heard from no husband." He started walking back down the hall.

"Wait!" Heather said.

The jailer turned around, a look of pure malignance clouding his face. "Yeah?" he said.

"I need my phone back," Heather said. "They took it when they put the handcuffs on. And I need it back. I need to make some calls."

"She needs to make some calls," the jailer said to no one in particular. "How about some fine stationery? You need that too? Or maybe you'd just rather have a nice little laptop with a high-speed Internet connection so you can catch up on your e-mails."

"E-mail would be nice," Heather said. "But I really do need the phone. It's urgent."

"It's urgent," the jailer mimicked.

The woman in the opposite cell let out a throaty laugh. She sounded like a heavy smoker or an alcoholic. Heather got the feeling that this wasn't her first time in the clink.

"Now, wait a minute," said Heather. "I know my rights. I know I get a phone call. I've seen it on TV."

"TV." The jailer let out a whistle. "And I suppose you know how to operate too, from the doctor shows. Listen, lady, you tried to bite Officer Pasquale on the way over. You resisted arrest. You assaulted an officer. You're considered dangerous. I'm under strict orders not to let you out of the cell, not even for one minute to come use the phone on my desk."

"But my cell phone!" Heather wailed. "If you just gave me my cell phone, I wouldn't have to leave my cell."

"Sure, lady," the jailer said. "Cell phone. Need anything else? Maybe you'd like a cappuccino from Starbucks too?" He turned and walked back down the hall.

Heather plopped back onto her blazer. She was cold. She was tired. She wanted to go home. She had to go to the bathroom.

But she wasn't defeated. Oh no. Heather didn't like the guard's attitude, not one little bit. She rubbed her arms, freezing, and plotted all the ways, once she was again a free woman, that she would seek her revenge.

Kevin sped away from the school, his heart pounding but his mind focused and alert. What the hell was going on? And what kind of husband, not to mention lawyer, was he? He couldn't get the image out of his mind: Heather being dragged, kicking and cursing, down the hall of Pine Hills Elementary, as he ran alongside, vainly trying to figure out what was happening. Nothing made sense! But he would get to the bottom of it. He would. Something about Connor and the babysitter. Something about a game warden. Something about rattlesnakes.

Why had Heather wanted him to go home instead of following the police car straight to jail? Oh yes. The sitter had fainted. Strange. Kevin frowned, trying to think how Connor might have scared or tortured the babysitter. Could he have put a frog in the microwave? Duct-taped the poor woman to a chair? Anything was possible.

Well, the key was to get home quick, see what was going on with the sitter, and then go to the jail. If the babysitter had regained her senses, she could stay with Connor a little longer. But what if she'd hurt herself? She was elderly. Isn't that what Heather had said? If she'd fallen, she might have broken a bone. That could be quite serious. There might be issues of liability. Kevin might have to take her to a hospital. Then what would he do with Connor?

And what about Heather? Heather, who abhorred lines, who ranted about doctors who kept her waiting, who fumed in restaurants when the waiter brought the wrong salad dressing. Shit, if she had to wait for more than half an hour in jail, he'd never hear the end of it.

Kevin pressed his foot down on the accelerator. It was exhilarating to hug the curves on the country roads in pitch black. It was, for all the commotion, a beautiful night. Clear and crisp, but not cold, the stars splashed like Christmas lights against the sky. He wished he had the leisure to roll down the top of the convertible.

Kevin was so intent on whipping down the road that at first he thought the loud insistent whining behind him was coming from his own brain, the beginning of a tension headache. He didn't realize it was a cop until the siren was right up on him. He pulled over and sat in the car, waiting for the cop to come up and ask him to roll down the window. That's what you were supposed to do when a cop pulled you over. This, he thought, was where he differed from his wife. Sure, Kevin was impatient to get home, to check on Connor and to get Heather sprung from jail, and yet—unlike Heather—he was able to keep his impatience under control.

As Kevin waited for the policeman to come up, he rehearsed his excuses. His eight-year-old was home and the babysitter had fainted. He was urgently needed. His wife was in jail, waiting to be bailed out. Well, maybe he'd skip that last one. He'd stick with the babysitter.

A crew-cut officer, looking young enough to deliver newspapers, walked up. Kevin memorized the name on the cop's tag: Patrolman Meyers. His brass badge was still shiny, like it had just come out of the plastic bag. The uniform was so new, it still bore creases. Meyers could be a kid in a Halloween costume.

"License. Registration." Meyers wore a stern expression, like he was playing a grown-up in a school play.

Kevin reached into the passenger seat for his suit jacket. That's where he always kept his wallet, on workdays at least. Only, he suddenly realized, patting the leather upholstery next to him, his jacket was missing.

Then he realized, he must have left it at the school. Of course! He'd been in such a rush after the cops came that he'd left his jacket on one of the seats. He turned to Meyers. "My jacket—"

"Yeah, yeah, you left your jacket. That's where your driver's license is. I've heard it before. Registration?"

Kevin resented Meyers's world-weary tone. He thought about dropping some names of people in the prosecutor's office, letting this—this *child*—know that he had powerful connections all over the state. But he didn't want to take the risk. The uniform was the thing that mattered, and it was the young ones—full of their own power—who you had to watch out for. Kevin reached into the glove compartment. He took out the manual and the service receipts and found the plastic folder that he kept his registration and insurance card in. Only it was empty. Damn it, Heather, he thought. You're so damn organized when it comes to boxes. What happened to getting new registration cards after we moved?

"Um," he said. "You see, we moved recently. And my wife is very organized. Anal, you could even say. And here's what I'm guessing—"

"Save it for the judge," Meyers said, eying him with suspicion. "Do you know how fast you were going?"

Kevin thought. Route 381 was—if memory served—a forty-five-mile-per-hour road. He'd been barreling along at a good clip.

"Fifty-five?"

The officer shook his head.

"Sixty?"

Another shake.

"Seventy?"

"You were going eighty," the cop said. "Dangerous and reckless. I could take away your license right now. That is, if you had a license."

"Oh, shit," Kevin said. "Listen, I know this sounds strange, considering. But I've got to go. Really. I'm in quite a mess."

"You sure are," Meyers said.

"No, you don't understand," Kevin said. "My son's home alone."

"How old is he?"

"Eight."

"Child endangerment," said Meyers, again shaking his head with disgust.

"No, there was a babysitter. But something happened. And I don't even know what."

The policeman wasn't listening. "Name and address," he snapped. "Or don't you know those either?" Kevin identified himself, enunciating clearly and politely, and Meyers repeated the information into a walkie-talkie. Then he walked to the front of the car and read Kevin's license plate number. "Run the plates," he said to the voice on the other end.

"Really," Kevin said. "I can't wait." He pictured Heather in jail, getting angrier by the minute.

"Oh, you'll wait," the policeman said, walking back to his car. And Kevin would wait. Heather wouldn't wait, of course, given similar circumstances. She'd screech off, damn the consequences. But he wasn't Heather. He was a member of the New Jersey bar, obliged to uphold the laws of the state and to respect its officers.

It didn't seem like a good sign to Kevin when Meyers came back smiling like the cat who caught the canary.

"It's very interesting," Meyers said. "But the address you just gave isn't the one that matches the plates. That address is 82 Herring Lane."

"Oh," Kevin said, laughing. "That's easy to explain. I told you, we just moved."

"Could be," said Meyers. His nose wrinkled and his mouth turned into a snarl. "Or it could be a stolen car."

There was another squawk on the radio. Meyers listened.

"Holy moley. The wife too? What are the chances of that?" He turned to Kevin. "Listen, buddy, I don't know who you are. But the guy who owns this car, his wife is in the county jail, as we speak. Something's fishy here. You better come with me now. Back to the station."

"But, but," Kevin said. "My son."

"Up against the car," Meyers said, pushing Kevin against his BMW and into a spread-eagle position. He frisked him quickly. Kevin was surprised that it tickled. For all his experience defending corporations against tort claims, he'd never been on this side of the law before.

"Okay, you're clean," Meyers said. "Backseat."

"What?" Kevin said. "And leave an M3 convertible just sitting on the side of the road?" Now he was mad.

"Tsk, tsk, tsk," said Meyers. "I guess you're a man who knows his priorities. Forgot all about your son, huh?" He used air quotes on the word *son*.

Kevin pointed his remote at the car, watched the lights flash as it locked itself, and climbed into the backseat of the patrol car. He hadn't exactly forgotten about Connor. It's just that the M3 looked so vulnerable sitting on the side of the road like that.

Well, at least Heather wouldn't accuse him of dawdling, Kevin thought. It was just like Monopoly. Go directly to jail. Do not pass Go. Do not collect two hundred dollars.

Back at 63 Giant Tortoise Drive, Sally Jo had come to. But she seemed more dazed and confused than usual, so Agnes had called an ambulance.

After the ambulance left with Sally Jo, Agnes sent Connor to go watch TV and cleaned up the mess. She found an old rag and tenderly wiped the banana-cake icing off the dead rattler, which she then put in her specimen cooler, insulated with ice-gel paks. Then she crushed the real estate section, threw it into the trash, and hosed off the garage floor. When that was done, she went into the Peterses' kitchen and looked around. Her dinner, after all, had been interrupted by Professor Artemus, and it had been a long evening. There was another Sara Lee banana cake in the freezer.

Agnes defrosted it in the microwave, and then carefully divided it into halves, one for herself, the other for the little boy. Then she went into the family room, where the boy was watching some show with a really grating laugh track. She handed him his half of the cake, which he accepted with wide eyes, and then she sat down and stared at the television herself.

Watching a human cub wasn't so bad, she thought.

Although the phone rang several times, Agnes ignored it. The boy was safe, she knew, and she didn't want to deal with that horrid woman. If the child wanted to answer the phone, that was his business, but apparently getting half a banana cake and being allowed to stay up as late as he wanted was his idea of bliss. He avoided the phone, as if its only purpose might be ending the party and ordering him to bed.

Agnes stretched out on Heather's leather sofa. She'd been repelled by the idea of it—the fact that it had started out as an animal, and was new enough to still have a fresh leather smell—but it was the only piece of furniture that was big enough to sleep on, unless she went creeping around looking for bedrooms. Agnes stretched an afghan over the sofa to prevent her skin from making contact with the leather, fell into a deep sleep, and dreamed she was Peter Rabbit, stealing carrots from Mr. MacGregor's garden.

Chapter Nine

Heather heard Kevin's voice down the hall. Her prince! Her knight in shining armor! Her lawyer! He would spring her from this rotten place, he would. She'd walk out, with elegance and style, past that bigmouth in the cell across from hers and that, that despot with all the keys. She'd put on her little Italian heels, gather up her jewelry, and leave this scummy place every bit the lady that she was.

But, it suddenly occurred to her to wonder, how had Kevin taken care of Connor and Sally Jo so quickly? True, it felt like she'd been in jail for years, but it couldn't have been really any time at all. She looked down at her wrist, to check the time. She kept forgetting that they'd taken her watch. She estimated: twenty minutes? Well, maybe the man was more resourceful than she'd given him credit for. Maybe he'd called the house and discovered that everything was fine. Maybe he'd found some neighbor who could watch things until they got home. Only, they didn't know any of their neighbors, did they?

Heather heard Kevin's voice again, then the jailer's, and a third voice she didn't recognize. They were arguing. Kevin's voice got louder, like he was losing his temper, then softer, like he was pleading. The voices bounced off all the metal surfaces of the jail, bending, refracting. But the words were not distinct. Oh, it was so frustrating. Not to be able to hear what they were talking about. Not to be there to clarify whatever points Kevin was trying to make. To have to leave all the negotiating to . . . other people.

Finally, Heather could stand it no more. "Kevin!" she called. She tried to make her voice neutral, but it came out like an order, as if she were yelling down to the kitchen for him to bring coffee.

The voices continued, oblivious. That was really galling.

Eventually, Heather heard footsteps heading down the hallway toward her cell. Finally! She stood up, lifted her jacket from the bed, tried to smooth out the wrinkles. She pressed up against the bars, looking toward the left, to see Kevin.

But just short of her cell, the jailer stopped. He took out his keys, unlocked another cell, held the door. Kevin glanced at her, shrugged, and then disappeared into the cell.

"Kevin!" Heather screeched. "What's going on?"

But his cell was on the same side of the hall as hers, and since there were bars preventing them from sticking their heads out, they couldn't see each other.

Kevin and Heather spent the night in separate cells, having been informed that no judge was available to set bail until morning. It was not the happiest night of their marriage. Kevin tried to communicate the basic story of his imprisonment from down the hall—"speeding," "jacket," "registration"—but Heather wasn't getting it. Both the jailer and the woman across the hall told them to shut up.

In the morning, Kevin managed to clear his case up quickly. He was able to persuade the jailer to call Maryanne, at Galapagos Estates, and Maryanne came down to the jail to establish his identity and explain that he had indeed just moved. Once the car-theft charges were dropped, Kevin was dismissed with a ticket for speeding and driving without a license and registration—though he knew he would pay dearly in points that wouldn't come off his license for three years and, this being New Jersey, there would be a huge increase in his car-insurance premium.

But Heather was going to have to go before a judge in order for charges to be read and bail to be set.

"Like this?" she shrieked.

It was true: she wasn't looking her best. Her hair looked like a yellow fright wig, and black mascara was smudged all around her left eye. Her jacket, which she'd used in lieu of bedsheets overnight, was a mass of wrinkles. She hadn't showered, of course. She hadn't even gone to the bathroom. Heather couldn't see any of this, of course, because mirrors were no more part of the state's idea of overnight accommodations than were marble bathtubs.

"This is outrageous!" she said. "I can't go into court like this. Look at my jacket!"

"Oh, you don't have to wear that," the jailer said with a malicious smile. "You can wear this." He pulled open a closet and took out an orange jumpsuit.

"Orange?" Heather said. "I never wear orange. It totally clashes with my complexion. I'm a Winter."

Harlan liked to get an early start when he went fishing, but he'd spent the morning cleaning up his henhouse and nailing some boards around the baseboard. He didn't get to the general store to buy his worms until almost lunchtime. Still, it was a beautiful Indian-summer day, and he deserved a break, what with having to deal with that Heather woman and that rattlesnake business, plus the henhouse on top of it.

He walked through the store without really paying attention, the way you walk through your own house. He knew every aisle, every shelf, where you could find the Hostess Ho Ho's and the pancake mix. But when he got to the cooler where the fish bait was supposed to be, he stopped dead. Instead of the usual jumble of worms, there were neat rows of plastic packages. At first he thought that maybe Ray, the owner of the store, had packaged the worms in some newfangled attempt to make things more hygienic and convenient.

But the packages didn't contain worms. They seemed to contain . . . fish. Cut-up fish, some of it coral-colored, some dark red. Raw salmon, raw tuna. There was some light green paste that looked like lobster guts in the corner of each box, and a little plastic package that looked like a ketchup container with strange writing on it. Harlan looked at the printed label on one package. "Spicy tuna roll," it said.

A bubble of queasiness rose up in his throat. Sushi. Harlan felt like he might be sick.

Sure, he was used to putting worms on fishhooks and pulling squirming, writhing, struggling fish out of the water. He could gut a bass in the time it took most people to tie their shoes. But eat raw fish? Never. That was something birds did.

A tall, angular woman dressed entirely in black came up behind him and leaned into the cooler. "Is there any eel left?" she asked. She squealed and pulled out two packages. Apparently there was.

Harlan remained there, in front of the cooler, for a good five minutes; perhaps, if he waited long enough, the fish would magically turn back into worms. But it didn't. Some things changed. New Jersey changed. Hebron Township changed. Route 381 changed. The general store changed. But sushi didn't turn back into bait.

Where, he wondered, would he get worms now? When he was a boy, you could pick them up at any gas station in town, or at the John Deere store. But the gas stations hadn't carried worms since gas had cost thirty-three cents a gallon and they gave out free jelly glasses. And the John Deere store had been replaced by a Planet Honda. Harlan wondered briefly if he could use the raw chunks of sushi as bait, but then he looked at the price—$6.50 for a small package. He snorted, amazed. He might as well serve the fish some caviar.

He guessed he'd just have to dig some worms out of the garden.

Harlan was still contemplating when he heard footsteps approaching. A sturdy hand landed on his shoulder. It was Ray. "Sorry about the worms, Pops," Ray said. "But you were the only one who bought them anymore."

Harlan hated when people called him Pops. It was an old man's nickname. He'd gone in his lifetime from Boy to Buddy to Sir to Pops. Harlan looked at Ray and felt as if he were seeing a stranger. Yes, he looked the same, with his plaid shirt and his green feed cap, but it was like one of those pictures that changed shape if you squinted your eyes long enough. An optical illusion. Ray suddenly looked like a politician on a TV commercial, the kind who told you all the campaign promises his opponents had broken. Or maybe a used-car salesman. Sure, he was selling. That's what he was doing.

Harlan turned around, avoiding Ray's eyes, and walked toward the side of the store. It was then that he noticed other changes. A large area in the milk case had been cleared away for fresh flowers. Next to the old coffeepots was a cappuccino machine.

Then his eyes landed on a sign: FRESH ORGANIC EGGS, SUNNYBROOK FARMS.

Harlan blinked.

The general store had never sold organic eggs before. Regular eggs, sure. But if anyone in these parts wanted organic eggs, they always came straight to Harlan. Now the general store was selling them? And from a competitor?

Harlan opened the case and felt the cold, refrigerated air. It had always been a sensation he liked, opening the refrigerator case in the general store, feeling the supercooled air bursting free. It brought back memories of being a boy, of playing ball in the summer and coming into the store hot and dirty, drenched with sweat, to buy a five-cent bottle of Coke. In those days, pulling a Coke out of the refrigerator case was as close as anyone got to experiencing air-conditioning.

It wasn't the same. Nothing was the same. Harlan took out an egg carton and inspected the writing on it. "Sunnybrook Farms, Shohola, Pa., 100% Organic. No Antibiotics." He put it back.

Ray had followed him. "Harlan," he said, putting his hand on Harlan's shoulder again.

Harlan shook it off. "I don't have no business here," he said, walking toward the door.

"Pops," Ray said, and his tone of voice was like an apology.

Harlan stopped.

"The eggs. People were asking for them. I'm sorry."

"What about my eggs?"

"Well, you know," Ray said.

"Know what?"

"What they're saying."

"What the hell are you talking about?" Harlan asked.

"The salmonella," Ray answered. "They're saying your eggs have salmonella."

Rodney Campbell had been covering the Burlington County Courthouse for fifteen years. It was long enough to know everything and everybody: the lawyers, the prosecutors, the bailiffs, the judges, the filing clerks, the guys who ran the X-ray machines to check for guns and bombs when you came in. It was also long enough to be completely bored.

He'd been ambitious once. He'd been drawn to journalism by the legend of Woodward and Bernstein bringing down Nixon. He'd dreamed, as a young man, of having his own Deep Throat, of bringing down his own president. Instead, he'd married too young, divorced, and gotten stuck covering the court beat for a small South Jersey regional newspaper. Occasionally, there was a good case, like the rabbi accused of murdering his wife. But then the paper would send down one of their hotshots, and Rodney would be reduced to a mere tour guide, pointing out the bathrooms and where to pick up filings. Most of the time, it was routine. Wife beaters, crooked car salesmen, DUIs. He spent most of his time trying to get the new court stenographer to go to bed with him.

When a petite blond housewife came into the courtroom in handcuffs, complaining loudly about how she'd just spent the worst night of her life in the county jail, Campbell perked up. The lady's hair was messy and her makeup was smeared and she was wearing a terribly wrinkled blazer, but she looked a whole class higher than the usual customer. She looked, in fact, like someone from one of those new developments, the kind where all the houses looked like they were on steroids. What could she possibly have been hauled in for?

He took out a pen and moved closer.

"Bail hearing of Heather Peters, 63 Giant Tortoise Drive," intoned the bailiff.

Campbell smiled. He was right. Galapagos Estates.

Judge Smiley looked at Heather and read the charges. "Killing a rattlesnake, which is an endangered species. Refusing to cooperate with a game warden. Resisting arrest. Assaulting an officer."

Campbell heard a whisper a few rows behind him. "And being a general pain in the ass." It was the jailer, hands resting on his generous stomach, sitting with a few of the cops.

The judge slammed down his gavel and threw the jailer a dirty look. "Order!" Then he turned his attention to Heather. "That's a heap of trouble for such a little gal," he said. Finally, he looked at the prosecutor. "Flight risk?"

"I don't think so, Your Honor," the prosecutor said.

Judge Smiley looked at Heather again. "Young lady," he said, "I'm going to set bail at two thousand dollars. A court date will be set for your trial. Until that time, I'd like your promise that you won't be killing any of our fine New Jersey wildlife. And I don't want you going near a police officer. No speeding tickets. No jaywalking tickets. Got that? Is there anybody here to post your bail?"

Heather looked at Kevin. "Yes, Your Honor," Kevin said.

The judge slammed his gavel down. "Okay, Officers, once bail is posted, you can release Mrs. Peters from her handcuffs. Mrs. Peters, is there anything you'd like to tell the court?"

Heather stood up. "Just a question, Your Honor," she said. "Where are the little forms?"

"Little forms?" Judge Smiley said. "I don't know what forms you're talking about."

"You know," said Heather. "The ones they have in all the hotels. 'We want to know how you rate our accommodations. How was the housekeeping? Did the air conditioner work? Is there anything we could have done to improve your stay?' "

"A room-evaluation form?" the judge asked.

"Exactly," Heather said. "I have a thing or two to say about the way you people run a jail."

Campbell shook his head in amazement. He didn't know which was stranger—a woman getting arrested for killing a rattlesnake, or the imperious way she was treating Judge Smiley. It didn't matter. For once, he'd found a half-interesting story. And a scoop. There wasn't another reporter in the courtroom.

Quietly, he followed Heather, Kevin, and the policeman to the clerk's office and waited for them to post bail. He observed Heather closely, taking mental notes about her hair, what she was wearing. When she turned around to leave the justice center, Campbell stepped forward. His press-ID card hung around his neck, and he lifted it slightly. "Rodney Campbell," he said. "*South Jersey Eagle*." Then he tilted his head and composed his face into a look of intense sympathy. "I was just in the courtroom during your bail hearing. And I'm just amazed at what I heard. Killing a rattlesnake? They put you in the slammer for killing a rattlesnake?"

Heather drew back. She looked at him like he was a panhandler, a suspicious character to be avoided at all costs. But then Campbell saw her glance quickly at his ID, and he noticed her face soften ever so slightly. He was from the press. That gave him power. He could almost see the scale inside her head, tilting one way and then the other as she weighed the pros and cons of acknowledging him.

"I don't know, Heather," said the lawyer standing next to her. Like most lawyers, he seemed innately suspicious of the fourth estate.

Campbell looked back and forth at the two. The woman was curious, but her lawyer could snatch her away in a second and the opportunity would be gone. He had to think quickly.

"It sounds like a real travesty of justice," he said.

Heather brightened. Instantly, she stood straighter—like a flower perking up after a long-overdue watering. She pulled away from the lawyer and turned her face up toward his.

Campbell reached his hand out to shake Heather's. Touch, always important. Then he added his left hand, the way one does with a mourner at a wake, as a way of showing extra concern. Inwardly, he smiled. *A travesty of justice.* He did have a way with words.

Chapter Ten

Sitting in the stranger's lime-green car, on the way to school, Connor reviewed the events of the previous night. A strange lady had come to the door. His mother had gone to Back to School Night. He saw a dead rattlesnake. The babysitter fainted and had to go to the hospital. The strange lady stayed with him all night, feeding him half a Sara Lee banana cake and letting him stay up as late as he wanted. His parents never came home.

Weird.

It had, actually, been kind of cool—especially the part with the snake. And the lady who had taken care of him was pretty cool too. She'd let him fall asleep in his clothes, without brushing his teeth or taking a bath, right on the floor in front of the TV. She let him eat cake there too and didn't complain about crumbs or getting icing on his face. When he walked into the kitchen pantry and came back with potato chips, she didn't say anything about eating healthy food or putting on weight or it being almost bedtime. She just asked him to pass her the bag every once in a while.

This was very different from Connor's mom, who was always following him around, giving orders and complaining about every little thing. In fact, this lady didn't seem to give a hoot what he did. He probably could have played with his remote-control airplane right inside the house for all she would have cared. And when they were watching TV, she didn't even answer the phone. That was really strange. Connor had never seen a grown-up ignore a telephone.

Then came morning. This time, when the phone rang, the lady jumped out of her chair and answered it. "School!" she said, after hanging up. "We have to get you to school!" And then, "Clytemnestra! Oh my poor, poor Clytemnestra. You must be so hungry."

She didn't seem to care if Connor was hungry.

Suddenly the lady who'd been so laid-back the night before began zipping around the kitchen. "Coffee?" she asked, walking around in circles, opening and shutting cupboards and drawers. It almost sounded as if she were pleading. Finally she found his mother's jar of instant "gourmet" hazelnut coffee and mixed it with boiling water. She took a sip and made the kind of face Connor made when he had to eat brussels sprouts. "Instant gourmet?" the lady muttered. "Swill!" She took another sip and then poured the rest into the sink. "Vulgarians!" She set down her mug and looked at Connor. "Come on, kid. Put on your shoes." Then she was out the door and honking her horn.

Connor knew he wasn't supposed to get into cars with strangers, but then this stranger had spent the whole night in his house, and she had a really cool car, a bright green Volkswagen Beetle. Anybody who drove that kind of car couldn't be a bad guy, could they? Besides, as everyone knew, bad guys were men. And if she had wanted to kill him, wouldn't she have just done it while he was sleeping?

The lady pulled into the circular driveway in front of Pine Hills Elementary, heedless of the sign that said it was illegal to park there, and waited for him to get out. She didn't offer to take him into the office and explain why he was late. She didn't even say good-bye. As soon as he was out the door, she sped off.

When Connor got halfway up the stairs of the school, he realized that he'd been rushed out of the house so fast he'd forgotten his backpack. Without thirty pounds of math and science books, Connor felt strangely light and half naked, like in those dreams where you go to school in your pajamas. It wasn't a good feeling. He looked down and was relieved to find that he was actually wearing the clothes he'd fallen asleep in the night before. Well, he would go to the office to check in, because he was late, and then he'd ask to use the phone so he could call his mother to bring his backpack.

That's when it hit him. His mother wasn't home. She hadn't been home all night. And neither had his dad. The phone would ring in the empty house. And ring. And ring. And nobody would bring him his backpack.

Connor trudged toward the office, big tears brimming in his eyes. He would not cry, he told himself. He would not cry.

Rodney Campbell sat on Heather's patio, drinking an iced tea. He'd just gotten the mini-tour of the Peterses' house, at least the first floor, complete with the story about the Roman shades and the incorrect window measurements. He'd been surprised to see the big circular staircase, topped by a rotunda, when Heather had first let him in the house. It looked a bit pretentious, but then what did he know? He'd driven by places like this but never been in one.

Campbell lived in a little apartment on top of a pool hall in what used to be the center of town but was now just a tired-looking section of two-story brick buildings. Campbell's apartment was hot in the summer and cold in the winter, and the stove didn't work, but he put up with it all because the neon sign below his window flashed on and off all night, making him feel like a 1940s gumshoe. Because of that sign, he could say things like "I had this skirt over the other night" and not feel foolish. Atmosphere. Who needed a stove when you could spend your nights living in a noir film?

Most of the people he knew—the court stenographers, waitresses, secretaries, and a few other divorced reporters—lived in apartments too, although the gals had nice little garden apartments with air-conditioning and patios. He'd even dated a gal last year whose apartment complex had a swimming pool. But this, this monstrous house, which came off as a sort of combination French Country chalet and the White House, he didn't know anyone who lived in a place like this.

Campbell was sitting on Heather's patio now by virtue of his quick thinking. After Heather's bail had been posted, she'd had a hushed argument with her lawyer and the man had rushed off, in a cab, talking about an important deposition. "And how am I supposed to get home?" she had demanded, stamping her foot. That's when Campbell, smooth as a gin and tonic on an August afternoon, had offered her a ride. His "travesty of justice" line had gotten her attention. Now, by coming to her rescue, he had his scoop almost in the bank. He'd keep her interested all the way home by letting her talk about herself. He knew the type. It wouldn't be hard. "What you said to the judge," Campbell asked, tossing a month's worth of fast-food containers and old newspapers into the backseat of his Chevy Cavalier. "About the accommodations at the county jail? How bad was it?"

It wasn't until the tour of Mrs. Peters's house that he discovered that the lawyer was actually Heather's husband. There were pictures of the guy all over the place—along with Heather, of course, and a chubby little redheaded boy. It looked like they led a swell life. There were pictures of them on boats and on tropical islands. Expensive lifestyle. No wonder the guy had to run off to work.

Heather had gone upstairs to change, and when she walked back to the patio, she was in jeans, her face scrubbed and her hair pulled back in a ponytail. She looked ten years younger, Campbell thought. She plopped down on a chair and sighed deeply—as if to exhale the indignities of the previous night's incarceration.

Campbell almost felt guilty making her go through an interview. But when he mentioned the word *rattlesnake,* she instantly perked up.

"I was standing right here," Heather began, jumping out of her chair. "I'd just brought out my nice Willow Ware because I was going to be having a tea party. You know what Willow Ware is, don't you? The blue-and-white stuff? I've been collecting it for years. And then, anyway, I saw it. Big, nasty, ugly. *Ugh.* I just dropped the Willow Ware on the ground. It all broke. What a shame. And homeowners insurance wouldn't even cover it. Can you believe that?"

Campbell, scribbling furiously, shook his head. That was all he had to do. Shake his head when she wanted him to agree that something was horrible, nod when she wanted him to agree with something that wasn't. He was beginning to feel a little like a bobble-head doll, but it sure beat having to draw information out of people. No, he didn't have to talk, much less formulate questions. Interviewing Heather was like turning on a spigot. She wouldn't stop until he got up to leave.

"And then," she said, "I called—" She stopped.

"And then," Campbell prompted.

"I called," Heather said. "I called out for a neighbor. But nobody was there. Nobody heard."

"So you were all by yourself. With this huge rattlesnake? What was it—three feet?"

"Oh, no," Heather said. She stretched out her arms to suggest the length of the snake. "Five feet. Six. I don't know. It was huge."

"And then?"

"I killed it."

"You killed the rattlesnake all by yourself?"

Heather nodded vigorously.

"But how?"

"Well," she said, taking a deep breath. "There was this vase that I kept on the patio. A very big, heavy vase. Ming dynasty. I got it on eBay. And I threw it at the rattlesnake." She looked very satisfied with herself. "It was a shame, though. Having to ruin a perfectly good, valuable vase like that."

"You threw the vase—the Ming vase—at the rattler," Rodney said, taking notes. "And that killed it."

"Well, I would say it stunned it," Heather said. "So then I walked over there and picked up a croquet mallet and clobbered the thing to death."

Campbell put down his pen and looked at her appreciatively. "Wow," he said. "Killed a rattlesnake yourself." This story would play well. Page 1. He'd call the photo editor when he got back and set up a shoot. He could see the picture in his mind, the petite blonde, standing on her patio, holding her arms out to indicate just how big the rattler was. He wished he'd had a picture of her in handcuffs.

"And of course you didn't know anything about it being an endangered species?" Campbell said.

"No, of course not. Except for what—" She stopped.

"Except for what?" prompted Campbell.

"Oh, nothing," Heather said.

"No, you started to say, except for something."

"Except. Well, later my handyman told me."

"I see."

"He helped me clean it up."

"Ah," Campbell said. He jotted down the word *handyman*. "And so the jail thing. How did that come about? I mean, how did they find out you killed it? It wasn't the handyman who tipped them off, was it?"

"Oh, no," Heather said. "No no no no no." She seemed quite agitated at the idea.

"Well, how, then?"

"You know, it all happened so fast, I'm not quite sure," Heather said. Her face got this faraway look, and Campbell could tell that she was thinking. It seemed like she really didn't know how they'd found her. But then she seemed to remember something. She opened her mouth again. "There was this strange woman who came to my door with a machine, and the machine was beeping. I was heading out for Back to School Night." Her expression suddenly changed. "School!" she said. "Oh my God! Connor! Shit! Shit shit shit shit shit!"

"Connor?" Campbell asked, hoping to nudge her along. But by then Heather had run into the house.

The office of Pine Hills Elementary was like Hong Kong at lunch hour. Phones rang, children waited for mothers to bring forgotten sandwiches, teachers lined up to use the photocopier, secretaries put mail in slots, deliverymen arrived with packages, sick kids waited for the nurse. But when Connor Peters walked in, a hush descended. The two secretaries exchanged glances. Mothers bringing in book reports or coming to pick up children with earaches stopped in their tracks. The silence was finally broken when a little girl with skinned knees pointed a pudgy index finger and said loudly to her mother, "That's the one!"

"Ssshh," her mother said.

The little girl meant, that's the one who runs around after girls on the playground and hugs them, who looks up their dresses when they go on the swings, who barges in front of people in the cafeteria line.

But the mothers and the secretaries recognized something different. Word had spread fast through the halls of Pine Hills Elementary, and by now everybody knew. This was the boy whose mother had been led away from Back to School Night in handcuffs.

Mrs. Haggarty, the head secretary, would normally have looked at a boy who was an hour and a half late to school, without a note or even a backpack, with a practiced attitude of official scorn. But she was beginning to feel sorry for him. As bad as he was—and he'd been to the principal's office three times already, and it was only September, and he was only in third grade—he clearly had problems at home to contend with. She tried to speak to him as kindly as she could.

"Mr. Peters," she said. "Can you tell me why you're late to school today?"

Connor shrugged and dug the toe of one of his shoes into the floor.

"Well, can you tell me where your mother is?"

Connor shook his head.

"Then, that woman who answered the phone this morning. Who was she? A babysitter? An aunt? Your grandma?"

He shook his head again.

"Who was she, then?"

"I don't know."

"How did you get to school this morning?"

"The lady drove me."

"What lady?"

"The one who answered the phone."

"You got a ride from a stranger?" Mrs. Haggarty said.

"Um," said Connor, looking at his feet. "I guess so."

"Okay, I've heard enough." Mrs. Haggarty scribbled something on a notepad and tore off the top sheet. "Here's a pass to get back into Miss Kindermack's class."

Connor trudged out of the office, his head low. He'd looked forward to telling all the kids about the rattlesnake. But he'd already missed recess. And the secretary in the office made him feel strange. Where was his mother? And who was that lady? And would he get in trouble for taking a ride from a stranger?

After Connor was safely down the hall, Mrs. Haggarty turned to the other secretary, Mrs. Snodgrass. "Child Services?" she said, arching an eyebrow.

Mrs. Snodgrass looked down. She enjoyed gossip as much as the next person, but she didn't like talking about a parent in a room full of students and other parents.

"And you know the worst of it?" Mrs. Haggarty continued.

Mrs. Snodgrass looked up.

Mrs. Haggarty lowered her voice to a whisper. "She's a class mom."

Chapter Eleven

"Oh my God," Kevin said. It was Saturday, and on weekends he allowed himself the luxury of sleeping in an hour before taking his morning run. He'd picked up the paper on his way back in, planning to read it in the kitchen with his first cup of coffee. But when he sat down and unfolded the paper, expecting the usual stories of off-duty policemen who'd killed their ex-wives, he saw instead the picture of his wife, her arms outstretched, looking like a skinny blond Christ, minus the crucifix. "Jesus," he exclaimed.

"What?" asked Connor, who was watching cartoons in the great room.

"Mom," Kevin said. "She's a celebrity."

Connor ran into the kitchen and looked at the newspaper. "Wow," he said. "We're famous. Now those kids won't make fun of me."

Kevin chose not to respond to Connor's remark. He didn't like self-pity, no matter what Connor's $175-an-hour "worry doctor" said. Yeah, maybe he could have said, "What kids?" and heard some sob story about Connor's chilly reception on the school bus. But there was his goddamned wife on the cover of the *Eagle,* and he didn't feel like getting into it. He filed the remark away under the subject of Connor's self-esteem, then read the article, including the jump on B-4, with the same absorption he would give to a brief.

When he was done, Kevin drummed his fingers on the kitchen table several times and stared out the bay window into the backyard. Then he folded the paper, poured the coffee into Heather's favorite mug, and walked into the master-bedroom suite.

"Well," he said, walking into the bedroom and tossing the paper on the bed. "It appears that somebody in our household is famous."

Heather came to consciousness slowly, rubbing her eyes.

"Or should I say infamous?"

Heather picked up the newspaper, blinking when she saw her own image.

The picture, she noticed immediately, made her arms look fat. How could she ever have agreed to such a ludicrous pose? There she was, on her patio, her arms stretched out, her face in a scowl. At the time, it had made perfect sense. She remembered that fellow, that journalist who'd given her a ride home—Rodney what's-his-name?—prompting her to show the photographer the size of the rattlesnake. She'd been happy to oblige, to demonstrate the sheer magnitude of the danger she'd faced. But to see that gesture frozen, and that flab on her arms, on the front of the *South Jersey Eagle,* that was completely different. And the caption. "How Big?" Was that supposed to be facetious? Were they making fun of her?

Well, at least the flagstone patio in the background, with her new Restoration Hardware black-mesh dining set, looked attractive.

She looked up at Kevin, about to complain about the picture, and noticed that his face looked dark and angry, like a midwestern sky before a twister. That's when she remembered. She'd forgotten to tell him about the interview, and about the photo session the following day. But had she really forgotten? Or had she failed to tell him because she was still pissed off that he'd left her standing outside the courthouse after the night she'd spent in jail? Maybe giving the story to that journalist fellow was Heather's unconscious way of punishing Kevin. Especially since he was so suspicious of reporters. That's probably what Dr. Phil would say. She half smiled, trying to imagine Kevin's face when he first opened the paper, and then immediately returned her mouth to a neutral expression, not wanting to make him any angrier.

It was just that she hadn't quite pictured the results of the interview or the photo session.

Heather read the newspaper article slowly, frowning from time to time as she took sips of coffee. She liked Rodney Campbell's description of her as a "perky blonde" but was annoyed at his depiction of her house as a "mausoleum of upscale egoism." What in the world was that supposed to mean? She swallowed hard when she came to the part about killing the rattlesnake herself. She hadn't meant to upstage her handyman. She was just trying to keep him out of trouble—that was it. But the part about her "imperious demand for a room-evaluation form" in Judge Smiley's courtroom stopped her cold.

"That makes me look like, like—"

"An idiot?" Kevin suggested. "Girls who play with snakes shouldn't complain when they get bitten."

"But I didn't play with the snake," Heather said. "I killed it."

"I was talking about that reporter," Kevin said.

The phone rang. It was her mother. Almost as soon as she hung up from that call, it rang again. Someone in Kevin's firm. Then again. One of the mothers from Connor's class. The phone didn't stop for hours. Each time, she had to explain. Yes, a rattlesnake. Yes, Back to School Night. And, she'd ask the caller, no matter who it was, didn't the picture just look hideous? She sighed deeply every time she hung up, as if genuinely exhausted by the attention, but each time she heard another ring she perked up, leaning toward the telephone like a plant toward sunshine.

Clytemnestra bounded onto the kitchen table and padded right across the newspaper that Agnes was reading. She stretched, bidding Agnes a good morning and inquiring gently about her breakfast. The bowls on the floor were all empty, and the other animals were milling around the kitchen, waiting for their morning meal. Clytemnestra, the favorite, didn't care to wait. "

Scat," said Agnes, giving her a gentle shove.

Clytemnestra jumped down, looking gravely offended, and sought out a corner where the other animals would not stare at her disgrace. Agnes went on reading.

The article was outrageous, human-centric, ridiculous. *"I'm the one who's endangered," Mrs. Peters said. "Not the rattlesnakes."* Agnes wrinkled her nose. Endangered, my ass, she thought. Entitled is more like it. *"This awful woman came to my house and demanded that I show her the rattlesnake, right then and there," Mrs. Peters said, her voice filled with annoyance. "On Back to School Night!"*

"Awful woman!" And the reporter hadn't even come to get her side of the story.

This Rodney Campbell, whoever he was, had succeeded in making the state's attempts to protect endangered wildlife appear ludicrous. It was the typical bias. Humans good, animals bad. Humans important, animals inconsequential. And this Heather character, dimwit though she clearly was, came off like some kind of hero. She'd killed the "poisonous predator" herself, "sacrificing a valuable Ming vase in the process." Ha. That bludgeoned snake was killed with more than just a vase. It was hammered with a blunt object. Brutally. But of course the snake hadn't been around to tell its side of the story.

Agnes turned to the jump. Oh there it was. *She finished the job with a croquet mallet.* So that's how the snake had met its end. Sad.

The phone rang. Agnes practically stepped on Clytemnestra as she went to answer it. Leroy Adams from Friends of the Fauna. "Did you see that outrageous article in the *Eagle*?" he asked.

"Yes," said Agnes. She started opening cans of cat food.

"And that was you, I suppose, the 'awful woman'?"

"Guilty as charged." Agnes beckoned Clytemnestra to come to the bowl, but the cat stayed in the corner, sulking.

"And what are we going to do?" he asked.

"Do?"

"Well, you're not going to just stand for that, are you?"

"Leroy, I've only had one cup of coffee. I haven't filed a libel suit yet, or whatever it is you'd have me do. For Christ's sake, I haven't even fed the cats."

"I think we should call a meeting."

"Let's wait a couple of days," Agnes said. "Maybe this whole thing will blow over."

"It won't," Leroy said. "Just wait and see. This Heather lady, she's going to become a folk hero. A legend."

"Oh, I don't think so," Agnes said. She stooped to pick up

Clytemnestra, who fixed her with the cold, withering expression of a leading lady who'd been stood up for dinner. "Listen, Leroy, I've got to go." Agnes hung up, pulled the snarling feline onto her lap, and caressed her with long, smooth strokes.

Real tuna for Clytemnestra today, Agnes thought. Sometimes you had to suck up to your favorite cat.

Jack Barstad was on the third fairway when he felt the vibration of the cell phone in his pants pocket. Damn. What the hell did Barbara want? Hadn't he signed her up for a whole Elizabeth Arden day of beauty just to make sure she stayed out of his hair today? Her heels should be getting loofahed right now, or maybe they'd be moisturizing her double chin. Besides, didn't she know what was at stake? It wasn't just that he was playing with three members of the Burlington County Board of Zoning Adjustment, men he'd need in his pocket to make sure that all the *i*'s got dotted and the *t*'s got crossed for Galapagos Phase 2. It was also the fact that he was playing at Timbers, the most beautiful, difficult, and exclusive golf club in the state. Not only would talking on his cell phone screw up his concentration, it was a breach of green etiquette.

It wouldn't be Dana, he knew that. She was too much of a pro to call him when he was out on business rounds.

"Yes?" he said with irritation, turning away from his partners and walking toward the rough.

"It's Maryanne."

"Crap, Maryanne. I'm playing golf. With you-know-who."

"I know," she said. "Sorry. It's just that there's something I think you should know. This morning's *Eagle,* page one. It's a story about Galapagos Estates."

"Galapagos Estates? What about it?"

"Do you remember that Heather woman? The one near Walden Pond? Who gave us a hard time about the window measurements?"

Barstad turned around. The next foursome was approaching the tee, and the zoning czars were starting to look annoyed. He smiled wincingly at his companions and pointed at his phone, then held up his finger in the one-minute sign. "Get to the point. They're waiting."

"She found a rattlesnake in her yard. And killed it. Endangered species. Went to jail. Now they're making her out to be a big martyr."

Barstad didn't say anything.

"I have a feeling there's going to be a feeding frenzy about this. More stories. More media. And Jack?"

"Yes."

"There's a line in the article about your rattlesnake report for Phase One. You know? Where you said that this wasn't a known refuge for any endangered species?"

"Shit," Barstad said. Maryanne had been right to call. He was with the zoning czars, for Christ's sake, the ones who'd accepted his bogus environmental impact statement in the first place. He doubted any of them had seen the paper, because nobody had said anything. But who knows? Somebody could come up to them in the clubhouse afterward and make a joke about snakes. Barstad would have to finesse it. And what crappy timing. Just as he was going forward with Phase 2. He'd have to schedule another planning session with Dana and plot a new public relations strategy. She'd know what to do. "Okay. Thanks for letting me know."

Barstad pasted a big smile on, turned around, and walked toward his golf partners. "Whoops, sorry," he said. "Better get going." He winked in the direction of the foursome behind them. "Sherman's troops are advancing."

Barstad approached the ball, removed his four iron, swung—and dug a divot the size of an ironing board. His ball dribbled a few yards down the fairway.

Harlan gathered up the morning's eggs, examining the henhouse for any more signs of intrusion. As far as he could tell, there were none. The day after he'd discovered the bloodbath, he'd patched the old structure up as best he could, installing new screens, hammering up plywood, checking for holes where nocturnal predators might have gotten in.

The hens spared in the previous week's attack clucked contentedly until Harlan moved them to remove their eggs—a procedure that always miffed them. But there was no blood and no hens missing, no sign that the hens were particularly stressed. So far, so good.

He wished he could say the same about the human side of things. As he sat at his kitchen table, getting ready to put the eggs into wire baskets, he went over the delivery list. There'd been twelve order cancellations on his answering machine just last night, and eleven others had trickled in the previous week. The voices sounded embarrassed, awkward. Not one of them mentioned the word *salmonella.* Instead, they made vague excuses, polite, well-meaning, and not entirely believable. "Um, Mr. White, we won't be needing our eggs this week. Or, well, next week either. Paul's doctor told him he has to cut down on cholesterol." "Hello? This is Edie McNeil. I'm calling to cancel our order for a while. Problem is, we're having an addition put on our house, and it'll be kind of hard for you to park with all the trucks outside. I'll let you know when the work's done."

Bullshit, thought Harlan.

He took the morning paper from its plastic wrapper. He always took the stock section out and laid it on his table before he divvied up the eggs. It was neater that way, in case one broke. Saved time.

But something caught his attention first. There, on page 1, was a picture of that Heather woman. Holy shit. Why was she in the news?

Harlan reached for his glasses, sat down, and began to read. Son of a gun. It was about the damn rattlesnake. She hadn't gotten rid of it after all—like he'd warned her—but had left it in the yard bag in her garage. Endangered species. Somehow Fish and Wildlife had discovered it. She'd spent the night in jail. Harlan chuckled, imagining the spoiled princess behind bars. That was a good one. He took a sip of coffee, content knowing that there was indeed justice in the world.

But the next sentence made him spit the coffee out. *An unlikely executioner, the petite 35-year-old said she killed the rattler by throwing a Ming dynasty vase at it. "I'd called out but no one heard me," she said. "So I just grabbed the first thing I could find. I was scared to death, but it was either me or the snake."*

Well, Harlan thought. She's rewriting history now. He didn't quite know what to think. On the one hand, she'd robbed him of his moment of heroism. But on the other, she was the one who'd spent the night in the county jail. She was the one facing charges. It was true, she was a little shit who couldn't even clean her own lawn chairs, let alone kill a rattlesnake. But this was her problem now. He could wash his hands of it entirely.

He'd enjoy it next time she called for help around the house. He wouldn't say a thing. He'd just look at her with a knowing smile. It would drive her crazy. That is, if she had the nerve to call him again.

Harlan took a kitchen towel and gently wiped off the eggs he'd accidentally spit his coffee on. It looked like diarrhea. Damn. That was the last thing he needed, with these stupid rumors about salmonella: people thinking that his chickens had diarrhea.

Chapter Twelve

"Come on, old man," teased Dana, turning around on her bike. She was a good fifteen yards ahead, but even from that distance Barstad could see how good her butt looked in those little khaki shorts. But his penis—which he knew was down there somewhere—couldn't salute. He hadn't biked since he was a kid, and now he knew why. His shirt was drenched in sweat and glued to his back, and his bum knee was hurting. But worst of all was the pressure of his crotch up against the saddle. It had started with a feeling of pins and needles, turned into a constant burning pain, and finally, all sensation had disappeared. He was bicycling on the towpath alongside the Delaware and Raritan Canal—the sexiest girl in New Jersey in front of him, a night in a bed-and-breakfast ahead—and he'd turned into a goddamned eunuch.

And here she was teasing him because he couldn't keep up. He tried to gain speed, but the path was clogged with pedestrians, strollers, and bicyclists of varying skill, and it was too narrow to pass. In certain sections, near the bridges, some guardrails were missing, and it was a good twenty-foot drop down to the canal. Well, he'd catch up when the throng cleared and the path widened a bit.

At least it was a beautiful fall day. Indian summer.

Lambertville had been Dana's idea. Jack had wanted, as usual, to hold their planning session in a high roller's suite in Atlantic City. There was something about the bright lights, one-armed bandits, and flashy stage shows with the long-legged dancers—not to mention the Atlantic Ocean—that filled the atmosphere with electricity. Jack was convinced that the very air there charged him up, made him stronger, sharper, better in bed—even if it wasn't true, as sometimes rumored, that casinos actually pumped extra oxygen into their gambling floors to keep their customers from falling asleep. Besides, Dana had been good luck the last time he'd played blackjack. Why not try again?

But Dana had heard about Lambertville from one of her friends. Then she'd read a story about it in *New Jersey Monthly*. As soon as he mentioned another planning session, she brought it up. "It's cute, Jack," she said.

"I don't do cute," Barstad replied.

"It's got antiques, art galleries."

"You're starting to sound like Barbara."

"Excellent restaurants."

"I like the restaurants in Atlantic City."

Dana pouted. "And bed-and-breakfasts make me horny. I don't know what it is. It reminds me of doing it in my parents' house. It makes me crazy."

So he'd given in. She was right about the horny part. At least, he had a vague memory of the previous night, back when there'd been some sensation in his nether regions. But he was dubious about tonight. He'd read somewhere that bike riding led to erectile dysfunction, and he was inclined to believe it.

They still hadn't spent any time on the planning portion of their weekend: what to do about the dramatic appearance of an endangered timber rattlesnake in Galapagos Estates and the even more dramatic consequences for the home buyer who had killed it. It had come, as problems usually do, at the worst time. He was already having to butter up the zoning czars on the issue of traffic. Route 381 had been widened once—luckily no one had been smart enough to make him pay for it—and the addition of two hundred houses was going to put even more pressure on the road, not to mention the water, sewers, and the school system. The traffic engineers were saying they would have to install a new traffic light to handle all the left-hand turns out of the development. But people in Hebron Township didn't like change, and there'd be complaints about how a light was going to slow down the morning rush.

And he still hadn't bought the land he needed from Harlan White, although he had seen signs that his rumor campaign about Harlan's eggs was starting to work. It had all been so simple, especially for a man of Barstad's cunning. What was the most efficient way to spread gossip in a small town? Well, where was there the greatest foot traffic? The general store, of course. And Ray, who owned the store, was more than obliging as a vector of unsubstantiated rumor, and totally unconscious of his role. Ray knew everybody in town, and loved to talk. Anybody who came in for a quart of milk ended up shooting the breeze.

For a master like Barstad, it was child's play. He'd dropped in to Ray's store one morning on the way to the Galapagos Estates sales office, poured himself a cup of coffee, and was waiting for his change when he nonchalantly dropped his little bombshell. "Heard anything about some egg farmer around these parts selling eggs with salmonella?" he'd asked, stirring his coffee.

"No," Ray said with a gasp, his voice filled with genuine concern. "Not Harlan White?"

"White, Gray, Black, I don't remember," Barstad said. "I think some color name. Green, maybe? I heard some little kid got sick and had to go to the hospital."

Perfect. Subtle. He hadn't even named White directly, so he couldn't—even if anybody was able to trace the source of the rumor—be accused of slander. White, Gray, Black, Green. Sometimes Barstad amazed himself with his own brilliance.

Now all he needed to make his plan work was time. Eventually, Harlan's egg business would go under, and the old farmer might decide that a tidy sum of money would come in handy. Then he'd sell his farm. Barstad just hoped it would happen sooner rather than later.

He swerved to avoid a kid on a training-wheel bike and pumped harder, trying to catch up with Dana.

But what to do about the rattlesnakes?

He'd made that issue go away once. It wasn't going to be so easy this time.

There'd been talk, before he'd built Phase 1, of a rattlesnake den near the little pond in the section of Galapagos Estates where Mrs. Peters lived. At first he'd been worried that the snakes—if there really were snakes—might pose a risk to the people who lived there. Well, he wasn't worried about the residents so much as he was about lawsuits and bad publicity. But the kooky environmentalists who brought it up at the public hearings were worried about the opposite: that home owners posed a threat to the rattlesnakes! The snakes had certain daily commuting patterns, they said. They'd surely get smashed by cars as they made their way from their basking spots back to their dens. Well, boo hoo hoo, Barstad thought. Besides, he hadn't seen any rattlesnakes. Not personally. And he'd spent good money to find a herpetologist who shared his opinion to write the environmental impact statement.

But now this stupid Peters woman and her rattlesnake were all over the news. It had been in the local paper, then been picked up by *The Philadelphia Inquirer* and even the Jersey section of *The New York Times*. There'd almost been an aviation disaster when two of the local news channels had sent helicopters up for aerial shots of Galapagos Estates at the same time and they missed each other by just a matter of feet. That had bumped the story from the inside pages up to the front again. And the rattlesnake killer, that little blond bitch at 63 Giant Tortoise Drive, was reveling in all the publicity. Just eating it up.

Suddenly, traffic on the narrow bike path seemed to slow. Barstad eased on his brakes. A few feet ahead, a gaggle of ducks had begun to walk across the path. Okay, he saw it. He was a little wobbly, but his balance held. It wasn't until a little girl, about three years old, rushed out of nowhere to pet the ducks that Barstad lost his balance. His bike skidded sideways, and he fell, scraping knees and wrists and elbows, and then realized that he was flying through the air. Like the coyote in the Road Runner cartoons, he rolled down the pebbly bank of the canal, the bicycle twisted around him.

Barstad tried to get up, to maintain his dignity, to show how hardy he was. But he was, after all, a man in his late fifties, and extricating himself from such a fall wasn't just a matter of springing up. Bones from his shoulders to his ankles throbbed, and he felt every ounce of his two hundred pounds when he tried to lift his body. When he finally managed to heave himself up on his elbows, he saw two dozen concerned faces looking down. Please, not Dana, he prayed. Let her be far up the path. Don't let her see me like this. But there she was, graceful as a gazelle in her hiking sandals, already halfway down the embankment.

They decided to ditch the bike, which was pretty much a total wreck, but even without the tangled metal to contend with, it took twenty minutes to get him up the hill. With his clothes torn and covered with blood, Barstad didn't look much better than the bike. By the time he limped back onto the towpath, an ambulance was waiting and the medical technicians already had a stretcher out and ready.

"I'm not going to the hospital," Barstad said. "I'm fine." He turned toward Dana. "Do you see what happens when you don't go to civilized places like Atlantic City?"

"Come on, sir," said an EMT who looked young enough to be his grandson. "You could be in shock."

"I'm not in shock," Barstad said, trying to sound like the powerful man he really was, at least the powerful man he'd been until twenty minutes ago. "I'm merely in a state of utter humiliation."

"But those abrasions," said another EMT, a girl. "They're all over your body."

"I'll take a couple of Band-Aids," Barstad said. "And some Bactine."

The first EMT fixed Barstad with a grave look. "Sir, the shock of your injuries is providing a natural anesthetic at this point. You might have sprained or even broken something. If you could look at yourself in a mirror right now, you would see that a hospital is where you need to be." He nodded toward Dana. "I'm sure your daughter agrees."

"Young man," said Barstad, puffing up his chest, "if you so much as touch my little finger without my permission, you will face the biggest lawsuit of your life." He began hobbling away, leaning against Dana.

"If you're going to refuse medical treatment, you'll have to sign—"

Barstad quickened his pace, straightening his back and holding his head high. If they wanted to take him to the hospital, they'd have to tackle him. But he paid dearly for the gesture, with shooting pains up and down his right leg. Dana leaned over and gave him a playful little smooch on the cheek. "Hey, Daddy," she cooed.

"Ouch," said Barstad, jerking his head away. Even his cheek hurt.

When they'd booked a room on the third floor of the Victorian, it had seemed to make sense. It was one of the largest rooms in the bed-and-breakfast, and certainly the most private. Unlike most of the guest rooms on the first and second floor of the B&B, it did not share a bathroom. This was an absolute requirement, as far as Barstad was concerned.

Who knew that he and his bike would plummet down an embankment of the Delaware and Raritan Canal and that merely getting to the third floor would be like scaling Everest? And who knew that it would be such a hot mid-September day, with highs in the low nineties, and that these places didn't have air conditioners? At seven o'clock, when Barstad and Dana had planned to be eating at the Merry Widow, a roadside tavern from the 1700s that promised "Colonial charm," "stunning river views," and "a French onion soup to knock your socks off," according to Zagat's, they were in bed. Barstad was moaning, but not with delight, as Dana took towels filled with ice—which she'd had to get at a 7–Eleven, since B&Bs didn't provide ice buckets like normal hotels—and positioned them on different parts of his body.

At one point she leaned down to the opening in his boxers and gave him a provocative lick. As if to say, Sorry, can I make it up to you?

"No," Barstad winced.

"Well then," said Dana, sitting up in a cross-legged position. "Do you want to discuss the snake problem?"

"Snake problem," Barstad said tonelessly. "Snake problem."

"How to spin it," Dana said. "I've been thinking—"

"Forget the snakes," Barstad said. "What the fuck do I say to Barbara? I told her I was going to scout some property this weekend down in Maryland. How the fuck did I end up like this?"

Chapter Thirteen

Heather was sitting on the patio, lovingly turning the pages of her press scrapbook. There was the first article, the one by Rodney Campbell, with the unfortunate shot of her arms. Then there were a series of follow-ups by Campbell; also stories from the *Inquirer, The Times,* and *Newsweek,* and a handwritten thank-you note from Katie Couric. Heather wondered whether it was time to get a publicist. Hollywood? Maybe she could get a spot on Leno. Somebody had mentioned a show called *Politically Incorrect,* but it turned out that it had been canceled.

Her reveries were interrupted by a strange sound.

Heather put down the scrapbook and sat still, listening hard. It sounded like tiny teeth chattering. Or, no—like the unwinding motion of some children's noisemaker. Was it to her left? Her right? Behind her? Her body tensed, carrying the physical memory of having heard this sound before. This was not a benign sound. This was no toy, no noisemaker. It was a . . .

Out of the corner of her right eye, Heather saw it move: a baby rattlesnake. It was slender, only a foot or two long, not as big as the other one. But it had the same distinctive pattern covering its skin. She opened her mouth to scream, but nothing came out. Her vocal cords were frozen. The rattlesnake came closer, slithered up to within a foot of her patio chair, then did something strange. It lifted its neck up and rose, like a serpent in the Bible, facing her. Even more strange, it opened its mouth and began to talk. "You killed my mother," the baby rattlesnake hissed, its voice both sweet and terrible, and it pointed its head at her the way a person might point an index finger. "You killed her. And now I must have my revenge." Then the rattlesnake emitted a hideous laugh.

Finally, the scream was released from Heather's throat. It came out like the wail of a fire engine: long, shrill, and seemingly without end.

"Heather, Heather," said Kevin. "Wake up." He shook the bony shoulder of his wife, who was screaming, writhing, kicking, and sweating, rolling around like a person possessed, in their king-sized bed. "Heather, you're having a dream."

Her eyes popped open, and she looked at him with terror. "The snake," she whispered.

"What snake?" Kevin asked. "The one you killed?"

"No," said Heather. "Its baby. It's come back to . . ." She looked around. She was surprised to see that it was her bedroom. But there were her walnut plantation shutters, the French Country armoire in which they hid their forty-five-inch TV, and Kevin! She was not outside on the patio, with her media scrapbook. What media scrapbook? She didn't have a media scrapbook. Although maybe that would be a good idea, something to give to Connor when he grew up. She wasn't outside, with a baby snake seeking to avenge its mother. She was in her bedroom, with her husband, safe. It had been—yes, it had been, thank God—only a dream.

Kevin reached over and began to stroke her arm. "Shhhh," he said. "It was just a dream." Heather pulled away, as if singed by a hot coal.

"I know that," she snapped, and seeing his pout, she immediately regretted her tone of voice. It was just that her mind was several steps ahead of her body, which was still in fight-or-flight mode. Every ounce of her 110-pound frame was buzzing like a high-voltage wire; every nerve felt raw and exposed. Her heart was still pounding. "Shhhh," she said.

"What?"

"I heard something."

"Heather."

"Under the bed! Kevin, look under the bed! A snake! I hear a rattlesnake."

Kevin rolled his eyes.

Heather knew that look, and God, did she resent it. Kevin always treated her like this, as if she were a hysteric. She was more finely attuned to danger than her husband. She had better hearing and a canine-like sense of smell. But did he ever believe her when she smelled gas leaking from the oven? Did he listen when she shook him awake at night after hearing strange noises in the kitchen? No. He mocked her.

Connor walked into the room, his face still soft and blubbery with sleep. "What's going on?" he asked. He was sucking his thumb, something he did in times of stress. Regression, the worry doctor said.

"Mom had a bad dream," said Kevin. "She wants me to look under the bed and make sure that there's not a snake there, waiting to get her."

"I'll look," said Connor, dropping to the floor with surprising alacrity. Heather opened her mouth to protest but said nothing. She should stop him. An eight-year-old! This was Kevin's responsibility. It was the father's job to protect his family. But when Heather saw Connor on his hands and knees, and lifting up the bed skirt, her fears suddenly seemed, well—as much as she hated to admit it—a little absurd.

Still, it was nice to see Connor willing to help out. For someone who couldn't even be counted on to brush his teeth without repeated nagging, he was certainly taking to the assignment with gusto.

Connor slithered under the bed and began throwing things out from underneath. First, some used tissues. Then, a paperback book. After that, a skinny object, about three feet long.

"Connor!" Heather screamed as the object flew upward. Then she recognized it as a bathrobe belt, covered in dust.

"Yuck," she said. "I knew that cleaning lady was doing a crappy job."

Then there was silence. Heather and Kevin looked at each other. Connor wasn't often silent. They smiled. Heather's heart had finally slowed to its normal rate. It was a Saturday morning, and here she was, in her very own house, with the people she loved most in the whole world. She'd been unkind to Kevin. But there he was, looking at her with an expression of tenderness. They kissed. Still no noise from under the bed.

"Connor?"

He came up with a *Playboy* magazine, which featured Miss October, who was sitting, spread-eagle, atop an enormous pumpkin. "What's this?"

Kevin grabbed the magazine and quickly jammed it into his nightstand drawer. He turned to Heather. "I read it for the stories," he said.

She looked away, disgusted.

"Really," Kevin said.

Connor sat on the floor and looked back and forth at his parents. "Can I see that magazine again?"

"No!" they shouted in unison.

"Well," Connor said. "How about pancakes? After all, I risked my life for you people."

Kevin had put on fresh coffee and was stirring the pancake batter for Connor, who was already watching Saturday-morning cartoons. Normally, he might have been irked by Connor's demand—where did he think he was, IHOP?—but this morning he was happy for the diversion. Happy to get out of bed. Happy to get away from his wife. It had been exactly one week since the story had broken about Heather and the rattlesnake, and he was, frankly, sick of it. Sick of it, and sick of her. They hadn't had sex for going on six weeks now. They'd hadn't even done it the night they'd signed the contract on the house. And she'd been a total nutcase for weeks. The move, the school, the snake, jail. And now the press.

It had been an onslaught. Since last Saturday, when he'd thrown the paper on their bed, the phone hadn't stop ringing, even into the wee hours of the night—when reporters from places like Sweden and South Africa called. And never mind that he or Connor was trying to sleep, Heather was just as loud in the middle of the night as she was any other time. Even though Kevin would cover his head with his pillow, he would still hear "ON THE PATIO . . . WITH A VASE . . . MING DYNASTY"—over and over.

Worst of all was the invitation for her to appear on the *Today* show. The call had come on Monday morning, just as Kevin was shaving, and Heather's scream had caused him to nick his chin. He'd come running, only to discover from the manic smile on her face that it was one of her rare good screams. She cupped her hand over the phone and mouthed, "The *Today* show!" When she hung up, she jumped up and embraced him. "With Katie! The car's coming for me tomorrow at four A.M."

"Four A.M.?" Kevin asked.

"Well, yes," Heather said. "It takes more than an hour to get there. And then there's makeup. And the pre-interview. And—oh shit! What am I going to wear?"

When he came home that night, there were four outfits spread over their bed. Heather was wearing a pink Chanel suit with oversized gold buttons, and Sally Jo was kneeling down, pins in her mouth, hemming the skirt.

Kevin walked over to the bed and looked at the price tag on one of the outfits: $245! He looked at another one: $400! "Heather," he said, "what do you think this is? Your coronation?"

"It's national television," she said. "Seen by millions and millions of people. Including my mom."

"But five outfits!"

"Well, I couldn't decide, you know, what look to go for? I can't just wear blue jeans. Well, I could, I suppose. I saw Daryl Hannah in jeans on *The View* last week, but I'm sure they were five-hundred-dollar designer jeans. So I thought, maybe Chanel. Hence this." She executed a small turn, forgetting about Sally Jo, who almost toppled over. Heather didn't appear to notice.

"But now I'm thinking that's a little too, I don't know, suburban matron? Right now I'm leaning toward a more urban look." She pointed to a black pants suit on the bed. "What do you think?"

"So you'll take the other ones back?"

A voice floated up from the floor. "Not now, she can't," said Sally Jo.

"How come?" Kevin asked. He felt his blood pressure start to rise and loosened his tie before it could become a noose.

"Because I shortened them all."

Kevin looked at Heather. "What the hell were you thinking?"

"Just like a man," Heather said to Sally Jo with a dismissive shrug. "Kevin, you can't expect me to decide what outfit to pick out with the hems down around my ankles. Can you?"

He envisioned next month's Visa bill, already jacked up with purchases for the house: garbage pails, toilet scrubbers, full-length door mirrors, teakettles, and the like. Now a new media wardrobe for his wife. This snake thing was getting to be a major liability.

That night Heather, who had insomniac tendencies under the best of circumstances, insisted on going to bed right after dinner. But of course, she didn't go to sleep. She kept popping out, demanding that Connor turn off the sound on the PlayStation, then asking Kevin to turn off the Phillies game in the twelfth inning with the bases loaded. Every time he flushed a toilet, even on the other side of the house, he felt Heather's annoyance. The phone couldn't be unplugged—it could be the *Today* show, or the car service—so it was Kevin's job to answer it on the first ring. There was a press call from Botswana—he supposed that snakes had their advocates there, or maybe just enemies—and he tried to take a message, but Heather popped up and took the call herself. When the alarm rang at 3 A.M., she jumped up and started rummaging through her closet noisily. Kevin lifted his head and opened a sleepy eye.

"Oh, you're up," she said brightly. "I didn't sleep a wink! I guess it's just the adrenaline carrying me now."

Kevin couldn't say the same for himself. Hours later, when his secretary came running into his office to tell him that Heather was coming on after the next commercial, Kevin's forehead was resting on a volume of New Jersey case law from 1993. He blinked and walked slowly to the conference room, where all the secretaries and paralegals were gathered around. Heather had chosen, in the end, to wear the pink Chanel, and the interview began swimmingly. To Heather's obvious delight, Katie Couric told her she bore an uncanny resemblance to Reese Witherspoon. Then Katie's face became serious and she asked Heather what it was like to face a rattlesnake alone. Heather had gotten up to the Ming vase when there was a commercial break. "We'll talk about your judicial nightmare when we return," Katie said.

But when they came back from the break, Heather was off the couch, and Katie's face had turned from serious to grave. The words "Special Report" were superimposed on the bottom of the screen. "This just in," Katie said. "There's word from Washington about an ongoing hostage situation."

The secretaries at Brockman, Brockman & Liebowitz let out a collective groan.

The picture on the screen showed a government building, surrounded by a District of Columbia SWAT team, guns drawn. But Kevin was quite sure that, in the background, behind the set of the *Today* show, or possibly even in the greenroom, he could hear the plaintive tones of his wife. "But I'm not done," she said, before some technician remembered to turn off a microphone.

Kevin was barely back at his desk before his phone rang. "Did you see?" Heather's voice surged through the line. "I was booted!" He had to hold the headset about six inches from his ear. "Of all the days for some asshole to hold up the Department of Weights and Measures!" Heather began to sob.

"But," Kevin said, "Katie said you looked like Reese Witherspoon."

"I have a mind to bill them for the outfit!"

She vowed, later that night, that she wasn't going to fall for another big fancy TV-show invitation again—"I've played that game"—but when a producer from *Oprah* called on Thursday, she squealed with delight. A trip to Chicago, Kevin thought miserably. What poor government bureaucrats would have to be held at gunpoint this time?

It was Connor who heard it first. There was a drumbeat, first distant, then closer. It was followed by the deep wail of some brass instrument. "Turn that off," Connor said with irritation. "I can't hear." It was imperative, of course, that nothing interfere with Connor's enjoyment of *Dragonball Z,* his favorite Saturday cartoon show.

Kevin, reading the paper, arched an eyebrow. "Turn what off?" He didn't have the radio on and wasn't playing anything on the stereo.

"That stupid music."

Kevin listened closely and finally recognized the brass instrument as a tuba, originating somewhere outside the house. He walked into his living room, which afforded the best view of Giant Tortoise Drive, marveling, as he always did, at how he had come to be the owner of such a room. The room was entirely unused—unless you could consider consultations with a decorator a "use"—and sparsely but expensively furnished. He didn't quite get the point of having a room that nobody ever used—that Connor was absolutely forbidden to enter and that he too was discouraged from being in—or why Heather was so obsessed about how it was furnished. The room was grossly impractical, with a white rug, sofas covered with off-white muslin, and the couple's only pieces of what Heather called "real art," two large abstract oil paintings that the decorator had picked out for a grand apiece. Kevin had made a crack about the paintings in front of the decorator, something about having seen better art come home from kindergarten. That had been a mistake. The decorator had narrowed her eyes and looked at Heather coldly, and then, with pursed lips, started taking the paintings down. Heather practically had to beg the woman to hang them up again. Needless to say, the customary reward for his purchase of a big-ticket-item was not forthcoming that evening.

Kevin walked over to the window. The tubas were getting closer—clearly there were more than one—and together they sounded a low and mournful tune. He couldn't see anything yet, but he placed the music around the corner on Wild Egret Way. He stood and watched, hoping that Heather had fallen back asleep and wouldn't find him drinking coffee in the living room. Soon he was presented with the most astonishing view.

Several rows of horn players, wearing black suits, top hats, and white gloves, rounded the corner onto Giant Tortoise Drive. The tuba players were followed by trumpeters and saxophonists. In the middle of it all was a long narrow box—about one foot by six feet, Kevin judged—draped in purple-and-black bunting and held aloft by four people. Bringing up the rear were people wearing strange, garish hats and twirling bright, fringed umbrellas, alongside a set of drummers.

Kevin rubbed his eyes, clearing them of their morning gunk, and stared again. Yes, that's what he had seen, all right. And now he thought he recognized one of the people holding the box—the coffin, that's what it was—and the music: it was a dirge. And the person he recognized—it was, it had to be—the woman he'd nearly run over the day they'd first visited Galapagos Estates, the woman who had crossed Route 381, followed by all those crazy animals.

Kevin put his coffee down on the cherry end table and tried to open the living room window so he could better hear the music through the screen. His eyes remained riveted on the parade—for yes, it was a parade of sorts—while his hand searched for the window latch. But there was none. The living room window didn't open. The developer, in his infinite wisdom, had decided that people wouldn't need to open their windows, and that must have saved him a few bucks on screens. It made perfect sense, Kevin had to admit, since nobody ever went into these rooms in the first place.

Kevin raced to the front door and went outside to see what the commotion was about. It was—yes it was—a real New Orleans–style jazz funeral! Right here in Galapagos Estates! What a funny thing. And then, even more shocking, the funeral procession stopped right in front of their house. The musicians stood there facing him, keening their sad, slow lament, reminding him of Christmas carolers waiting to be invited in for hot cocoa. How strange.

That's when he noticed the signs: R.I.P. OUR RATTLESNAKE FRIEND and SNAKE KILLER. And racing alongside the strange musicians and parasol twirlers were television cameras, microphones, and reporters with notebooks.

Kevin thought he recognized the melody. "What a Friend We Have in Jesus," only the mourners were singing "What a friend we have in nature." Then he noticed another sign, whose message sent a chill through him: LEAVE EDEN.

My God, Kevin thought. They're having a New Orleans–style funeral for the snake. The one that Heather killed.

Suddenly he was rushed by a throng of reporters, all thrusting microphones, cameras, or notebooks into his face.

"Mr. Peters! What do you think about the funeral?"

"Mr. Peters! Mr. Peters! Can we have a comment?"

"Mr. Peters! Do you plan to move out of Galapagos Estates?"

"Mr. Peters! Where is your wife?"

Kevin's heart clattered inside his chest like a jackhammer. A minute ago he'd been sitting quietly in the living room, reading the paper, and now this crowd, this pack, this mob of bloodthirsty hyenas had him cornered. Right here, on the threshold of his own castle, where he should be safe. Fight or flight, Kevin would realize later when he relived the scene. It was as simple as that. He chose flight.

Kevin turned away from the pressing crowd and reached for the front door. He was prepared to go in, slam it, bolt it, and close all the blinds in the house. To hide.

But just then Heather came out. She was wearing a light blue, satin baby-doll nightgown, and she planted herself right in front of him, preventing him from opening the door. "What is this?" she asked. Her tone was accusing, as if the commotion was something that Kevin had purposely cooked up just to cheat her out of beauty sleep.

Then she took it in, all at once. The New Orleans music, the outlandish funeral attire, the signs, the press. Camera shutters snapped.

Later the pictures would show her with her mouth open and one of her boobs almost hanging out of her nightgown.

But Heather had, in just one week of her celebrity, developed some media savvy.

The hyenas were braying: "Heather! Heather! Give us a comment! What do you think!"

She satisfied them with a sound bite that would lead the local news that night and appear in large type as the next morning's headlines.

"I am the victim here!" Heather shouted. And with that, she reached right past her stunned husband, grabbed the handle of her front door, and marched into her house.

Chapter Fourteen

The Rolling Hills Nature Center, which Agnes ran, consisted of four rooms. The heart of her operation was her office, where she waged campaigns on behalf of endangered species, ordered snake food, paid bills, and even dealt with that necessary evil, booking children's birthday parties. Hanging from each wall and cluttering all horizontal spaces were calendars from the Nature Conservancy, the Sierra Club, and similarly green-minded organizations. The calendars, which came in various shapes and sizes, were all gifts from friends who thought they knew Agnes better than anyone else did. A dorm-sized refrigerator accommodated Agnes's two small dietary fetishes: Diet Snapple (she knew people who would be shocked at her use of aspartame) and the old-fashioned, pre-Nutrition Facts variety of Dannon yogurt, the good fattening kind, with all the goop at the bottom. In the corner, next to a metal desk piled high with papers, stood a fifteen-year-old photocopy machine, gigantic by today's standards and without any of the useful newer features. On the cover of the machine's scanning bed were a stapler, a paper clip dispenser, and scissors, which had to be moved whenever copies needed to be made—a setup even Agnes knew wasn't efficient.

But then organization had never been her strong suit. If she had more money, if the nature center had more money, she would hire a secretary, at least part-time. As it was, she alone had responsibility for changing the toner in the copier, opening mail, replacing lightbulbs, and putting the message on the answering machine whenever the center closed for a snow day or a holiday.

Next to Agnes's office was the Reptile Room, where two corn snakes lived a comfortable if uninspiring life and several turtles sloshed lazily about in oversized petri dishes. Here, Agnes kept all her books on reptiles, biology, conservation, Darwin, and related subjects. Next to that was the New Jersey Ecology Room, with five touch-screen computers, and then the Children's Learning Center, a lime-green space with a fancy jungle mural, a dry-erase board, art supplies, and a dozen small chairs in primary colors.

It was this room Agnes presided over now, only it was night, and there were no children. Childish people, perhaps, but all of them old enough to vote, many old enough to have voted for FDR. It was an emergency meeting of Friends of the Fauna, an organization dedicated to protecting and preserving the diversity of local wildlife, and Agnes was its leader. A thankless job. The Friends, who could agree in principle only that Birkenstocks were preferable to Manolo Blahniks, and that ponytails were appropriate for women and men, was not what anybody would call a Robert's Rules of Order type group. Boisterous and opinionated under any circumstances, they seemed even more out of control in these tiny chairs, as if perhaps the mildest breeze might topple them, and the discussion, into a free-for-all.

A thin man, about thirty-five, with a prominent Adam's apple and the scars of an unfortunate case of teenage acne, was holding up a copy of the *South Jersey Eagle* and ranting. "I can't believe it! Again! She stole the headlines again!"

The man, named Nate, was pointing to a picture of Heather in her blue baby-doll nightgown, in front of her McMansion, a photograph that covered a third of the area above the paper's fold. That Heather was clearly distraught, that her Barbie-doll face was distorted into something out of *Phantom of the Opera*, seemed to offer no consolation to Nate—or anyone else in the room, for that matter. There she was, in all her self-righteous glory, the words I AM THE VICTIM in thirty-six-point type. And the pictures of their New Orleans–style jazz funeral, a photo opportunity if there ever was one, were hidden inside the paper, on page B-26, with the jump.

"I told you we should have brought a horse," said a woman whose salt-and-pepper hair bore more than a small resemblance to a used Brillo pad. She was knitting a scarf with expensive heathery yarn and didn't look up when she spoke. Her voice was almost a whisper, and everybody had to lean a little forward—and risk teetering off their seats—to hear her.

"Diane," said Agnes, "I told you before. That would have been exploitive."

"But, it would have made for better pictures," Diane said. "And besides, a horse would have enjoyed it. The music and all. The attention. It would have been fun."

"And as you recall," Agnes said, "nobody volunteered for pail-and-shovel duty."

"Maybe," came another voice, "we should forget the snakes and champion some animals that people like. Eagles or something. Porpoises. Dolphins."

Agnes took a breath, deeper than strictly necessary. Okay, a sigh, an audible sigh. "Persephone," she said, struggling to keep her annoyance as understated as possible, "we don't have any porpoises or dolphins in Burlington County."

"But we do have eagles," Persephone chirped.

Sometimes these meetings gave Agnes a worse headache than the children's birthday parties, where she reluctantly allowed the grubby, cake-smeared wretches to pet her corn snakes. For a bunch of people whose politics were in the right place, it was surprising how exasperating they could be. Nobody, Agnes excepted, seemed to get the big picture. Some of the members, like Diane—who sent out a Christmas card every year featuring a picture of her two Yorkshire terriers, Yin and Yang, wearing silly Santa hats—only loved animals they thought were cute. Nate, on the other hand, didn't have any domestic animals at all. He was a hiker and a bird-watcher and, as an owner of a small advertising company, fancied himself an expert on the press. So it was natural that he would opine under the current circumstances. It was he, after all, who had dreamed up the idea of the jazz funeral and hired some musicians from the gospel band of a local AME church.

Agnes had never been fully convinced that the funeral was a good idea. Not that she had anything against publicity. It's just that the issues were subtle, especially when it came to a creature like *Crotalus horridus*. And when you created a media event, you were always handing control of your message over to, well, the media. A group of people that in general you couldn't trust any more than you could trust, say, a snake.

But distasteful or not, Persephone had hit upon a truth. Nobody liked rattlesnakes. That was the crux of the whole thing. Few people liked snakes even of the nonpoisonous variety. But rattlesnakes! All the PR in the world wasn't going to save their reputation. And until that happened, Heather Peters would keep coming out on top.

Agnes, on the other hand, had a certain undeniable affection for snakes. It had started when she was about twelve, a year or so after her brother died. Maybe it was the way her mother always tried to protect her after that, to keep her inside the house, in dresses, playing piano, in her stupid room with the stupid pink floral wallpaper, when she wanted to be outside, scampering about the woods. Yes, certainly that was what had started it all. Sneaking outside on a Sunday morning when she was supposed to be in church was certainly a pleasure. But bringing a pet snake into the house and hiding it under your bed, now, that was something else. Sweet adolescent rebellion. Agnes had to smile, thinking of it. And of the time her mother, God rest her soul, had accidentally come upon the snake while sweeping under Agnes's bed. "Well, that's it!" her mother had shrieked. "That's the end of maid service!" The snake, of course, had to go, and from then on, Agnes would clean her own room. Then, just to make sure that her point had been made, Agnes's mother forced her to go to Elsie Potter's charm school, where she spent the most boring twelve Saturdays of her entire life.

None of these measures, however, had done anything to staunch Agnes's affection for reptiles. Snakes began as a secret and forbidden pastime, but over time she grew to admire them on their own terms. She liked the way they moved, the way you could see whatever prey they'd swallowed move through their bodies like a lump under a mattress, the way they glistened and looked slimy and slippery but really weren't. It was fascinating to watch them, how they patiently observed their surroundings and then pounced. A snake's eyes always looked ancient, as if they were staring out of hundreds of millions of years of history. Agnes couldn't shake the feeling, when beholding a snake, that she was in the presence of a very wise and elemental being.

Rattlesnakes, of course, were a bit different. She didn't like rattlesnakes. Couldn't possibly. Not after what had happened so many years ago. But she protected them, their rights, on principle—even going so far as to help Richard Artemus track them in the field. They were animals too, part of the grand fabric of life, and the fact that their natural defense mechanism could inflict a slow, painful death—characterized by profuse bleeding, paralysis, loss of breath, and ultimately total kidney failure—well, that wasn't exactly the rattler's fault. Particularly when they didn't go out of their way to attack, humans at least, unless they'd been disturbed. Maybe nobody was going to put a picture of a timber rattlesnake on their Christmas card, but still, they deserved the same consideration as any other creature that walked or crawled or swam the earth. That was Agnes's belief.

A young woman whom Agnes had never noticed before raised her hand. When had she slipped into the room? She was astonishingly beautiful, thin and chic with blunt-cut black hair, and as out of place in this crowd as an orchid in a patch of dandelions. And who in this group waited for recognition before speaking?

"Yes?" Agnes said.

"Well," the young woman started, "I know I'm new here. But I do wonder if we're all perhaps focusing on the wrong thing."

"The wrong thing?"

"Well, perhaps this rattlesnake thing is just a battle we're not going to win, in the media anyway. I think maybe that lady—Persephone?—is right. Maybe we should focus on some other animals, animals that need our help. And that would take the attention away from this Heather Peters for a bit."

There were murmurs around the room, and Agnes couldn't help thinking that they were cooing over the woman's beauty as much as her ideas.

"What animals did you have in mind?" Agnes asked.

"Have you heard about that man who sells organic eggs?" the stranger said. "There's a rumor going around, something about salmonella. And I heard too that his chickens aren't really free-range. They're all cooped up in this tiny little shed, walking around in their own—pardon my language—shit. And he's passing it off as organic! Maybe we should look into that."

The murmurs had turned into a palpable stirring. Nate's Adam's apple bobbed several times, and it wasn't clear whether he was unsuccessfully framing an argument in his head or simply smitten beyond words.

"Harlan White," Agnes said. "The farmer."

"Yes," said the young woman. "That's his name, I believe. White."

"I don't think—" Agnes began.

"Oh, sure, I know him," said an elderly man sitting in the back of the room with his wife. The man was holding a pipe and sucking on it, though it wasn't lit, naturally, this being, like almost everywhere else in New Jersey and in fact America, a nonsmoking zone. The man and his wife looked a little brainier than the average member of the group, Agnes thought. Probably had regular tickets to the Philadelphia Philharmonic. "Seen him down at the general store. Hunts. Fishes. Probably a card-carrying member of the NRA. I never understood why he sold organic eggs."

"Supposedly organic," the young woman corrected.

"Maybe you're right," said Nate, who had recovered his ability to speak. "Maybe that's just the tack. Change the parameters of the debate. Reset the agenda."

"But—" said Agnes. They all looked at her. She stopped. She knew Harlan, of course, from way back. And he wasn't any particular friend, it was true. He did hunt, he did fish. Agnes and Harlan had never seen eye-to-eye on the subject of animals. And maybe she did blame him, a little, for that rattlesnake bite her brother, Kit, had gotten five decades earlier. After all, he'd been there that day, just as she had. And she'd seen him, with the stick, poking at the rattlesnake, just before it leaped—yes, leaped—and bit Kit in the leg. Agnes's intestines began to roil at the memory, and for the first time she realized how much intestines were like snakes, and how peristalsis, however invisible inside a human body, was a process that connected Homo sapiens to their reptilian ancestors. A small dot of sweat broke on her forehead.

"Excuse me," she said.

Agnes ran to the bathroom. The pain in her gut made her double over. Was it merely the mention of Harlan White that had made her feel so ill? Or was it something else, some other instinct? If so, she couldn't imagine what. When the pain passed, she looked in the mirror, washing her hands, and then threw a little cold water on her face. She was surprised to see how pale she looked. And really old. When had she gotten so old? Which made her think again of Harlan. And then she remembered what she had been thinking, what she had been about to say. Yes, she was about to tell them, his politics are all wrong. But he was also as honest as the day was long.

When she got back, Agnes found the group vibrating with energy and resolve.

"I agree," Nate was saying, nodding vigorously. "I absolutely agree."

It was not like Nate to agree, Agnes thought. But then there usually wasn't such an attractive young woman to agree with. Leroy Adams, the group's most radical member, who'd been strangely quiet this evening, had his chin cradled in his fists and was listening to the proceedings intently, like a judge in chambers.

"Then that's the plan," the young woman said. "I'll take care of everything."

"Take care of what?" Agnes asked.

"Dana's going to do her own little inspection of Harlan White's henhouse," Nate said, winking awkwardly.

The old man in the back of the room explained. "He has a very identifiable car. Light blue '72 Ford pickup with a white cap and rust all around the driver's-side door. A real antique. And he likes to fish. Pond near my house. I'll call Dana next time he's out there, and she'll go over with a camera. Document the whole thing. Liberate the chickens, if need be."

"Sony digital camcorder," Dana said helpfully.

Agnes opened her mouth to object. "But I don't think—"

"Forget those damn rattlesnakes," Persephone said. "They're yesterday's news. Move on."

But it was Leroy Adams, concentrating fiercely, who worried Agnes the most.

Agnes felt her intestines clench again. She bolted for the toilet. By the time she came out, the lime-green room had entirely emptied. Someone, in fact, had even turned off the lights. Agnes walked to the front door of the nature center and looked out into the parking lot. She saw two sets of taillights leaving. Only her VW Bug remained.

Chapter Fifteen

"You did *what*?"

It was Atlantic City again. Barstad still had scratches and bruises on his arms and legs, but at least he was back where it was safe. He'd managed to finesse his story with Barbara last weekend, to create an explanation for coming home full of abrasions after a land-prospecting trip to Maryland. He'd stayed in one of those cheap two-story motels (he told her) and had fallen down the stairs at night while looking for the ice machine. No, he wasn't going to sue. The guy who owned the motel was the same guy who was selling the land he'd gone down to look at.

Getting out this time had been even easier; he didn't even have to lie. He was a judge in the Miss America pageant. Not bad work if you could get it, all in all—and a good networking opportunity. He told Barbara it didn't make sense for her to come because the judges were so tightly scheduled he'd have to ignore her the whole time. Naturally he didn't mention to Barbara that he was going to eke out a minute here and there for his mistress.

But that was turning out to be hard. There were competitions and stunts for days leading up to the main event on Saturday night. Judges were handed a ream of rules and regulations the size of a telephone book. Lawyers were all over the whole thing, Jack could see. The judging instructions they gave him had fine print that made the legal language in Barstad's own sales contracts look like something out of *Dick, Jane, and Sally.*

He was sitting next to the bed, going over the rules for judging the talent competition, when Dana emerged from the bathroom enveloped in a lavender-scented cloud of steam and nothing else. Well, that was one way to get a man's nose out of the fine print. Then she climbed onto the foot of the bed and faced him, finally telling him the little "surprise" she'd been teasing him about since they got to Atlantic City. What did she say? He must have heard wrong. Maybe the lavender scent had addled his brain. Or was it the sight of those perfect breasts?

"I infiltrated that group," Dana repeated. "Friends of the Fauna." She stretched one leg out provocatively and gently nestled her foot into Barstad's crotch.

"You?" Barstad snorted. "Posing as a nature lover?"

"I like fauna," she said, pretending to pout, her voice just on the edge of baby talk.

Barstad smiled and wondered how he would ever be able to rank one Miss America contestant over another. None of them could compare to Dana. "So? What did you learn?"

"It's not just what I learned," she said. "It's what I did."

"Did?"

"Oh, you know, just a little simple agenda swapping. They're whining and crying like a bunch of babies about Heather Peters and all the damn press she's getting, and I just suggested—nicely, politely, of course—that they place their attention somewhere else. Like on Harlan White's shit-encrusted henhouse."

Jack whistled appreciatively.

"But that's not all."

"What else?"

"A little stealth run."

"What?"

"I'm going to go over there, to Harlan's, and mess things up a little."

"Mess things up?"

"In the henhouse. Spread some chicken shit around. Foul the nest, as they say."

"You?" He tried to imagine her in overalls, up to her ankles in chicken shit, but the picture kept dissolving in his brain. Cunning, yes. Subterfuge, yes. But rummaging through a chicken coop? His Dana?

"And there's more," she said.

Jack raised an eyebrow. "Oh?"

"I'm going to bring a video camera. We'll have some nice footage, afterward, of all the crap."

Barstad could see that Dana had spun herself a clever little plan, and that she was immensely proud of it. Guerilla tactics, media manipulation. All good thinking, granted. But breaking and entering? It was true that Barstad felt that the law was malleable and, with the right lawyers, a sort of optional guide to human interaction, yet he knew that Dana's plan could—in less generous eyes—be seen as a felony. For the first time it occurred to him that perhaps he ought to be a little protective of this sublime creature. He suddenly pictured her as a daughter, a risk-taking, storm-the-world kind of girl in her twenties, dipping into waters that might be darker, murkier, more dangerous than she appreciated. It was a disturbing thought, especially with her naked like that.

"But Dana," he began.

"Don't you see?" she said. "It's brilliant, if I must say so myself. Two birds, one stone. We screw Harlan and stop all our animal-loving friends from making a federal case over this stupid snake thing."

The snake thing. It had moved up high on Barstad's list of problems. Aerial shots of Galapagos Estates with voice-overs about dangerous rattlesnakes, that little blond Peters bitch spreading hysteria everywhere she went. One of Barstad's zoning-board cronies, Mike Kawalcek, had even made a joke about it the other night, when Barstad had taken him to a late-season Phillies game—part of the oiling of the gears to launch Galapagos Phase 2. "Hear there are some serpent problems over in Eden," Kawalcek had said. "Been eating forbidden fruit?" he'd kidded, jabbing Barstad with his elbow. Barstad had laughed it off, but it looked like Kawalcek had guessed that he'd fudged his last environmental impact statement and might even have some inkling about Dana. Barstad's problems never seemed to end: traffic, water, sewer, whether that son of a bitch Harlan White would ever sell. Now snakes. And the possibility that his secret mistress wasn't so secret.

"Well," Barstad said to Dana. "You certainly have thought of everything."

He gazed at her and noticed that her nipples were hard; clearly being bad turned her on. Barstad had forty-five minutes until the Miss America contestants took their annual stroll down the Atlantic City boardwalk. He leaned over, kissed Dana, and allowed her to pull him onto the bed.

But even with her legs straddling his neck acrobatically, her cunt as wet and dense as a tropical rainforest, and her nipples stiff as bullets, his dick couldn't get any higher than half-mast. It was that damn thought of her as a daughter. It was the first time Barstad failed to perform with her—hell, she could make the pope hard—and he was humiliated. It made him think of his childhood dog, Frank, who peed on the rug when he got old and then would hide under a coffee table in shame. His parents had put the poor dog to sleep not long after that started.

Dana extracted her legs, sat up against the headboard, and looked at him with a mixture of pity and contempt. "That's okay," she said. "It happens to everybody."

Then she reached down between her thighs and touched her own button, expertly, and with her other hand fondled her breast. Barstad looked on with awe. He had never seen a woman give herself an orgasm. He couldn't imagine Barbara doing it, in front of him no less. Not in a million years. Dana came loudly, without any apparent embarrassment, in what felt to Barstad like a demonstration of his own irrelevance.

Now that the general store had shown its true colors, Harlan no longer felt like hanging out on the bench. Hadn't really been much of a point in a while anyway, since none of the guys Harlan liked happened by. But even if his own rear end was the only one to have warmed the bench lately, at least it was a tie, a tie to history and the community and the remote possibility of companionship. Now the only place he felt truly comfortable was on his own porch glider. Sad.

Then there was the strange deal with Heather Peters. First the papers, then TV, now everywhere you looked: the amazing lady who had single-handedly killed a rattlesnake! Only he (and Mrs. Peters herself) knew the truth—that she was as incapable of killing a rattlesnake as he was of doing cartwheels up Mount Everest. A coward was what she was, and a bossy little bitch. But he supposed that the way things had turned out, it was just as well. After all, it was Heather Peters, and not he, who was facing charges of killing endangered wildlife. And it was she who faced all the additional charges he'd read about in the paper: failing to heed a game officer, resisting arrest, assaulting an officer. Not that any of that would have happened to him. It was that lady's damn personality that got her into so much trouble. She was a walking land mine.

Sure, it irked him that she took credit for his bravery, but he was glad she hadn't told the truth and named him as the rattlesnake killer. Because the media circus that had sprung up around the case would have done him in. Harlan abhorred attention. He didn't even like it, as a boy, when his parents and aunts and uncles sang "Happy Birthday" to him. He could see it in his mind, all those years back, his mother walking slowly into the dining room with a chocolate cake, little candles marking his years plus one for good measure, all eyes on him. Being the center of attention, even for something as basic as his own birthday, made him feel like he was up on a stage, naked.

He was sitting at that same dining room table now, only it had been ages since anyone had carried in a birthday cake. In a way, everything remained the same—the fancy cherry sideboard, the chandelier that dripped pieces of crystal, the glass-covered bookcase crammed with his mother's old cookbooks, the old Philco he was listening to now, which still worked just fine. Everything the same, except his parents were missing—his father, who'd died in 1964, and his mother, who'd made it all the way to 1972. Harlan had never had the heart—or the need—to part with any of the old furniture, and so it sat, like relics in a museum, the Museum of Harlan White's Early Life, a museum without admission or guides and not a single visitor but him.

There were no Sunday dinners in the dining room anymore. What would be the point, with just one mouth to feed? So now the dining room table was merely a place where he spread out all his bills and his correspondence and notices from the town and whatnot, and where he worked on the puzzle of who to pay first and who second and how to make the money stretch. There was one stack of bills that absolutely had to be paid: the telephone, the electric, the infernal tax bill. Then there were the bills with some give, lots of give in fact, like the hospital bill from a year ago when he'd fallen down in front of the Stop & Shop and some people had called an ambulance even after he'd tried to wave them off. There'd been the emergency-room charge, the doctor's charge, and a bunch of other tests, including a very expensive MRI. Medicare paid for some of it but not all. The doctor's bills came every month, with increasingly dire threats, and every time Harlan looked at them he thought to himself: But I never asked to go to that hospital, I never wanted to be examined, I told them not to give me an MRI.

Then there was a third pile, bills that had to be paid but not necessarily in full. Like the Visa. He couldn't believe he'd actually gone down that crooked plastic road, but here it was with a balance of $17,693, and growing steadily, inexorably, like a tumor. At first he'd convinced himself that it was an investment. He needed to tear down his daddy's old henhouse when he decided to go organic, and he didn't have the cash to build a new one. But then it had also come in handy for other things, like fixing his old Ford pickup, which he'd bought from some of the money that came when his mother died. It had been a good truck, a comfortable truck. But it was old, and things kept breaking down. It was in the shop right now, in fact, because of a rattle he'd been hearing coming from the front right wheel, and the heater didn't work and winter was coming. You thought maybe you could live cheap, sleeping in a house that had been paid for decades ago and driving a thirty-year-old truck. But the world just kept reaching out, slapping you with bills.

Across from the stacks of bills was another pile of papers, the letters from Jack Barstad, each with a progressively higher offer for his land. Each month, when the Visa bill came in, Harlan would look over at the Barstad letters as if they might hold his salvation. It was simple, in a way. Problem and solution, weight and counterweight. The easiest way to dig out of debt. But then he'd look around the room, look at the old buffet and glass-faced shelves, and think of his parents and all the history in his house, and he'd vow: Hell, the only way I'm leaving this place will be feet first. Salvation from the devil, that was what those letters offered.

He was staring at the Visa bill, wondering how much he would pay this time, when the phone rang. It was a black rotary wall phone in the kitchen, the only phone in the house, and its solid, mechanical, old-fashioned clang was the same one he'd been hearing his whole life. Harlan walked slowly into the kitchen. He didn't believe, like most people, that you had to leap up and fly headfirst just because someone rang a bell at you. Just as with most everything else, he didn't rush. If it was important, they'd wait.

"Hello," came the voice. "Is this Harlan White?"

"Yes." He didn't like phone calls like this, calls that sounded like someone was working a list.

"This is Rodney Campbell of the *South Jersey Eagle*."

"Sorry," said Harlan. "Already subscribe." He hung up and started back toward the dining room. It rang again.

"Mr. White, wait! I'm not trying to sell you anything. I'm a reporter. I just want to talk to you. About a story."

"The Heather Peters thing, I suppose," Harlan said.

"Why yes! Exactly. She told me that you'd cleaned it up for her—the snake, that is—and that you told her about it being endangered and all."

Harlan suddenly realized that he'd been caught, hook, line, and sinker. Why had he opened his fat mouth? Why hadn't he just said he wouldn't talk to the press, or that his dinner was getting cold? Or just hung up? The man had put a hook into the water, and Harlan had bitten, like a stupid bulge-eyed perch. And now he was on the line, about to be reeled in.

It must have been those letters from Barstad, which had made him think about Galapagos Estates. Or maybe, deep down, he wanted to set the record straight. He was the hero who'd killed the rattlesnake, not her.

But, shit. He didn't want anyone to know that. Shut up, he told himself. Shut up, shut up, shut up. Don't say another stupid thing.

The reporter was yapping away when Harlan thought he heard a noise outside. Yes, he did, the sound of a car door slamming. Even though it was a couple of hundred yards down the road, it was a rare-enough sound on Harlan's farm. Could it be Sam or one of the other mechanics at the shop bringing his Ford back? It was possible. But then he'd have heard two cars. His own, being dropped off, and another one, to take Sam back. Was there a second car? He couldn't tell. At least not with the phone to his ear. He wished the stupid reporter would just shut up so he could concentrate.

"So I was wondering if, maybe, tomorrow I could come by," the reporter said.

"Yeah, sure," Harlan said. "Fine." Anything to shut him up. He hung up and walked quickly into the living room, where his shotgun hung over the fireplace. The phone rang again. Harlan didn't answer it. He didn't have time. Probably the damn reporter again, asking for directions. Well, he could just buy himself a Burlington County map and look it up. Right now Harlan needed to look, to listen. And if there was someone outside, he didn't want them to hear him talking on the phone.

He stood by the window, looking out to his backyard, where the sky had just turned a rich shade of cobalt, that last stop on the color wheel before dusk would dissolve into the color of India ink. He saw nothing, nobody. He strained to hear, but he'd left the radio on in the dining room. A car commercial. Come in now, and pick up an '04! End-of-the-year clearance before the '05's come in! Zero percent financing! Extraordinary values! Only three days left!"

Oh shut up, Harlan thought. He felt his heart thumping double-time and realized that this emotion—this fear, excitement, whatever you wanted to call it—was a rare event. He'd always prided himself on being calm, unflappable, but suddenly he saw that it didn't mean a thing, except that his heart had shrunk up like a hard little raisin, that he'd closed himself off to just about everything. In a flash he saw his life, small and pathetic, nothing to make his heart pound, ever, nothing but bills and radio commercials to remind him that he was still alive. He might as well be a piece of the furniture. His life was so empty that a simple noise outside his house had him acting like a crazy person, standing in his TV room and looking out into the dark, holding a shotgun.

It could be anything. There were people around these days, lots and lots of people, and lots and lots of cars. Developments, stores, restaurants. Maybe the sound just carried farther than he thought. Sure, that was it. He was just an old fool.

Harlan turned away from the window and sank into his favorite chair, an old La-Z-Boy. He set the gun down. The radio had finally stopped trying to hawk things and had settled into a Frank Sinatra song. Harlan felt his heart begin to slow. He pulled the lever that made the footrest of his La-Z-Boy come up, and he stretched his legs. He closed his eyes, heard the very faint sound of crickets, the last few that hadn't died yet.

And then, distinctly, he heard a car door slam again, and this time the sound of an engine starting and car wheels crunching gravel.

It had been a splendid September afternoon, sunny and bright but with a hint of autumn in the air, and following fifty Miss America contestants wearing bathing suits and high heels down the Atlantic City boardwalk wasn't bad work, if you could get it. If you could call it work. There'd been little of consequence for a judge to note. Miss New Jersey had been cracking gum—she'd get points off for that—and Miss Georgia had twisted her ankle and lurched awkwardly but managed to avoid an embarrassing fall. Barstad and a few other judges had muttered quietly about how that should affect her score. A few people thought that she demonstrated character by going on with the show and not crying, and even suggested that she get extra points for showing grace under pressure. Barstad, however, subscribed to the notion that Miss Georgia was a klutz, best kept off the runway. Compared with Dana, he thought, she was a country bumpkin in a potato sack.

Ah, Dana. Barstad pictured her naked and pouty on the hotel bed. Then he winced, thinking of his problem rising to the occasion. That was rare, in his experience. He hoped it wasn't a sign of aging, or some reaction to their recent bike trip. And, now that he thought of it, Dana's reaction had been strange. She'd said it was okay, but the way she masturbated like that, right in front of him, was—to say the least—a bit disconcerting. Well, he'd make it up to her. He'd pick up a diamond necklace in one of the hotel gift shops. He'd slip it on her, take off all her clothes—just leaving the necklace—and then make love to her. If he couldn't get it up then, well, they might as well take him out and shoot him.

Barstad remembered to put the necklace on his corporate card.

Maryanne would see it, but Barbara wouldn't. That's what mattered. The saleswoman, a buxom woman who looked old enough to have worked the gift shop on the *Titanic,* complimented him on his good taste. And she was the soul of discretion, studiously avoiding the words "wife" and "lady friend" and sticking with the more neutral "her" and "she." She tucked the necklace into a small turquoise box, clearly meant to resemble one from Tiffany's. Smart marketing, Barstad thought. He put the box into his jacket pocket and walked to the elevator. When he pressed "up," he wished he had a button like that to operate his dick.

While swiping his key into the electronic pad, Barstad mentally rehearsed what he would say when he saw Dana. "I've got a surprise!" (Too ordinary, too apologetic.) "Honey, I'm home!" (Ironic and witty, but it might remind her what a fuddy-duddy he was.) "Oh, chicken-coop girl?" (Appropriately private, but dumb.)

He settled on the cool, playboy-like "Hey, baby" as he opened the door.

Dana wasn't on the bed.

Barstad walked over to the bathroom, the only other place she might be. Another shower? Another bath? Was she servicing herself again? "Baby?" he said again, slowly opening the bathroom door.

The bathroom was empty.

Barstad felt like an idiot looking in the small closet. It wasn't like she'd be standing there planning to say *boo*. That's when he noticed that her long black dress, the one with the plunging neckline, which she was planning to wear to the pageant, was also gone.

Chapter Sixteen

Mrs. Gupnick, the principal at Pine Hills Elementary, had decided that things had sufficiently settled in during lunch hour to allow the third- and fourth-graders, who took their meal at the same time, to choose their own tables. For the first few weeks of school, each class was assigned a specific table in the cafeteria. But after that, if they could prove to the lunch ladies that they could "behave appropriately," they would be allowed the privilege of open seating. For most kids, this was a particularly jubilant day on the school calendar. Cliques that had been wisely broken up at the end of each school year were allowed to flourish again, at least within the context of a thirty-five-minute lunch.

On the menu that day was the food known throughout the ages as mystery meat. It was a rubbery patty, about three eighths of an inch thick, marinated with grease, and it smelled like a cross between a burning tire and socks at the bottom of the hamper in summer. Connor liked it anyway. It was, in fact, one of his favorite cafeteria dishes. It came with whipped potatoes (actually reconstituted flakes from potatoes harvested during Jimmy Carter's administration) and a beet-colored slice of candied apple (more candy than apple, but enough to satisfy some basic government criteria on serving fruits and vegetables to kids), and it could be counted on to keep Connor's appetite at bay at least until three-fifteen, when he would settle down to a Pop-Tart and some serious video-game violence in the comfort of his own home.

Connor paid the cash-register lady, picked up his tray, and marched out into the cafeteria. He walked toward the table where he usually sat—the table set aside for Miss Kindermack's class—but found it populated by a strange group of fourth-grade girls. He stood there, his eyes bulging, not quite able to process what was going on. Then he remembered the announcement that had been made on the PA system that morning, about open seating in the cafeteria. So that's what it meant.

Connor's eyes scanned the room, searching for a familiar face. He spotted two boys, Billy and Thomas, from Miss Kindermack's class. He moved a foot or two in their direction before remembering that they were the cool kids. And sure enough, he saw that they were indeed surrounded by the other alpha males of Pine Hills Elementary, trading sandwiches and snorting like the cruelly popular high school football players they would become. When Connor caught Thomas's eye, he was rewarded with a look of withering contempt. Thomas leaned down and said something to Billy, and the two of them—staring at Connor with malicious smiles—began to cackle.

Connor spun around. Most of the faces were new to him. The few kids he did know—from his class—seemed happily ensconced with friends. A few tables away, he saw Chloe, the girl he liked to chase on the playground, and he looked hopefully in her direction. She quickly turned her head, pretending not to see him. He continued to scan the room, beginning to panic, as other kids with trays walked past him and found seats.

It began to dawn on him: he was in the middle of a gigantic game of musical chairs. The kids with the bagged lunches got to the tables first. The other kids, the ones buying lunch, raced to get in line and, while they were waiting, memorized the seating arrangements so as not to be eliminated. And then there were the kids like Connor, with no strategy and no friends, who stood in the middle of the cafeteria, scanning the room miserably, as the grease on their mystery meat began to congeal. Kids like Connor, who had failed to use their time in line effectively.

Connor, in fact, had been daydreaming in line about his mother's recent fame, and how that might lead to him meeting some cool Hollywood stars.

But now he was getting desperate. In addition to the social ramifications of standing there holding his tray and showing all the kids in Pine Hills Elementary what a loser he was, there was the simple fact that he was really, really hungry. He had to make a move, some move. He walked to the first table he saw with an empty seat and started to put his tray down, but one of the kids sitting there—a fourth-grader—quickly stretched his arm out, blocking the tray, and shouted, "Saved!" Connor spotted another empty seat a few tables down and rushed there, but the same thing happened.

Finally he looked across the room and saw the table closest to the trash bins. There were three or four seats available. He exhaled, feeling palpable relief. But as he approached, he recognized the other kids. They were the special-ed kids, the ones pulled out of class and sent to the Resource Room. Some of them even spent the whole day in a separate room. There was one boy, with strange protruding eyes, who was accompanied by an aide. It was the aide who now smiled at Connor and offered him a seat.

Connor sat down, knowing that in the intricate game of Pine Hills Elementary musical chairs, he had lost, and lost badly. He took his knife, cut off a piece of mystery meat, and took a bite. It tasted awful. He took a second bite. Even worse. He tried the candied apple, but even that tasted cloying and too much of cinnamon.

He suddenly felt a change in the molecular structure of the air, indicating that a popular kid was in the vicinity. He looked up and saw that it wasn't just one popular kid but two—Billy and Thomas, coming to throw their garbage in the trash bins. Billy looked at Connor and mouthed the word *retard*. He didn't say it aloud because that, of course, would get him into trouble.

But later, in the boys' room, without any grown-ups around, Billy exercised no such restraint. "Retard," he began to chant. "Retard. Connor is a retard."

Even in the privacy of the bathroom stall there was no relief. Connor had to pee but couldn't possibly consider using one of the urinals, so he went into the stall and pretended to make a bowel movement. But knowing that on the other side of the wall there were boys, who were his enemies, waiting for him to come out, made Connor's bladder freeze. He sat there hating himself, hating school, wondering if he could possibly pee before the bell rang, when suddenly something long, black, and rubbery flew over the top of the door and landed at his feet.

He screamed, and the boys outside let out a collective howl of laughter. The thing that had landed next to him was a toy snake.

Then the bell rang, and the boys' room emptied of everyone but Connor. He sat there, staring at the snake. He tried to urinate, but the more he tried, the more impossible it was. Finally he heard the door of the boys' room open. "Connor Peters?" a voice asked. Thank God it was a grown-up voice, that of the assistant principal, Mr. Padlovsky.

"Yes?" he said quietly.

"It's time for class, son. Everything okay?"

Connor came out of the stall. His bladder was still full. He allowed Mr. Padlovsky to lead him to Miss Kindermack's room and waddled after him, keeping his knees as close together as he could.

The ultimate humiliation didn't come until recess, when one of the boys, out of earshot of recess monitors, called him "retard" again. Connor wet his pants, and at the same time huge, salty tears poured from his eyes. The playground went silent and the children gave him a wide berth, the way people do on the subway when a wild-eyed and urine-stained wretch enters the car.

Heather had been out for a day of waxing. Her Land Rover had needed waxing, her legs had needed waxing, and her eyebrows and her blond peach-fuzz mustache had needed waxing. It was one of those sparkling fall days, and now her SUV gleamed and she felt clean, almost virginal, purged of all errant body hair. To top it off, she'd stopped at the mall and hit Bloomingdale's on the way home. There'd been a special on Clinique. Buy fifty dollars' worth of makeup and get a free tote bag filled with moisturizer, toner, antiwrinkle cream, and eye cream. The tote bag was even cute. Black-and-clear vinyl, very chic.

It had been nice, Heather thought, to treat herself. Her sudden involvement with politics had been quite draining, and her media schedule—ridiculous! She drove into Galapagos Estates and up Giant Tortoise Drive nervously, prepared for an onslaught of reporters. But there were none. Thank God. Except, well, did that mean she was yesterday's news? They would come back, wouldn't they? There'd be more appearances? More invitations? Her fifteen minutes of fame had been exhausting, granted, but she wasn't quite ready for it to be over.

Heather went into the house, dropped her Bloomingdale's bags, and poured herself a glass of iced tea. Then she dialed Answer Call for phone messages.

There were two. The first was from Kevin, wanting to know if she'd gotten the Visa bill yet. Heather's newly waxed eyebrows knitted themselves into a knot of annoyance. Why was he bothering her about that from work? Was he still worked up about those little outfits she'd bought to go on the *Today* show? She looked guiltily over at her Big Brown Bag. Kevin wasn't going to like that. Well, she'd just hide it. Put all the makeup away and stow the Bloomie's bag at the bottom of the recycling before Kevin got home.

The other call was from Miss Kindermack. Heather sighed, reached for a pen, and sat down. Certainly this was going to involve some kind of chore. What did she have in mind now? A field trip to Batsto Village? A dreadful day of watching blacksmiths forge nails for Revolutionary War reenactors? Or a trip to the Camden Aquarium, so they could all get mugged in the parking lot? Then suddenly she remembered. Halloween was coming up. Heather must be in charge of the party.

But the tone of Miss Kindermack's voice was sad, drained, even apologetic. "Mrs. Peters," she said. "Something happened to Connor at school today. I think you should come down."

Come down? Just what she needed! After waxing day! She'd been planning to sit out on the patio—it was so lovely—and read the copy of *People* that she'd "borrowed" from the waxing place. (She couldn't very well leave it there, could she, halfway through an article about Kirstie Alley's pork-out?) Well, Heather thought, this was probably something that could be taken care of by phone. They were always exaggerating everything—teachers were and therapists were—always worried about children's fragile self-esteem. Connor probably fell down at recess. That was it. He had a boo-boo on his knee. The school, worried about litigation, was calling her to let her know, so she wouldn't slap a lawsuit on them a week later if the boo-boo got infected.

Heather slipped her cordless under her arm—she'd make the call as soon as she got settled—picked up her *People* magazine and her iced tea, and walked out to the patio. She took the most comfortable chair, the chaise longue, and stretched out her legs to admire them. It had been nippy at night, but it was still warm enough to go bare-legged during the day, and she wanted to hold on to whatever tan she still had going into winter. She opened up the magazine and started looking for the Kirstie Alley story. Mechanically, she punched the number of Pine Hills Elementary into the phone.

One of the secretaries was just answering when out of the corner of her eye, Heather noticed some movement. When she saw the baby rattlesnakes—three of them!—she screamed, tossing the phone, the magazine, and the iced tea into the air.

It was just like the dream. Except there were three baby snakes, not one, and of course they were not talking. And this time, unlike with the first rattlesnake, she was all alone. There was no handyman in the basement, no handyman to kill these snakes, bag them, and clean up the mess, along with the thousands of shards of glass from dropping the iced tea. She'd been embarrassed to call Harlan White ever since that first newspaper interview with Rodney Campbell. But she suddenly remembered his words. The snakes. She mustn't frighten them.

Heather hiked herself up the lounge chair and tried to make herself as small as possible. She held herself perfectly still, hoping to blend into the background. Maybe, if she didn't move an iota, the snakes wouldn't notice her and would go back to wherever they'd come from.

But unfortunately, when she'd screamed and dropped her iced tea and the cordless phone, the phone had skidded right in their direction and landed on one. That was bad enough. Even if the phone had miraculously managed to kill that snake, which even Heather could see was unlikely, the other two would surely be angry, and attack her. But then, compounding matters, came the disembodied, somewhat nasal voice of Mrs. Haggarty. "Hello? Hello? Mrs. Peters?"

To the snakes, Heather thought, this must seem as strange as her dream in which the serpent had stood tall and talked. She also made a mental note: they must have caller ID at the school. Maybe they'll send somebody.

"Mrs. Peters? Is everything okay?"

Heather studied the snakes, their reaction to the phone. Then she focused all her powers of concentration—which were considerable, even under normal circumstances—and willed Mrs. Haggarty to hang up the fucking phone and call the police.

It seemed to work, the first part, at any rate. The voice on the other end of the phone stopped.

Heather sat there, scrunched up and terrified. If only, she thought, her own PR were true. If only she were the fearless snake killer that she had told Rodney Campbell and Katie Couric she was. If only Harlan were here, fixing the automatic garage-door opener, which Kevin had been complaining about.

Lacking the courage to either fight or flee, she waited.

She began to go through the stages that Elisabeth Kubler-Ross had attributed to dying—denial, anger, bargaining, and depression—and got stuck in bargaining. If only the snakes would go away, Heather thought, I will be a good wife, a good mother, a good neighbor, an upstanding, law-abiding member of the community. If only the snakes would go away, I will never want another material thing in my life. She squeezed her eyes tight, making her silent bargain. I'll cut up my charge cards, take the makeup back to Bloomingdale's. I'll give half the clothes in my closet to charity. The size 4s, anyway.

Heather opened her eyes and, wincing, looked down. Damn. That hadn't done it.

She sucked in a hard, impatient gulp of air and scrunched her eyes shut again. If only the snakes would go away, she thought, upping the ante, I'll be more considerate of my husband. I'll appreciate how he supports me, stop complaining about where he leaves his shoes. I'll even—she wrinkled her nose, imagining the indignity—give him a blow job once in a while. If only the snakes would go away.

She looked down again. Gone!

A miracle. But . . . yuck. Did she really have to make good on that last promise?

Cautiously, Heather put her feet on the ground. There was glass everywhere. And she didn't 100 percent trust that the snakes had really gone away. Maybe they'd snuck closer, by her chair.

But the patio was clear.

She ran into the house, slammed the French doors, and bolted them. Then, safe, she finally exhaled—and realized she hadn't breathed properly since the snakes had arrived. She looked for the phone, and remembering that it was outside, walked into the great room to pick up the phone by the sofa. But there was only silence. The phone, not hung up, was disengaged.

She looked for her purse, which had her cell phone in it. A great and terrible thing had happened. And yet, like the tree falling in the forest, nobody had been there to witness it. How brave she'd been! How utterly fearless! She had to call Kevin.

She found her purse and scrambled in it for the phone. The battery indicator showed that the battery was low. She had only pressed the first four digits of Kevin's number when the phone beeped and went dead.

So she did the only thing she could think of. She opened the refrigerator, took out a bottle of chardonnay, and poured a glass. Then she kicked off her shoes, went into the living room, lay down on the sofa, and let the room's regenerative whiteness wash over her.

Kevin was cleaning up after dinner, rinsing dishes and putting them in the dishwasher, and Heather was talking to his back. It was seven o'clock and Connor should have been doing his homework. But Kevin and Heather both felt so bad about what had happened in school that day that they didn't have the heart to make him open up his books. They said he could play with his video games but asked him to use his old Nintendo 64 system back in his bedroom so they could talk.

"Three of them," Heather was saying. "Three! Not one. Not two. But three snakes."

"I know," Kevin said. "You mentioned that."

"But they were babies."

"You mentioned that too."

"I think they know their mother was killed here. And they're coming back to haunt me."

Kevin turned around, wiped his hands on his pants, and folded his arms across his chest. "That's the most idiotic thing I've heard you say for at least"—he glanced up at the kitchen clock—"five minutes."

"No. It's not. I went online. And I looked up timber rattlesnakes. And I discovered that they have their babies in late August, and that the babies can follow their mothers by scent."

"So now you're an expert on rattlesnakes." He turned back to the sink, banging plates and mugs into their various dishwasher slots with more force than was strictly necessary.

"Don't patronize me, Kevin. And guess what. I found out something else."

"What?"

"They've always lived here."

"Who?"

"The snakes! They've been here for years. Before there even was a Galapagos Estates. This pond. Walden Pond. It's been a rattlesnake den for years."

"That's ridiculous."

"The *South Jersey Eagle*. It's online. You can search it. I looked it all up. There were zoning hearings, and it came up. All these crazy, vegetarian animal fanatics came to the hearing and complained."

"You mean like the people who put on that stupid rattlesnake funeral?"

"I guess so," Heather said. "But Jack Barstad filed some kind of environmental, um, environmental—"

"Impact statement," Kevin said. It disgusted him that his wife couldn't come up with the phrase. She spent so much time being cute, getting her legs waxed and buying expensive knickknacks for the house, that she didn't have much time or brainpower left to learn the words for things.

"Right! Environmental impact statement. And he said, in that environmental impact statement, that there were no rattlesnakes. So the zoning board passed it."

"Probably had a few of them in his pocket," Kevin said. "That's the way it works."

"Rattlesnakes? In his pocket?"

"No. Members of the zoning board. Listen, can we talk about Connor for a minute?"

"Wait!" Heather said. "This is important. We're not safe in our own home. There are rattlesnakes that live right in that pond. In our backyard. And that bastard, Barstad, probably knew all along. Hey, don't put the knives in the dishwasher like that. Put them downward. Someone will cut themselves."

"Here," said Kevin, slamming the dishwasher shut. "Put the fucking knives in any way you want."

"Kevin." Heather pouted. "What's wrong?"

"Rattlesnakes, rattlesnakes, rattlesnakes. That's all I ever hear anymore. Fucking rattlesnakes."

"Kevin!"

"And I can tell you one thing. It's fucking up our son."

"What do you mean 'fucking up our son'?"

"His mother's prancing around all day, going on one TV show or another, and not being a mother. So consequently, at school, he pees in his pants."

"But that's not fair!" Heather wailed. "I wasn't on TV today."

"But you weren't there either. When they called."

"Kevin. Did you listen to a single word I said? I was outside, trapped by three rattlesnakes, when I tried to call the school."

Kevin's eyes flashed at Heather. "All I can say," he said, "is that you better stop being Heather Peters, Rattlesnake Wrestler Extraordinaire, and start being Connor Peters' mother."

"I am Connor Peters' mother!" she protested. But Kevin had already left the room.

Chapter Seventeen

Rodney Campbell had a feeling about Harlan White. He was an old guy—he could tell by the voice—which meant he might be able to give the story some historic context. And the guy was apparently pretty savvy. He had known, after all, that rattlesnakes were endangered. That's what Heather Peters had said. White was also the one who'd cleaned up the dead rattler. At the very least, there could be some interesting details in that. But most promising was the fact that White had brought up Heather Peters even before Campbell had—almost as if he'd been expecting a call from a reporter all along. That had taken Campbell aback. It meant something. He might have been stuck on the courtroom beat for two years, covering whatever human catastrophes happened to parade into the Burlington County Courthouse, but he still remembered a thing or two about tracking a story down out in the field. And he had a feeling now that this White character might hold the key to something. At the very least, the guy would add some local color to his piece.

But it was strange how White had rushed him off the phone. Like he'd seen a rattlesnake himself.

Campbell was glad to be out of the courthouse. When the story first broke nationally, getting the final "funny story" slot on both the CBS and NBC nightly newscasts, the *Eagle* had assigned it to one of their hotshots, Bob Hampton. But when the story grew whiskers, Hampton had gone back to doing whatever award-winning crap he usually did. Campbell had practically had to beg the managing editor to pick up the story again. In fact, he'd had to do something he hated: he'd had to whine.

"But I broke the goddamn story," he'd said. "I got all that good color. Her asking the judge for the room-evaluation form."

"Well, you were there, weren't you?" the ME had shot back. "Any reporter with a pulse would have had that."

"But I gave her a ride home," Campbell had gone on. "Remember? She spilled the whole story."

"And you were there to mop it up. Now you want a Pulitzer?"

"Please," Campbell had said. "I was made for this story. Endangered species, damsel in distress, media circus—"

"Save it for your memoir," the ME had finally said. "I surrender. Cover the damn story. God, it's like running a fucking nursery school—"

"You won't be sorry," Campbell had said, and hung up the phone. Quick, before the asshole could change his mind.

The next day, as Campbell drove down Harlan White's gravel driveway, he looked for details he could memorize and put in his story. It was really country, like Iowa or something. Just off Route 381, but a whole world unto itself. The way all of Hebron Township must have looked once, he realized.

Cambell drove past the remnants of what must have been a damn good vegetable garden. The main house was plain, the kind of house his grandparents lived in: white clapboard, green shutters, a friendly front porch with a glider. Then he saw—actually smelled, first—a chicken coop. A farmer. A goddamn actual farmer.

It was all such a contrast with the Peterses' house in Galapagos Estates, where every detail—from the mailbox to the in-ground sprinkler system—practically screamed money.

But there was no car. That was strange. Had he gotten the day wrong? Well, how could he? He'd just called the man yesterday.

Campbell parked, walked up the front steps, rang the doorbell, and waited. He looked at his watch: eleven o'clock. He was on a feature deadline—he didn't need to file a story today at all—but if he didn't get

White, he'd have to figure out what to do for the rest of the day. Who was next? The nature lady, the one who'd organized that parade?

Campbell had almost given up when the old guy finally came to the door. White's expression—a scowl that looked as if it were carved permanently into his face—offered no welcome, no solace. Maybe he'd forgotten the interview. Or maybe he was just one of those types who hated reporters. This wasn't going to be like interviewing Heather Peters, Campbell realized. No iced tea on the patio. Nobody spilling forth while he, scribelike, merely took notes.

"Hi," Campbell said, pulling out his press card. "Rodney Campbell. The *Eagle*." He extended his hand.

Harlan squinted at the press card and said nothing. He didn't move. Or shake Campbell's hand. Or, for that matter, invite him in.

Campbell shifted his weight from his left foot to his right, and tried again. "Um," he said, "we were going to talk? Today?"

"Go ahead," said Harlan.

This was going to be harder than he thought. "Can we go, um, in?" Campbell asked, gesturing toward the screen door.

"Here is fine," Harlan said. "You said it wouldn't take long."

Campbell pulled out his pen. So, he'd do the interview standing up. Okay. He didn't want to push the guy. "So. Heather Peters, the lady who killed the snake—"

Harlan chuckled.

Campbell looked up, puzzled. "What?"

"Nothing," said Harlan.

"But you laughed," Rodney said.

"Nah. Go ahead. What about her?"

"Well, she told me you cleaned it up. And that you told her that it was endangered."

"Uh-huh."

Campbell wondered if he was going to get more than two words in a row from this guy. It wasn't promising. He pressed on. "Well, I just wondered how you knew."

" 'Course I knew," Harlan said.

"Because?"

"Because I read the damn papers. And because I grew up around here. I fish. I hunt. I have to know what to do when I run into a wild animal if I'm out in the woods. And because there've always been rattlers around these parts."

If Campbell wasn't mistaken, White had uttered two, maybe three, sentences in a row—a speech by the old guy's standards. He struggled to take notes faster. He was aware of the possibility of screwing up, of somehow missing the story altogether—like the AP reporter who, at the dedication of Gettysburg, ended his story with the sentence "President Lincoln also spoke." If anything was to be gotten from this geezer, now was the time. He had to come up with the next question, before he lost the guy, but it was awkward scribbling in his notebook standing up.

"Always been timber rattlers here?" he said, his hand moving furiously.

"Oh, yeah," Harlan said. "A friend of mine died of a snake bite when I was growing up. And that pond—they call it Walden now—right near Heather Peters' place? That was pretty much Rattler Central."

"Really?"

"Oh, yeah. Stupid to build there. Even stupider to live there."

Campbell scribbled faster. It wasn't going to be a piece of cake like the Peters interview, but the guy was talking. Thank God for small miracles.

Chapter Eighteen

Heather had been making calls about the Halloween parade and party, a Pine Hills Elementary tradition that rivaled the Super Bowl in both buildup and letdown. It wasn't like Connor's old school, where the kids just dressed up in any old costume and marched around the playground after lunch. At Pine Hills, every class had to come up with its own theme—or at least its own variation on the schoolwide theme, which this year was "All Creatures Bright and Beautiful"—and each kid had to be fitted for a costume conforming to this theme. The costumes, of course, were sewn by the moms. After a procession that snaked around the school three times, all the classes met in the cafeteria for a giant, theme-related, and, of course, mom-catered feast. This was even harder to manage than the parade, as the class moms were expected to lay out a Halloween repast reasonably low in sugar and chocolate, and of course nut-free, while maintaining—as Principal Gupnick was fond of saying—the "festive feel" of the holiday.

It was, in other words, impossible.

As class mom, Heather had to orchestrate it all—at least for Miss Kindermack's class—and she had to coordinate this with all the other class moms as well. This involved numerous meetings, both in and out of school, each one presenting a lavish spread of figure-wrecking temptations—Danish, bagels, muffins, chocolate-covered strawberries—which, of course, nobody touched. A pity, really, to see so much lovely food go to waste, Heather thought, but she knew the stakes of mom-to-mom combat. Picking up a lemon Danish was like telling the world you'd given up. Besides, Heather had already bloated to a size 6, practically obese, and with all her television appearances, it was critical to get back to a size 4, if not a size 2, which is where she'd been just a year before. Television, as everybody knew, put twenty pounds on you.

Miss Kindermack's class had chosen as its theme the book, *If You Give a Mouse a Cookie.* So the children were all going as mice, cheese, cookies, or milk cartons. This would work nicely with the party portion of the event—milk and cookies, what could be more simple?—although some mothers complained that milk cartons reminded them of missing children. Not exactly what your typical exurban mom wanted to be thinking about on Halloween.

Heather went to bed each night with the class list beside her, woke up with it still there, and had cold-calling nightmares in between. The calls were not going well. There were exactly two moms who could sew, Betsy Staunton and Mary Sue McGee, and they were bitter rivals. Betsy and Mary Sue called Heather constantly, giving her seam-by-seam updates on their costume-making, pumping her for information on how the other was doing, and unabashedly fishing for praise. Unfortunately, they were the only ones in telephonic contact with Heather. The other moms seemed, well, a little icy. They were always running off, waiting for a doctor to call or about to sit down to dinner. They couldn't sew, couldn't bake, or already had Halloween committed away to their kids in nursery school. One actually had a C-section scheduled for that day. It was distressing how many young mothers there were these days. It made Heather feel old. But even more distressing to think . . .

. . . they hated her. Or they hated Connor. Which pretty much amounted to the same thing. Heather had drawn little frown faces next to all the people she didn't dare call, parents of children whom Connor had harassed or annoyed at school. She couldn't force herself to dial the number listed for Chloe, the girl Connor had been chasing around the playground, or to call that woman who'd come up to her on Back to School Night complaining about Connor and scissors.

She blinked back tears, going down the list one more time to see who she hadn't called, or who might have said they'd call back and hadn't. You'd think that Jean Kobel and Janet Parsons, who, after all, had volunteered to be class moms in the first place, might be willing to lend a hand, but their reactions had been among the chilliest. "I'm so sorry," Janet had said, not sounding sorry at all. "But I've got a merger that's closing the following weekend and I'm not even sure if I'll be in town." Heather thought for sure that Jean Kobel would bake for the event—the woman had, after all, been a finalist in the 1998 Betty Crocker icebox cookie contest, as she let everyone know—but there was a decidedly passive-aggressive aspect to her offer. "I make a swell *drei Augen,*" Jean had said.

"Dry what?" Heather had asked.

"*Drei Augen,*" Jean had repeated, pronouncing it "dry ow-gen," and lavishly rolling the *r.* "It means 'three eyes,' in German."

"I guess that's appropriately scary for Halloween," Heather had said. "What's in it?"

"Oh, nothing much," Jean had said. "Butter, flour, cinnamon, red currant jelly, finely ground almond powder."

She might as well have said "eye of newt" or "finely ground glass" for that matter. "Never mind," Heather had said quickly. "You know what? We have enough baked goods. But thanks. Can you sew?" Nobody was going to bring nuts to school under Heather's watch!

It wasn't until she'd related the conversation to Kevin later that she realized she'd been tweaked. Almond powder! Jean Kobel hadn't just accidentally suggested a pastry with hidden nuts. Her suggestion of *drei Augen* was retribution for Heather stealing the class-mom position out from under her.

Agnes was on the Internet, reading over the federal government's new rules on the gassing of nonresident Canada geese, when the phone rang. This had been a big issue in July, molting season, when the geese couldn't fly and were therefore sitting ducks for all the people who were angry and resentful over the fact that they pooped. Municipalities and counties across the state had been rounding up the poor creatures and murdering them wholesale in mobile gas chambers, which brought out the fury of anybody who'd ever sent a dollar to Friends of the Fauna or spattered red paint on a fur coat.

As usual, though, all the fair-weather animal lovers dropped out in August, as they drove their Volvos off to Martha's Vineyard and Acadia National Park. And by September, they were so frantic racing their kids to soccer games that they would have run over a goose that got in their way. As usual, it fell to people like Agnes to protect New Jersey wildlife once the headlines dropped off. The new federal regulations would give the goose killers a free hand next summer, and it would take some intense lobbying, or litigating, to turn things around. But try getting anyone interested in the issue now.

Agnes picked up the phone. "Rolling Hills Nature Center."

The speaker identified herself as Ida Gupnick, principal of Pine Hills Elementary School. "I understand you do wonderful work," she said.

Agnes nodded, knowing full well that the woman couldn't see her nod, but it was just vague pointless flattery and she didn't want to countenance it. Why didn't the lady get to the point?

"Are you there?"

"I'm here."

"Well, I heard that you do animal presentations for school groups. And I just wondered if perhaps—"

"Tuesdays and Thursdays. Ten o'clock or two o'clock. A hundred dollars for each class."

"Yes, I know. It says that on the Web."

Agnes looked up at the ceiling and rolled her eyes.

"I was just wondering if you might come here instead?"

"There?"

"Yes. To Pine Hills Elementary. The thing is, well, Halloween is coming, and every year we have a theme. This year's theme is 'All Creatures Bright and Beautiful.' "

How she hated that kind of thing, stupid sentimental animal worship. She wanted to throttle the woman, to reach her hands through the telephone headset, grab her neck, and shake her. She wanted to say, "And what about the animals that are dull and ugly?" but some inner censor, barely awake, held her back. Instead she said, in a voice she hoped sounded patronizing and unhelpful, "You want me to go there?"

"With the reptiles." Mrs. Gupnick's voice remained as cheerful as a kindergarten teacher's. "The children are all going to be dressed up as animals. They'll love it."

Agnes considered. She never did presentations outside of the nature center. It was a pain in the neck to travel with reptiles. The glass aquariums inhabited by her corn snakes were heavy—not to mention breakable—and water from the turtles' habitat would slosh all over the backseat of her VW. Not to mention the dislocation the animals themselves would suffer.

"Why?" Agnes said.

"Why what?"

"Why there? Why can't the children come here?"

Ida Gupnick laughed. "Oh, you don't understand," she said. "There's a lot going on that day. Halloween. A parade. A big party in the cafeteria. All the changing into costumes. There wouldn't be time to put the kids on a bus."

Agnes's eye fell again on the federal goose-killing regs on her computer screen. Money. They always needed money. "I don't normally do this," she said.

"I understand, but—"

"Twenty-five hundred."

"Twenty-five hundred?"

"Bucks."

"Oh." The phone went silent. Agnes imagined Ida Gupnick unlocking a school safe and counting what remained of the taxpayers' money. "Okay," she said, her voice still bright. "Twenty-five hundred."

"I'll send over a contract." Agnes hung up, feeling taken. Gupnick had agreed so quickly. Maybe she should have asked for more. Three thousand? Thirty-five hundred?

A navy blue Toyota Corolla from the mid-1980s rolled slowly into the entrance of Galapagos Estates. Its engine was a little noisy, but nobody noticed. It wasn't the kind of car you would notice, and besides, who was outside to notice it? The husbands were at work, the children at school, and the wives—most of them—were either at Pilates class or at the hairdresser, experimenting with new shades for their highlights. An unlucky few, who had volunteered for pizza duty at Pine Hills Elementary, were trying to dish greasy slices onto paper plates fast enough to satisfy the rapacious hordes.

Heather was home, but she didn't notice the car either. She had fired up the Jacuzzi in the master bath and was treating herself to a relaxing interlude. She needed it. She deserved it. Yes she did, after what she'd been through. She hadn't made any progress on Halloween. The only phone call she'd gotten that day was from the *Oprah* producer, canceling her upcoming appearance. The nation's attention, the producer explained sweetly, had shifted. There'd been that botched mastectomy case in Ohio—the one where the surgeon accidentally lopped off a thirty-two-year-old's left breast, instead of her right—and women across the country were hysterical. Unfortunately, the snake segment had to go. Oprah's viewers needed to hear about overworked doctors and greedy HMOs. Heather understood, didn't she?

And that wasn't all that had Heather moping. That morning, as Kevin was leaving for work, he had mentioned that they were going to have to consult an attorney about her case. "Case?" she'd said, rubbing her eyes.

"The rattlesnake?" he said. "Endangered species? Resisting arrest? Assaulting an officer? Ringing any bells?"

"But you're an attorney."

"Honey, I don't do criminal law. And even if I did, only an idiot would take his wife for a client. Oh, and by the way, that new love seat you wanted? I think we're probably going to have to put that off."

Heather poured a capful of mint-rosemary bubble bath into the Jacuzzi, inflated her bath pillow, situated her cordless phone next to the tub, put a Norah Jones disc into the CD player, and sank in.

Outside, the blue Toyota stopped in front of her house. A man in his late twenties quickly stepped out, opened his trunk, and unloaded three large slatted wooden crates. He pulled a piece of paper out of his pocket, checked the number on Heather's mailbox, and then crumpled the paper and removed the top panels of the crates. He smiled to himself, stuffed an envelope in Heather's mailbox, then got into the car and drove off.

Heather was fast asleep in the Jacuzzi when Connor got home from school. It wasn't really the doorbell that woke her—the ring could barely be heard above the Jacuzzi's jets—as much as it was the time of day. Something inside her was programmed to become alert at three-fifteen when the school bus pulled up. Some maternal instinct. Or maybe just her nervous system preparing for its daily jolt of postschool Connor.

She got out, rapidly toweled her prunelike skin, and pulled on Kevin's terrycloth robe, before checking the clock. Three-thirty. Connor had been waiting for fifteen minutes, probably ringing the bell the whole time. He was going to be furious. He might spit, he might hit. She might even have to use one of the negative-reinforcement techniques the worry doctor had prescribed, like cutting back his video-game time, and then she'd have to endure even more wrath.

But when Heather opened the door, she found her son sitting cross-legged on the landing, preoccupied with the contents of a wooden crate and looking quite content.

She squinted into the bright October sun. She'd drawn the blinds in the master bath, and her pupils were still wide like the mouths of baby chicks. What was this crate? Had UPS been by while she slept? She hadn't been expecting a package, had she?

As her eyes adjusted, she noticed that white things were streaming out of the crate. Styrofoam packing worms? But no, they were bigger than that. And they weren't just getting blown out of the box. They were . . . crawling out.

Connor reached into the box, gathered a dozen of the little white things in his hands, and held them up to her face. "They're so neat!" he said. "Can we keep them?"

They were furry, and if they hadn't been wriggling, you might have thought he was holding a bunch of tiny Beanie Babies. But they were wriggling. Writhing, crawling, falling out of his hands and onto the porch, near Heather's bare toes. "Mice!" Heather screamed, then lurched back, away from Connor, forgetting momentarily that she was wearing Kevin's robe. In the process, she managed to flash both her son and the rest of Giant Tortoise Drive. She slammed the door in Connor's face.

Heather wouldn't find out until later that she'd misidentified the little white furry things in the crates. They weren't mice after all.

They were rats.

Little baby laboratory rats. Many, many laboratory rats, five hundred per case. Eventually they'd be traced to a nearby pharmaceutical company, where they'd been earmarked for an experiment in which they were to be prematurely aged and then put into a state of constant sexual arousal. The pharmaceutical company was hoping to develop a product to compete with Viagra and reduce the symptoms of Alzheimer's at the same time.

Chapter Nineteen

Neither Kevin nor Connor had ever seen an eruption to match this one. Heather registered only two emotions—anger and fear—and she veered crazily from one to the other, heedless of anything in her path. Though she'd slammed the front door on Connor when she saw the rats—which she still thought were mice—that had failed to keep them out. Their spines were like rubber; they could squeeze through openings as thin as paper. It was October, there was a late-afternoon chill, and they wanted heat. They slid under the front door and crawled inside through the dryer vents.

"Close that door!" Heather screamed. She was standing on top of the kitchen table, wearing Kevin's terry-cloth robe and winter snow boots and wielding Connor's baseball bat.

She had, of course, called Kevin with the news, but she'd been shrieking so much he hadn't quite understood what was going on. Only that a plague of biblical proportions had descended on his house and that he'd better get home. Immediately. Connor, meanwhile, had retreated to his room, where he was lying in bed reading a book for a change. If he could, he would have gotten himself one of those invisibility cloaks, like Harry Potter had, because whatever was happening was clearly his fault. He'd found the crate out by the mailbox, brought it to the front door, and even held some of the mice up to his mom's face. He was lucky that she'd just screamed and slammed the door on him. If she'd fainted, like moms did in the movies, he really would have been in trouble.

"Heather," Kevin said. "Calm down." He held his hands in front of him, palms out, fingers spread—the way cops do in movies when they're talking to a crazy person with a gun.

"Calm down? Calm down! My house has been taken over by mice, and you say, 'Calm down.' That's the best you can come up with? Kevin! I can't even walk around in my own house!"

"Yes, I see. But let's try to figure out what's going on."

"What's going on? Some maniac left a box filled with mice on our front steps, that's what's going on!"

"Actually, Heather, I saw two more boxes out by the mailbox."

"What?"

"By the mailbox. They looked like wooden crates. I noticed them when I was driving up."

"Two more!" Heather wailed.

A baby rat climbed up the leg of the table and began crawling toward her. It was, of course, low and outside, but Heather swung for the fences. She missed. "Could you help?"

"What exactly do you want me to do?" Kevin asked.

Heather looked like she would take a swing at him next. Never had he seen her so worked up, not even the time that they'd lost their passports in Aruba, just an hour before their plane was scheduled to leave. Not even that time, right after she'd given birth to Connor, when the nurses in the maternity ward lost the baby's chart—and the young intern had come in and accused her of being an irresponsible mother. She looked positively demented, standing on that table, swatting at little rodents with a baseball bat. But then, Kevin thought, who could blame her? What woman wouldn't be in hysterics? Kevin looked up at his wife with his best expression of sympathy and kindness. He willed every corpuscle of his body to radiate calm. Rats raced between his oxfords and around his briefcase, but he didn't flinch.

Heather's face suddenly melted into a rubbery ghoul mask, her lips quivered, and she began to blubber. "Rescue me!" she said.

Heather was propped up against the pillows in her bed, struggling to remain vigilant and awake. Kevin had found a prescription bottle in the medicine cabinet with one Xanax left in it and ordered her to take it. She had, and now she was starting to fall asleep. The thought of falling asleep would have terrified her, but for the Xanax, which worked like a thick blanket to form a barrier between her thoughts and her emotions. She visualized little mice making their way upstairs—Pied Piper–style, in neat lines—wending their way to her bed, up her sheets, crawling on top of her. It was a grotesque thought, but she couldn't quite muster the energy to freak out.

The phone rang. With exaggerated slowness, like a movie zombie, Heather reached over and answered it.

"Hello?" She slurred a little.

"Heather? Heather Peters?"

"Yes?"

"It's Jean, Jean Kobel."

Jean Kobel? Heather tried to focus, but her head kept falling to her chest.

"From Miss Kindermack's class. *Drei Augen*?"

"*Drei Augen,*" Heather repeated, her mouth turning rubbery. She sounded drunk.

"Listen, I was going to offer . . . you sound tired. Were you asleep?"

At that moment, Heather was asleep. Her eyelids quivered.

"Look," Jean said, "I just wanted to, I don't know, help. But it seems like I woke you. I'll call back tomorrow."

The phone clicked off, but Heather let the headset drop onto the mattress, and she finally entered a dreamless void where, even if the rodents could get her, she wouldn't know.

Kevin kept a package of mousetraps in the basement. It was something his father had always done, so he did it too. It was as automatic as carrying an empty gasoline can in the trunk, in case you accidentally ran out of gas and had to walk to a gas station to buy some, or going out each spring to get new filters for the air conditioners.

He walked down to the basement to retrieve the traps, and when he turned on the light, he saw a dozen rodents scatter. The package contained three traps. Well, this was going to be like trying to empty the Atlantic with a teaspoon. Still, he didn't know what else to do. He took the traps, baited them with peanut butter, and set them up around the kitchen. Within seconds he heard a *pop, pop, pop,* and then he had three twitching balls of white fluff, with spots of bright red blood, to dispose of. And still dozens more live ones racing around.

Connor suddenly ran into the kitchen. "Dad!" he said. "What are you doing?"

"Getting rid of a few of our little friends," Kevin said.

"But, Dad. That's cruel."

Kevin wondered when Connor had developed an aversion to cruelty.

"Dad?"

"Yeah?"

"I found something."

"What?"

"I went out to the mailbox, earlier, when Mom was freaking out. Because you know, I sent away for that Blaster Rocket from the Froot Loops?"

"Look, Connor. It's late. And I don't know if you've noticed, but our house is overrun by mice."

Connor reached in his back pocket and pulled out a piece of paper, which he unfolded and handed to his dad. It was a computer printout of sorts, and as Kevin squinted, he could just barely make out that it was some kind of official receipt or invoice. It mentioned the name of a vendor, Ratland USA, Tacoma, Washington, and then the name of the payor, Soyoz Pharmaceuticals. The blocky computer type listed three crates of white infant laboratory rats, certified disease-free, with a quantity of five hundred to a case. The bill was for ninety-five hundred dollars.

Kevin whistled. So they were rats, not mice. And between the two crates by the mailbox and the one out front, there were fifteen hundred of them. Heather was not going to be happy.

"Did you see what it says, Dad?" Connor said.

"I'm reading it."

"No, Dad. The other side."

Kevin flipped the paper over, and then he noticed the words written in thick black marker. "Snake food. Enjoy."

Kevin dropped the paper as quickly as if it had just caught fire. He suddenly realized: the invoice was evidence. Now his fingerprints were on it. As were Connor's. He got a plastic sandwich bag out and coaxed the note into it. Then, staring at the piece of paper in the plastic Baggie, he began to feel ill. All the mice—no, rats—running around his house hadn't done it. The *pop, pop, pop* of the mousetraps and the red blood on the fur hadn't done it. He wasn't thrilled that his house had been taken over by rodents, but they didn't creep him out the way they did Heather. But this did. They had an enemy—a secret, malicious enemy—who was out there somewhere taking pleasure in their distress. He looked up at the kitchen window. Were they being watched? Was it possible this nut was outside now, looking in? He thought about the abortion doctor who'd been shot to death a few years ago, right through his own kitchen window.

"What do they mean, Dad? Snake food?"

"Connor, go to your room," he said.

"But, Dad."

"Now."

Kevin walked over to the kitchen phone. Who should he call? 911? It wasn't exactly an emergency, was it? One of his friends who worked in the district attorney's office? The nonemergency number for the local police? An exterminator? He looked up on the bulletin board, where Heather stuck take-out menus, notices of school events, and business cards from landscapers, upholsterers, and plumbers. He saw a little piece of paper with the name Harlan White written on it. Right. That was the handyman, the guy who sold the eggs. He used to be over a lot, fixing things around the house, although not much lately. He was the guy who cleaned up the snake that Heather killed. A local guy. Kevin just had a feeling. Harlan White probably would know what to do about the rats. He was a solid guy, with common sense. He'd figure out how to get rid of the rats. That was first. They couldn't live like this. Heather would blow an artery or something if they didn't get rid of them. His next call, after Harlan, would be the police.

Kevin picked up the phone, but there was no dial tone. The line was dead.

Connor had cupped one of the rats in his hands. It was soft. It felt nice. He could feel its little feet motoring around as it futilely tried to leave the shelter of his hands, and he giggled. It felt like being tickled. "You're not going anywhere, little ratty," Connor said. "You're mine."

He couldn't understand why his parents were making such a huge fuss over all of this. His mom was acting like the world had come to an end, and his dad looked scared. Yes, scared. That was weird. It was always his mom who overreacted to everything. But he'd seen his father drop that note on the kitchen counter and then wiggle it into a Baggie without touching it. You'd think he was dismantling a bomb or something.

Connor had always wanted a pet, just one creature in all the world to look up to him. But they wouldn't let him have one. His mom said they were too dirty. And his dad hardly ever went against his mom. But this! It was like a miracle or something. God had answered his prayers. And he didn't just have one creature to love him, he had hundreds. And rats! Wait till he told the kids at school.

"I'm going to name you Fluffy." He squeezed the rat, not meaning to hurt it. He only meant to hug it really, to show it affection, but Fluffy apparently didn't take it that way, and bit the soft, padded part of Connor's right hand. "Ouch!" Connor said. "You lousy rat!"

He flung the rat across the room. It slammed against the lifeless gray screen of the television set, bounced off, and fell to the floor, where it lay stunned but not bleeding, in a state of torpor that suggested hours of watching cheap animated cartoons.

Connor went over, picked the rat up by the tail, and walked into the bathroom. He dropped it into the toilet bowl and flushed. "Nobody messes with me," he said, wiping his hands together with satisfaction.

Connor found another rat, identical to Fluffy, trying to climb up the slippery incline of the bathroom sink. It was funny to watch. The rat scuttled up the porcelain, its claws looking like tensors of tiny hiking boots, but a few inches from the top it would always lose its purchase and slide back down. Connor watched this three or four times before he finally rescued the rat and cupped it in his chubby hands. The rat felt warm and soft, even though it was a little damp.

"I will call you Fluffy Two," he said.

Kevin paced around the kitchen, biting his lower lip and sucking in huge nervous breaths. There was no dial tone. No dial tone! Somebody had cut their wires.

He was outside, their tormentor, cackling maniacally and watching them. Kevin knew this, instinctively; years of watching TV thrillers had instructed him. He could almost feel the creep's eyes boring in on him.

He tried to think rationally. Heather was upstairs, probably asleep from the Xanax. The light was probably off. Which meant she was safe. What about Connor? Kevin had heard the toilet down the hall flush. That meant that Connor was out and about. He'd have to go down there, tell him to stay in his room, in the bottom bunk. He'd be safe there. Unless . . .

Kevin's stomach lurched. *Unless the flush wasn't Connor*. He sucked in another breath. His eyes darted around, casting about for unseen enemies. He strained to hear more. He thought he heard Connor's door close. Finally, he exhaled.

No, this was ridiculous. Murderers didn't usually stop in the bathroom on their way to killing you. Did they? And even if they did, would they flush?

Kevin felt trapped and powerless. What kind of husband and father was he? What kind of protector? Why couldn't he think of anything to do? Some creep had targeted his family—well, Heather really, that was pretty clear from the note—and was out there now, watching gleefully as Kevin twitched.

And then he remembered: his cell phone. He still had his cell phone.

Kevin went over to the chair that he'd laid his suit jacket on and pulled the cell out of his inside breast pocket. He ducked into the kitchen pantry, where there were no windows, and found refuge among the bottled water, Diet Coke, canned soups, and boxes of cookie and potato-chip snack packs that Heather stocked for Connor's lunches. He punched the numbers into his phone: 911.

Chapter Twenty

The police did not find a stalker or murderer in the Peters house. The wire to the telephone had not been cut. What they found, much to Kevin's embarrassment and to Heather's shock—when she was wakened from her drug-induced sleep by two cops, guns drawn, kicking open her door—was a telephone off the hook in the master bedroom.

The main consequence of Kevin's phone call to 911 was the efficient distribution of the news that fifteen hundred laboratory rats had been liberated in Galapagos Estates. The flashing lights and sirens brought out the neighbors, who stood across the street, pulling their windbreakers and leather jackets tight against the early-October night air, whispering, pointing, and trading theories. Their eyes were all on the Peters household until somebody accidentally stepped on a rat, and then suddenly their eyes were focused downward, on the sidewalk, where they began to notice, with growing horror, those little moving objects, iridescent in the moonlight, scrambling around their feet.

Rodney Campbell was leaving the newsroom when he happened to hear the dispatcher announce a possible "ten-seventy"—a prowler—at 63 Giant Tortoise Drive. He managed to race over, get the story, and file in time for the morning *Eagle*. His story would be picked up by an alert reporter in the Trenton bureau of the Associated Press, which meant that pretty soon, papers and radio stations from Sault Sainte Marie to Rangoon would be reporting the latest in the crazy animal antics of one

Heather Peters, aka the Snake Lady of Hebron Township, New Jersey. And that was how an off-the-hook telephone set off the second round of the media circus, complete with television satellite trucks, news helicopters, and press stakeouts on the Peterses' front yard.

Kevin did call Harlan White after all, when the police left. Harlan was surprised to get the call. And curious. He'd never even met the husband of the notorious Heather Peters. And Mr. Peters had refused to say over the phone what the problem was, only that it was serious, and there'd be plenty of money in it for him if he could solve it.

Harlan didn't like driving at night, and finding the Peters house in the dark was nearly impossible. All the damn houses in Galapagos Estates looked exactly the same. Then he noticed what looked like white spots blinking on and off all over the street. Was he going crazy? Or was it just time to get his eyes checked?

Kevin invited Harlan in, gestured to the kitchen table, put a mug of black coffee in front of him, and told him the story. Harlan looked around, watched the rats scuttle under the kitchen cabinets and over the countertops, using the toaster, blender, and microwave as gym equipment. The amount of rat poison needed to take care of an infestation this size would turn the Peters kitchen into a Superfund site. Traps? There'd be bloody messes, morning, noon, and night, and Harlan knew that Heather wasn't going to deal with it. He pictured himself on his hands and knees, picking up dead mice and cleaning the Peterses' kitchen floor over and over again, while the whiny Peters bitch yapped on and on about the latest crisis in her life.

That, he figured, was a pretty good definition of hell.

"So," said Kevin, who was still wearing his shirt and tie. "You're a practical man. You've been around, seen a lot. What should we do?"

Harlan, who'd been shaking his head and watching the rats, crossed his arms and looked up at Kevin. He was one of these hotshots with tons of money, the kind of guy Harlan usually hated. Rich, arrogant, young, handsome, the type of asshole who parked his car diagonally in a parking lot so nobody could get close enough to scratch it. But looking at him now, his face drawn and gray, his tie rumpled, Harlan almost felt sorry for him.

It all boiled down to one word.

"Move," Harlan said.

Barstad was in the den, watching the Phillies blow a 3–0 lead and sulking about Dana. She hadn't been answering her cell phone. She wasn't returning his e-mail. He'd canceled a reservation at the Taj Mahal when he didn't hear from her, because the idea of going to Atlantic City alone was too damn depressing. He'd even left her a message offering to take her to Lambertville. Nothing.

For days he'd been replaying the scene from Atlantic City in his head. The sudden protectiveness he'd felt when she started talking about her henhouse schemes, the mortification at his failure to perform. He'd wound up giving the diamond necklace to Barbara when he got back from Atlantic City—a guilt offering—and she'd looked at him suspiciously, as if she knew she was the second in line for the gift. But when he went down the next morning for breakfast, she had it on.

Depressing.

It wasn't like Barstad to sulk. He was an optimist by nature, a charmer, a schemer. If one bridge was down, his grandpappy had taught him, build another one. Yet here he was, in October, watching the Phillies let their chances of postseason glory slip through their fingers, doubting his virility and wondering if he'd ever see his mistress again.

Barstad's youngest son, William, the only child still at home, burst into the den. Without so much as looking at his father, he turned on the computer and started to IM his friends. That was grating. Here Barstad worked his ass off so Will could have a Fender guitar, the latest Nikes, money to color his spiky bangs yellow, and all the other jackass things teenage boys wanted these days, and the little shit didn't even have the common courtesy to say hello.

Barstad's jaw dropped as Bobby Abreu, the Phillies' right fielder, took the third strike—a fastball right down the middle—just stood there, like some wax groom on a wedding cake, and watched it sail by. "Hello?" Barstad said, his voice loud and sarcastic, talking to the TV.

"Those little things flying across the plate are called baseballs, and you're supposed to hit them."

Will turned around. "You talking to me?"

Barstad arched his eyebrows, forming an expression of exaggerated puzzlement. "Oh, Will? You're in the room? I didn't even notice you come in."

Will turned back to the computer.

The phone rang. Both father and teenage son lurched toward it. Barstad felt that jerk of expectation that the lovesick feel every time a telephone rings. There was nobody in the world he wanted to hear from, except for Dana. But at the same time it couldn't be Dana. She knew the rules. A mistress never called the home number.

Father and son jostled elbows, but Barstad beat Will out by a nanosecond. "Hello?" He could barely squeak it out, his heart pounding like a jackhammer.

"Jack?" came the voice. "Jack Barstad?" The caller was male, and though the voice was slightly familiar, Barstad couldn't quite place it. And who cared? It wasn't Dana.

"That's me," Barstad said.

"Kurt. Kurt Alexrod, Galapagos Estates Homeowners Committee."

"Oh, Kurt." Barstad's heart slowed down. He put on his good-old-boy voice. "Hey, what's up? I was just watching the game."

"Look. Sorry to call so late. But we have a little problem going on here."

Harlan pulled into his driveway, enjoying the reassuring rumble of gravel under his wheels. He got out of his pickup, stretched, looked up at the stars, took a deep breath—expecting to savor the crisp air of an October night.

That's when it hit him. The smell of manure.

He sniffed, testing the country air like a wine connoisseur inhaling the bouquet of a new Beaujolais. Manure. Harlan followed his nose like a hound, and it led him toward the henhouse. His nose puckered, unpuckered, puckered again. He knew the smell of chicken shit, but that was different. This was cow shit. Grade-A, minimally processed, authentic, fresh cow shit. And lots of it. Somebody had delivered fresh cow manure in the hour he'd been gone trying to help the Peterses!

When he opened the door to the henhouse, the smell almost knocked him to the ground. He pulled his cap off, held it over his mouth and nose, and tried to control the overwhelming urge to heave his guts. Cow manure had been dumped everywhere. It was caked on the floor, the benches, the walls, the gate, the nests. Harlan's best layers were flapping their wings frantically. They were hysterical, the smell literally asphyxiating them. Some had already succumbed, fallen over, their feet in the air.

He had to let them out, into the yard, immediately. If he didn't, they'd all die. But his farm wasn't fenced all the way around. Who needed it, he'd always thought. He didn't have any large animals. No steer. No horses. The chickens were always safe in the coop.

He swung the door open and let the birds flee. He tried to herd them into an outbuilding where he kept his riding mower and other farm equipment, but his knees were bad, and the chickens were running in all directions. They disappeared into the night, all but about a dozen that Harlan managed to corral into the shed. Gone. His business, half his livelihood, gone—just like that, in a matter of minutes. They'd run off into the woods, some of them, the lucky ones, or onto the deserted farms that Barstad had bought up for his new housing development. But most had headed to Route 381, just a few hundred feet away. How does a chicken cross the road? Harlan thought soberly. It doesn't. Roadkill.

When he'd gathered up all the chickens he could, Harlan returned to the henhouse to survey the damage. A few dead chickens and dozens of eggs all covered with shit. Harlan could imagine the E. coli counts. They'd be huge, enormous. He couldn't sell these eggs. Especially with the rumors going around about salmonella . . .

That's when it hit him. Someone was out to ruin him.

Clearly, he had some enemy, whoever had spread the manure in the hour he'd been gone. Now he was putting it together: the rumors of salmonella, the general store stocking eggs from a competitor, the bloody hens back in September. He had a long-standing enemy, Harlan realized, and he hadn't even known it.

Chapter Twenty-One

Heather had insisted on staying in a hotel. Kevin had of course given in. What choice did he have? If it hadn't been a hotel, it would have been the loony bin, and a hotel in the end would be cheaper. He couldn't blame her; the rats were even creeping him out. So they packed up, after the police and Harlan left, and found a room at the Embassy Suites. It wasn't expensive—Heather had managed to get an eighty-nine-dollar-a-night rate for a long-term stay—but it was going to add up. And the problem was that nobody could say how long it would go on. The rats seemed to be breeding like rabbits, and it wasn't just Kevin and Heather's house. It was most of Giant Tortoise Drive.

Exterminators who heard about the problem on the radio rushed over, hoping to get the job, then turned their trucks around when they saw just how big it was. Every mousetrap in every hardware store, grocery store, and Home Depot within fifteen miles of Galapagos Estates had been snapped up within the first twenty-four hours. All the cats up at the local animal shelter were adopted within days. But supply outstripped demand; the rats were so plentiful that the cats got stuffed and lazy and stretched out on rugs, their eyes glazed, while potential meals sprinted around—and sometimes even over—them.

Heather, pouring coffee one morning from the tiny carafe in the hotel's kitchenette, thought she had it solved. She ran into the bathroom, where Kevin was looking into the steamed-up mirror and trying to straighten his tie.

"Sweet'N Low!" she proclaimed.

He stared.

"It causes cancer in laboratory rats!"

"Yeah, if they consume a thousand times their weight," Kevin said. "And you have to wait a couple of years."

Things looked bleak. Television reporters, doing their stand-ups in front of the Peters house, were beginning to talk in serious hushed tones about Galapagos Estates having to be abandoned, like Love Canal.

Ultimately it was one of the secretaries in Kevin's office, concerned about the dark shadows under her boss's eyes, who found Mouse-Go-Bye by doing a Google search. Mouse-Go-Bye was a device that emitted high-pitched tones that humans couldn't hear, but that sounded to rodents like chalk scraping a blackboard. Kevin made a call to the Galapagos Estates Homeowners Committee, and someone from the committee made a call to the makers of Mouse-Go-Bye, who said that a device could be custom-designed—for $6,788—to distribute the sonic rodenticide over the entire acreage of Galapagos Estates. The committee reeled at the cost, even after it was explained that a radio tower would have to be built. Some objected on aesthetic grounds: they hadn't moved out to the country to look at something like that.

In the end, though, the Galapagos Estates Homeowners Committee voted to award a $6,788 contract to Mouse-Go-Bye.

There was only one problem. All the pet hamsters, mice, guinea pigs, and rabbits in the community would also be driven crazy by the noise. They would have to go. Mouse-Go-Bye wouldn't sign the contract unless this was guaranteed. Lawsuits, they said. Children wailed when they heard the news, hugged their guinea pigs to their chests, hid their hamsters under their beds. There was a general homework strike by the children of Galapagos Estates in protest of the plan. An enterprising ten-year-old, Chastity Jennings, even organized a lemonade stand to try to raise money for a guinea pig defense fund. She modeled her price structure on that of Starbucks, with a "tall" lemonade—the smallest size—going for $1.95.

In the end, special arrangements were made for children with these pets to put them on loan to their classrooms at Pine Hills Elementary, five miles away, and safely outside of Mouse-Go-Bye's sonic range. When Galapagos Estates was officially deemed rat-free and the "Mouse-Go-Bye" was turned off, the children would be able to retrieve their rodents.

The press, of course, was having a field day. The feature writers loved the fact that the animal kingdom was once again pitted against Heather Peters, and the local news stations couldn't get enough of little Chastity Jennings. The investigative reporters pursued the ecoterrorism angle. Who had broken into a pharmaceutical company to liberate fifteen hundred lab rats? Why? And how had they accomplished it? The science reporters were hot about the sonic rodenticide. There was even a small cadre of fashion reporters who chased Heather from her house to her hotel to the school, making alternately catty and approving commentary about her outfits.

Rodney Campbell, of course, was the greatest beneficiary of all—so much so that his editor sometimes jokingly accused him of having unloaded the lab rats himself. The Galapagos Estates story had turned into a whole beat, and Campbell was never happier than the day the *Eagle* hired a new reporter, a girl just out of journalism school at Northwestern, to cover the county courthouse.

Agnes knew. Of course she knew. She had seen Leroy Adams's face the night of the Friends of the Fauna meeting, had seen his eyebrows knit into an expression of private consternation, and she knew. He was up to something. There had also been that e-mail, back in August, in which he'd actually raised the issue, explicitly, of liberating laboratory rats.

She was in her kitchen, trying to clear the table of the bills, circulars, calendars, and magazines that accumulated daily and she kept picking up pieces of paper, hoping to be able to throw them away, only to discover that each one contained a date, a phone number, or an address that she might need someday. She was going in circles, moving stacks around like a Times Square con man offering up a shell game for the rubes, only there were no rubes—just Agnes and her own growing frustration. Normally the mess didn't bother her, but she fussed with projects like this when she was agitated, and she was agitated now. She'd been agitated ever since the news had broken about the rats in Galapagos Estates.

Leroy's e-mail. Had she deleted it? There were two stacks of paper in front of her: one that she planned to take into the office, the other that she intended to put into the bathroom for reading. But the urgency of the question, which she had not thought of until now, so jolted her that she threw both stacks onto the larger pile on the floor, thus wiping out her efforts of the past hour. She sat down and stared blankly at the mess as if she were looking right through it. This was serious. The e-mail. If it was still there, it was evidence. And what he'd done—breaking and entering, stealing laboratory rats (even though she agreed that animals could not truly be someone's property), and then depositing them so as to create maximum chaos in Galapagos Estates—that was a felony.

Should she turn Leroy in? This was really the issue she was struggling with, not which papers to throw away and which to keep. Or would that be bad for the animals? The dishonor it would bring upon the cause! And would failing to turn Leroy in make her a co-conspirator?

Suddenly she had to know. Was the e-mail still there? She ran to her desk in the living room and pressed the button that would rouse her computer from hibernation. It was slow, maddeningly slow, and while the thing was warming up, in the same old-fashioned way of the cathode-ray tubes in the early television sets, her eyes rested on the fortune-cookie slips she'd taped on the sides of her monitor. "The truth is your master," said one. "Lucky numbers 15-29-7-32-6." Another declared, "Your fearlessness is legendary." They looked down on her like stern Buddhas, and she felt judged.

The computer finally blinked awake. Agnes dialed in, another interminable wait, and when the mechanical voice intoned, "You have ten new messages," she ignored it, racing instead to inspect the older messages still in her in-box. When she didn't find the message from Leroy Adams there, she let go a relieved breath. But then she remembered: the file marked "Deleted." And there it was. Sender: Leroy Adams. Message: Intervention. Date: August 12.

She didn't even open it. Her right index finger leaped to the delete key, and when the question popped up, "Are you certain you want to permanently delete this message?" she clicked yes. Her finger was in charge, moving faster than her mind—or her conscience. She deleted Leroy's e-mail reflexively, protectively, the way you pull your hand away from something burning.

Then she remembered the next step. The computer's recycle bin. Was anything ever really permanently deleted without emptying the recycle bin? And when she hit "Empty Recycle Bin," she had to acknowledge—with the Chinese fortunes her only witnesses—that it wasn't a reflex. This was premeditated. She knew what she was doing.

She wasn't exactly sure why. She didn't want trouble, of course. She didn't want any connection to Leroy Adams. Maybe the police, the prosecutors, if they found the e-mail on her machine, would say that she should have prevented it, should have alerted the authorities earlier. Maybe that was it.

She didn't want Friends of the Fauna connected with this, either. Or the Rolling Hills Nature Center. She was a serious advocate of animals—who couldn't, after all, advocate for themselves—and now that work was compromised. All of them, all the people who cared about animals, were beginning to look like loonies. Why had she ever allowed herself to be talked into that ridiculous jazz funeral for the timber rattlesnake? How gaudy and out of character, and how it had backfired, turning Heather Peters into a martyr and a media darling. The whole world had laughed at the idea that rattlesnakes needed protection or deserved mourning. But this was even worse. Now it was little Chastity Jennings, with her lemonade stand, defending the rights of guinea pigs!

What had Leroy been thinking? Oh, yes, there was some poetic justice in leaving the rats at Heather Peters's doorstep, Agnes granted that, but did he think they'd just stay there, and have a great time? Didn't he realize that people would kill them? With mousetraps, rat poison, baseball bats, their boots, by running them over in SUVs? Was that liberation? Were the laboratory rats really better off running through Galapagos Estates than they would have been running mazes at Soyoz Pharmaceuticals? And it pained her to think of what the rats had yet to go through. Her eyes scrunched up at the memory of all the times she'd heard chalk scrape across a blackboard, and she couldn't imagine what it would be like for the rats, running to get away from such aural torture. Certainly Leroy hadn't thought of that when he'd dropped the crates off in front of Heather Peters's house.

Then she thought of Heather Peters herself, and though she despised the woman, or at least despised the type—rich, skinny, materialistic—Agnes did feel a little sorry for her. She had seen Heather on the news, running to the parking lot of the Embassy Suites, trying vainly to hide her identity with oversized sunglasses, and being swarmed by the press.

Agnes powered down the computer, then pulled the slips of paper with the Chinese fortunes off her monitor. She crumpled them up, threw them into the real recycling bin—the blue one with the arrows on it, the one for paper—then took some spray cleaner and a rag and worked off the grit that had been left by the Scotch tape. She wiped as if she were wiping out a witness to a crime, or scrubbing her soul clean.

But then, when she'd put the cleaner back under the sink and looked down at the mess in the kitchen again, she remembered. She'd heard—on NPR, probably—that nothing was ever really erased on a computer's hard drive. Kenneth Starr, Whitewater, Enron. It was coming back to her. It was impossible to truly erase a message permanently, unless you took a hammer to your hard drive. Hiding inside her computer, like an electronic shadow, was the proof. And it made her want to throw up.

It was bedtime, and so his parents had closed the door of the hotel's living room suite, opened the fold-out couch, and told him he had fifteen more minutes to watch TV. He could hear the whispers in the bedroom behind him.

This was the worst time of day for him. The lights were off, the TV glowed blue, and the only thing that stood between Connor and another day of torture at Pine Hills Elementary was one little night of sleep. It had been cool to stay in a hotel the first few nights, but after that its charms had worn off. It wasn't home. He didn't have his PlayStation. His parents were always telling him to turn the TV down. The bed was lumpy and tilted down to the right.

The kids at school blamed him, and his mother, for everything. Especially the kids who rode the school bus from Galapagos Estates. That was the only good thing about staying at the hotel. He got a ride to school from his mom instead of having to take the bus.

Connor reached under the sofa bed and pulled out the shoe box he kept his Yu-Gi-Oh! cards in. He took off the lid, pulled out the half-starved and dehydrated Fluffy Two, and rubbed him against his face. Fluffy Two had made a mess of the cheese-and-peanut-butter cracker Connor had left in the shoe box, and there were little orange clumps of reconstituted cheese food all over the cards. Connor had a mind to punish him—leaving crumbs like that—but the warmth and softness of the rat's fur felt so good.

But Connor hadn't thought to give Fluffy Two any water, and so the rat, parched beyond belief, leaped out of his hands in search of something wet. Connor's eyes bugged wide, trying to find the rat in the dark room, lit only by the flickering TV, and he would have shouted—but that would have gotten his parents' attention. Connor made a thorough exploration of his fold-out bed, patting the mattress, inspecting all the corners of his blankets, checking under his pillows, but Fluffy Two could not be found.

He turned off the TV, put his face against a pillow, and cried silently until he fell asleep.

In the middle of the night, Connor and most of the other guests on that wing of the Embassy Suites were awakened by a piercing shriek. Fluffy Two had been found—dead—in the glass of water that Heather always kept on her nightstand.

Chapter Twenty-Two

The hotel suite was dark and cramped, and for hours every morning Heather had to listen to the drone of vacuum cleaners and maids chattering in their tinny little Spanish voices. She tried to cover their sounds with the noise of morning TV, but each time they advanced toward her room, she'd grit her teeth and turn up the volume. An auditory war—not unlike the one going on at Galapagos Estates—only her adversaries didn't even know they were fighting. Finally, they'd knock on her door, wanting to make up her room, and always at the wrong time—when she was going to the bathroom or in the shower. And then, when she let them in, and they cleaned, leaving the door open, Heather felt exposed, like someone whose underwear drawer had popped open on a first date.

Heather thought of the vast clean expanses of her house on Giant Tortoise Drive—the light hardwood floors, the big bay window in the kitchen, her pristine all-white living room—and felt homesick. But then she'd picture the clicking of little rat claws on her hardwood and she'd want to retch. Could she ever go home? Would she ever feel safe there again? First the snakes. Not just once, but twice. Then the rats. Was God trying to tell her something?

It was two-thirty on a Friday afternoon, and she was still in her bathrobe, her hair a mess. She had no makeup on. That wasn't like her at all. When she was in labor with Connor, she'd reapplied her lipstick between contractions. But who could fight the fluorescent lights over the mirror, which made her makeup look clownlike and turned hairline wrinkles into deep ravines? This is what living in a hotel did to you, she thought sourly.

Everything seemed to be falling apart. Kevin was always miffed. Connor was doing disastrously in school. And being interviewed by TV reporters no longer seemed like fun. When they ran after her with their microphones, she felt like prey. They were hyenas, hunting in a pack, eager for blood. Her blood. And she wanted to spank that bitch from the E! channel who gave all her outfits a letter grade. Her pink plaid Gucci bag a C? It was beyond indignity.

Connor's class list sat on the nightstand—she was still supposed to be organizing the Halloween event—but it was hard to force herself to look at it. She'd come up with a code to remind her which names she shouldn't call to ask for help, and now just about every name had some kind of mark beside it. There was "WM" (working mom), "YK" (younger kids), "HC" (hates Connor), and "HM" (hates me.) Beside Jean Kobel's name, she'd just written the word "NUTS!" in a dark, almost brutally hard scrawl.

Miss Kindermack had called that morning, around ten, when her class went to gym and she had a break, and Heather had been embarrassed to be woken from a solid sleep. People could always tell when you were sleeping, even when you swore up and down that you weren't. Though she tried to pep up her voice quickly, Heather knew she'd been caught, a sloth, sleeping late—and by the very person she was supposed to be monitoring.

Miss Kindermack's voice was kind, concerned. She'd seen the news on TV, she said, and knew from Connor about the hotel. But she was also getting nervous about Halloween. The thing was—and Miss Kindermack sounded quite apologetic when she said this—she thought they might have to change their class's theme. *If You Give a Mouse a Cookie* was a darling book, of course, but—and this was awkward to point out, she said, but there it was—with Heather as class mom, and the rat incident, well, they'd be a laughingstock. If the press showed up, well, they'd definitely make the end of all the national newscasts again, that final wacky-story segment, and nobody wanted that. The school district's outside public relations specialist had, in fact, sent Mrs. Gupnick a memo on this very point.

Heather tried to gather her wits. "You mean, at this late date." She was starting to sputter. "With more than half the costumes already made, I'm supposed to get on the phone and tell the sewing moms to start all over again?"

"I'm afraid so," Miss Kindermack said. "Unless, of course, you want one of those other ladies who volunteered for class mom to take over. Jean Kobel—"

Heather cut her off. "No," she said curtly. "I'll handle it." In the hierarchy of failures, having Jean Kobel succeed her as class mom would have to be up near the top.

After she'd hung up, though, Heather had taken the DO NOT DISTURB, hung it on the door, and gone back to bed.

Now it was time to pick Connor up at school—this was another inconvenience of living at the hotel; no buses dropped off here—and she hadn't accomplished a single thing all day. As she pulled off her nightshirt, Kevin's oversized Rutgers T-shirt, and slipped into jeans, Heather looked in the mirror. She saw a puffy-faced, wild-haired woman with a bad attitude. She tried smiling at the mirror, but it just made her look deranged.

Heather laced up her sneakers, glanced again at the clock, took a deep breath, and braced herself. The press. She'd have to get by them to reach her Land Rover.

Harlan was more depressed than usual. His Visa bill was up past nineteen thousand dollars, and apparently last month he'd forgotten to pay it. He'd been wakened that morning by a call from a collection agent, asking politely if there was a problem. No, he'd said, just forgot. The agent had sounded cheery, polite, but Harlan had detected an underlying note of menace. Not fifteen minutes later the oil company had come to deliver a tankload of heating oil. He'd had a contract with them for years; they kept records of his oil use and delivered it when he was low. This was his first delivery of the season. Harlan walked out of the house and waved them off. It was at least five hundred dollars a tank, and he just didn't have it. The truck driver tried to argue. "You're almost empty," he said. "And we're expecting a frost this week."

"I'll wear a sweater," Harlan had said, walking back into the house.

Now that his egg business had gone bust, he didn't know how he was going to pay for anything.

There was a new letter from Barstad Enterprises on the table. What was the guy offering now? Last time it was four hundred thousand dollars. Month after month, the price had gotten higher and higher, as the jerk seemed more desperate to separate Harlan from his land. Maybe Harlan would have to rethink it. Maybe he was a whore, after all. He was just waiting for a john—or a Jack—to offer the right price. There were principles and then there was common sense. A man had to eat, didn't he?

But when Harlan opened the envelope and squinted at the print, he was shocked. Barstad's price had dropped. He was offering just $250,000. The tone of the letter was different too. It talked about last chances, about a possible "letter of condemnation" from Hebron Township, a final opportunity to make good on his family's lifelong investment.

For a moment, Harlan's heart fluttered in an involuntary spasm of fear. His chances were slipping through his fingers. His bills were going up. He'd just turned down a delivery of heating oil, and a frost was coming. He didn't even have hens to provide his morning eggs. He'd been eating cornflakes for breakfast.

Harlan took Barstad's letter and ripped it in half. Then he took the two pieces, put one against the other, and ripped it in half again.

Well, fuck him, he thought. And fuck Visa. And fuck the oil company. He didn't need any of them. He was resourceful. He had a fishing rod, didn't he? And a shotgun. He could live off the land. The woods were still full of deer and quail and possum, the streams still packed with trout and bass and walleyes. That's how his ancestors made a living, wasn't it? He had a shotgun. He knew how to use it.

Harlan looked down at the A&P circular sitting on the dining room table and saw the illustrations of pumpkins and candy corn. And that reminded him. Turkey season was coming up, just like it did every year, right at Halloween. Harlan smiled, for the first time in days, as he conjured the smell of turkey cooking in his mother's oven.

Heather was at the helm of the Land Rover, staring into the after-school traffic, looking for opportunities to pass slower vehicles, and trying to ignore her son. Connor had been whining about school, whining about not having his PlayStation, whining about how there were no good snacks in the hotel.

"When I was your age, I would have killed to stay in a hotel for a couple of weeks," Heather snapped. "It would have seemed like a vacation to Europe."

"What's Europe?" Connor said.

"Okay, Hawaii. Have you heard of that?"

Connor said nothing and began digging his nails into the car's leather interior. It was a habit, the worry doctor said, that indicated extreme anxiety. They were supposed to buy him a stress ball, but somehow they never remembered. When Heather noticed Connor clawing the leather through her rearview mirror, she swerved to the shoulder of the road, slammed on her brakes, and turned around. "What are you doing?" she said, glaring at Connor.

"Nothing." He quickly folded his hands on his lap and looked down at them.

"You're ruining a sixty-thousand-dollar vehicle is what you're doing."

"Well, if you knew, why did you ask?"

"Smart mouth." She turned back to the steering wheel and checked her side-view mirror for an opening. "If you do it again, we'll take it out of your trust fund."

Connor put his hands together and started kneading them rapidly.

"And I'll bind up your hands with duct tape."

"Like Abraham and Isaac?" Connor said.

"What are you talking about?" she asked. "Where are you getting this stuff?" They didn't go to church or send him to Sunday school. Were they teaching Bible stories in school? Had he made a little Jewish friend? It was vexing.

"Mom?"

"Yes." She hissed the word, her *s* more sibilant than necessary.

"Can we go by the house?"

Heather took a deep breath. The house. She hadn't been there in a week. Kevin had been stopping there every night, on the way home from work, to pick up the mail. She wanted to see the house too, but her stomach twisted at the thought of seeing another rat.

"Why?" she demanded.

"I left my goggles there. And the chlorine in the hotel pool hurts my eyes."

God, he was always whining about something. When she was kid, what she wouldn't have done to swim in an indoor pool at a fancy hotel. And she hadn't had goggles. Nobody did. Heather sighed. Well, if it kept him occupied, it was probably worth it. Besides, he'd been gaining weight. Whatever it took to get him to move his body.

"Okay," she said. "I'll give you the keys. But I'm not going inside."

Heather drove slowly down Giant Tortoise Drive, looking around warily for reporters. She didn't find any. But she was dismayed to see stacks of hay and corn stalks flanking half the doors, giant purple spiderwebs, dime-store witches, and, worst of all, Styrofoam cemeteries and tombstones with cutesy expressions like, "If you can read this, you're standing on my head." God, it was so low-class, so cheap and disgusting. Why did people have to ruin October this way? Mums—that was what you were supposed to have on your front steps this time of year, mums and only mums. Didn't the bylaws for Galapagos Estates outlaw such hideous displays? They regulated what kinds of trash cans you could use, and the color of your recycling bins. They had requirements for hedges, rules about trees. And of course the houses came in only two colors, beige and white. So this? She'd have to look into it, and send a letter.

"Cool," Connor said, as they passed a house with a gigantic spider hanging down from the front porch. "Can we have one?"

"God forbid," Heather said under her breath.

They rolled up in front of 63 Giant Tortoise Drive and from the outside it looked just the way it always had. There it was, her home, her Walden. Behind that door, she thought, was everything she loved and cherished. The window seat with the color-coordinated pillows. The great room, with the flat-panel TV, the Pottery Barn sectional, the silk ficus tree. Connor's room, with the bunk beds and the framed antique posters from the Ringling Brothers Circus. Her pride and joy, the all-white living room. And outside, the flagstone patio, which Barstad had extended, in exchange for that stupid snafu with the shades. That seemed so long ago, like ancient history. She sighed, handing Connor the keys.

Heather walked over to the mailbox—another regulated feature, she thought, making a note to mention it in her letter to Galapagos Estates—and pulled out the mail. There was quite a bit, so she returned to the car to open it. There were about a dozen mail-order catalogues, including the latest one from Restoration Hardware, the local rag they called a newspaper, promotional circulars from all the local grocery stores, and bills from Saks, Visa, American Express, and Verizon.

She shook the circulars over the passenger seat, because sometimes actual mail fell into them and got lost that way. She hated junk mail. Liked the catalogues but hated the newsprint circulars from the grocery stores and the drugstores. And sure enough, when she shook, two letters fell out.

One of them was one of those self-sealed jobs, with all the perforations and tabs and instructions for how to open it, and her name was typed in official-looking print. It looked like a jury summons.

She was half right. It was a summons, but not to be on a jury. It announced her preliminary court date, with a half dozen charges against her, ranging from killing a member of an endangered species to assaulting an officer. It was set for October 31.

"Damn," she said, tossing it to the top of the stack. Why didn't she have a lawyer yet? Kevin should have taken care of that by now. And what about the damn parade and party at Pine Hills Elementary? How was she going to be in court and do her class-mom duty at the same time?

The other letter's return address said Galapagos Estates Homeowners Committee. Well, she thought, maybe I won't have to write that letter after all. This is probably a notice telling people to remove those perfectly ridiculous Halloween decorations from their lawns.

But it wasn't a form letter. It was addressed to her and Kevin.

She glanced at it, taking in the key words rapidly. Rattlesnake. Media. Rats. Mouse-Go-Bye. She nodded, impatiently. She knew all this. Then her eyes rested on the last paragraph.

"The Galapagos Estates Homeowners Committee has decided that your presence in the community is disruptive to the other residents. For the sake of the majority, we are asking you to sell your residence and leave Galapagos Estates by March 1. If you do not vacate voluntarily by that date, we will contact your lender and begin foreclosure."

Heather was dumbfounded. Connor ran to the car, opened the door, and got in. "Ready!" he said, holding up the goggles.

Heather just sat there.

Connor looked at her and then, noticing the mass of papers on the front seat, unzipped his backpack. He rummaged through it and finally pulled out a piece of paper, in orange, which he shoved into Heather's face.

It was a school notice, and she could tell from the color, and the pictograms of pumpkins and witches, that it was about Halloween.

Then she noticed the drawing of a snake.

"We are proud to announce," the notice said, "that Agnes Sebastian of Rolling Hills Nature Center will be presenting her reptile demonstration during our Halloween celebration."

So, *If You Give a Mouse a Cookie* was bad PR, but Pine Hills Elementary could invite the same animal crazy who'd shown up at her house, gotten her arrested for killing a member of an endangered species, and then dragged the media in by organizing a dead-snake funeral to march up Giant Tortoise Drive. It was maddening.

Heather bared her teeth, snatched the keys from Connor, put the car in reverse, and screeched off.

When she got back to the hotel, she grabbed her suitcase from the back of the hotel closet and threw it on her bed. Then she took Connor's suitcase and tossed it onto the sofa in the suite's living room.

"Pack," she barked.

"Where are we going?" Connor asked.

"Home!"

Heather pulled open the dresser drawers roughly, throwing in her underwear, socks, pants, and shirts. She slammed the sliding door of the closet to one side and snatched her dresses from the hangers. She marched into the bathroom, not even glancing in the mirror, and began emptying the medicine cabinet of makeup, toothpaste, vitamins, and sleeping pills. She looked under the bed, found a few socks, a Danielle Steel novel she'd had trouble concentrating on, and the right partner of a pair of tassel loafers, which had been missing since the previous Wednesday. When she came upon the class list, with all her notations about the various moms, she looked at it with contempt—almost as if it were one of the animals that was always threatening to invade her refuge—and tore it in half. She didn't have time for this crap. Halloween! She was going to court and losing her home, and she was supposed to be calling people up to bake cookies?

In twenty minutes she was all packed and had made sure that Connor was too. She sat on the bed, arms crossed, and waited for Kevin. The two letters—the court notice and the letter from Galapagos Estates—lay neatly on the bed beside her. She stayed in that position for hours, staring straight ahead. She didn't pick up the phone or even turn on the TV.

Finally, she heard the swipe of the magnetic room key, which meant that Kevin was back. "Funny thing," he said, opening the door. "No mail today at all. Not even a catalogue." And then he stopped. Heather didn't know what tipped him off, the fact that her arms were crossed and she was tapping her foot or the suitcase sitting on the floor. "What—" he began.

"Oh, we got mail, all right," Heather said, and she grabbed the two letters and thrust them in his face.

He put down his briefcase and read the letters slowly. Then he read the one from Galapagos Estates a second time. It took about a minute. When he was done, he looked up as if awaiting instructions.

"Pack," Heather said.

"Pack?"

"We're going home."

"But I thought . . . the rats . . ."

"Kevin, do you understand? They want to take away our home! They want us to leave. Vanish. As if any of this is our fault. And I just won't let them have the satisfaction."

He reached over and put his hand on her shoulder, as if to talk reason into her. She anticipated the arguments. Galapagos Estates wasn't yet rat-free. They could still be anywhere—in her cabinets, under the sink, in the garage. Her neighbors would be hostile. The press would start another stakeout in front of the house, and that would piss the neighbors off more. Just hours earlier she'd wondered if she'd ever be comfortable in her home again, and here she was now, fighting to go back. Heather jerked her shoulder away from Kevin's hand, dismissing his arguments before he could even begin. "Pack," she said.

Chapter Twenty-Three

Barstad strode through the cool modern lobby of the Borgata, marveling at this new twenty-first-century version of Atlantic City. It was classy. Boy, it was classy. Polished wooden tables, polished marble floors, polished tinted glass. Just goddamned polished. You could buy a lot of class for a billion dollars. So much class that you'd never know—unless you were in real estate, like Barstad—that the place was built on top of a dump.

Barstad had always been partial to Trump's Taj Mahal, with the big white elephants that lined the driveway, its turquoise onion domes and massive crystal chandeliers. But he had to admit that the Borgata made the Taj look like a cross between a bordello and a Greyhound station. The Borgata—that's where all the players were staying these days, the real high rollers, and the celebrities, in from New York and Beverly Hills. He'd already spotted Bruce Willis and his entourage in the lobby. You practically had to make what Bruce Willis made to stay here, but who cared? Once you'd walked through the sleek chrome-and-glass doors, you wouldn't stay anywhere else in Atlantic City again.

And Barstad had the perfect accessory, a juicy piece of arm candy—a stunning, six-foot-tall platinum blonde who went by the name of Jessie.

Jessie wore a black sequin-studded gown tight enough to be shrink-wrap. Barstad had found her through an escort service—a Borgataquality service, and equally pricy—and though she wasn't exactly Dana material, Jessie's attractions were substantial nonetheless. She had returned his manliness to him that afternoon, under the three-hundred-count cotton sheets, and she could do things with her tongue that could get her into the Ripley's Believe It or Not, down on the boardwalk, as far as he was concerned.

Jessie wasn't stupid either. That was one of the advantages of paying up for these kinds of things. She'd graduated from Penn State and had planned to go into animal husbandry. But after graduation she'd taken a trip to Atlantic City and discovered the far more lucrative field of catering to the animal instincts of husbands. She was smart, and though she wasn't sharp or funny like Dana, her discussion of her senior research project—the sheep-mating harness—had its memorable moments.

When they walked through the casino, heads turned. Barstad liked it when heads turned. And it didn't matter whether the woman in the evening gown by his side was free or financed out of petty cash. Nothing was free anyway. Barstad's manhood swelled when he saw the looks that came their way. He noticed brief flickers of jealousy on the poker faces of men twenty years his junior. Some even tried to catch Jessie's eye. But she didn't look, bless her little heart. She was bought and paid for. A professional.

By the time he got to the blackjack table, Barstad almost felt as if Jessie were capable of conducting electricity. Wherever she walked, the ions spun and danced, setting off powerful eddies of magnetism and repulsion. Men looked, wives and girlfriends looked away, and even the dealers seemed unsettled. Which was just how Barstad liked it. It even gave him an inkling of an idea. Why not set up the whole Hebron Township zoning board with their own Jessies? An Atlantic City junket, his treat. He pictured that fat little jerk Mike Kawalcek marching into a casino with A-class material like this on his arm. The guy wouldn't crack stupid snake jokes then, Barstad bet. He'd be worried about keeping his hard-on from showing.

The first hand the dealer dished him a jack face up, and a six facedown. Barstad looked over at Jessie. Her face was as blank as a Barbie's.

"Hit," Barstad said. What the hell! He was fucking Barbie.

He was rewarded with a five—and a cool thousand bucks. And that was just the beginning of a wild string of good luck.

Barstad moved along to craps, to poker, to baccarat, and his winnings mounted. Now people weren't just staring when he walked in their direction, they were whispering as well. He strode through the casino like a lion, king of the jungle. No, like a god. He wasn't just on a winning streak, he was on top of fucking Mount Olympus. The assholes upstairs looking at the security cameras were probably wringing their hands, following his every step. Let them. He wasn't doing anything illegal.

As his luck mounted, Barstad began to let go of the damaged feeling he'd had since Dana had so mysteriously walked out on him. He was a winner again, a man of the world, and all his plans—he suddenly knew—would go well too. Galapagos Estates would soon be rid of Heather Peters—he and the Homeowners Committee were in complete agreement about that—and Harlan White, a broke and broken man, would soon accept his offer. Phase 2 of Galapagos Estates was practically in the bag, tonight's winnings would more than cover Jessie's fee, and Barbara would be none the wiser.

When he and Jessie cashed in his chips and walked back to the bank of elevators leading to their suite, Barstad studied the details of the lobby: the furniture, the carpeting, the lighting, the mirrors. All the lines clean, spare, modern. God, how could he have ever thought the Taj was the height of sophistication? And then he saw it, knew it. This was his future, his destiny. The Donald's father built places for people to live. The Donald built palaces. But even the Donald hadn't built this. Barstad would. He would build something even greater.

Agnes was listening to *All Things Considered* on the radio and sorting through the dozens of science experiments in her refrigerator. An omelet, that's what she wanted for dinner. But all she could find were jars of mango chutney crusted with mysterious white crystals, putrid containers of month-old soup, olives that looked biblical in provenance.

Where in the world were the eggs? She kept them in a little wire basket on the bottom shelf, because Harlan delivered them that way instead of in a carton. But even after emptying the entire contents of the bottom shelf onto her kitchen table, she couldn't find it.

Then she remembered. She'd used up the last two eggs making brownies earlier in the week.

Annoyed and growing hungrier with each minute, Agnes put all the items she'd taken from the refrigerator back inside. Then she went out to the back porch to see if Harlan had brought by some new eggs. It was already dark out. That was one of the things she hated about this time of year. And soon, when they rolled the clocks back, it would get dark even earlier. She looked around, hoping that maybe it was the dusk that was making it hard to find the eggs. But no, they weren't anywhere. No eggs, no basket, no sign anybody had been on her back porch at all.

She thought about calling Harlan, asking him where the hell the eggs were, but something stopped her. It was a feeling related to the one she'd had the other day, when she'd gone to the computer and deleted the e-mail from Leroy about liberating laboratory animals. And when she realized what it was, she felt a sickening pang in the pit of her stomach. Guilt, that was it. She suddenly remembered that Friends of the Fauna meeting a few weeks earlier, how the conversation had careened from Heather Peters and her snake problems to Harlan White's alleged mistreatment of hens.

What was it they were planning to do? She couldn't remember, exactly; she'd spent much of that meeting running to the bathroom. Her gut squeezed now, as she remembered. They were going to sneak into Harlan's henhouse. Inspect it. Something about salmonella. Or whether or not the hens got to run free. Videotape it, she thought they said. An exposé. Agnes hadn't heard anything since. Had they done it? Actually snuck into Harlan's henhouse? And if so, what had they found? And more important, what had they done?

Because if Leroy Adams had been capable of dropping fifteen hundred laboratory rats on Heather Peters's front lawn, who knew what he might have done to Harlan's henhouse? And that woman, Dana, too. There was something suspicious about her. She was too pretty. No, it wasn't that, not exactly. It was just that she had—yes!—too sharp a haircut! That was it. Agnes had run the nature center and Friends of the Fauna for years, and she knew the type of young woman who took to the cause. They had mops of frizzy red hair, or shaggy, badly cut brown hair. They bit their fingernails, wore overalls, eschewed makeup. And this Dana, whoever she was, wasn't one of them.

Agnes went back into the kitchen and started to think what else she might make, besides an omelet. She could heat up some frozen veggie burgers, or tofu dogs, she supposed. That would be pretty quick. But she was really disappointed. She'd been in the mood for eggs.

Poor Harlan. The more Agnes thought about it, the more sure she became: Harlan had been the victim of some kind of mysterious dirty trick. That could be the only reason, after years of delivering eggs, that he'd failed to put the basket of eggs on her back porch this time. Agnes didn't really like the man. They differed on so much, he being a hunter and everything. But they did go way back—to childhood, to the days when her brother was still alive. And in his own awkward, curmudgeonly way, he was kind of sweet. She'd never wished him harm.

She opened the freezer and took out a veggie burger, then poured a little olive oil into a pan. She should call him, she decided, she really should. She didn't want to, but she should.

Years ago, before the area codes had even changed, Harlan had had a little refrigerator magnet made up for his egg business. It showed a cartoonish hen laying an egg, and the hen's eyes looked big and surprised, as if stunned that this large object was coming out of her. The magnet had been on the fridge so long, she'd ceased to even notice it, but now, inspecting it for Harlan's phone number, Agnes felt a twinge of annoyance. What a dumb little cartoon. How insulting to chickens.

She dialed, and while she waited for Harlan to pick up, she walked with the long twisted cord over to the stove, to make sure the burger didn't burn. One ring, two rings, three rings. Then a recorded announcement: "This phone has been disconnected. Please check your number and try again."

Disconnected? She tried the number a second time, to see if she had indeed misdialed, but reached the same mechanical voice. Damn, she thought. What's going on?

"Mr. Barstad?" Jessie said, her voice tiny and schoolgirl-like. "Can we go see the tigers?"

Barstad quickly looked left and right, to make sure that nobody else had heard. He bent down and whispered in Jessie's ear. "Not Mr.," he said. "Jack. Jeez, if anybody heard that, they'd think you worked for me."

"But I do work for you."

He looked straight ahead, his smile pasted on his face, while he put his arm around her. "Jessie," he said, applying a little pressure to her right arm. "I don't want anyone to know you work for me."

He looked at his watch. Was it midnight? Was the charm over? Did he have to take her home? Why, oh Lord, why was she acting like a baby?

"Okay, Mr. . . . I mean, Jack," she said. "Can we go see the tigers?"

She was, he supposed, in her own way, an innocent. Sexy. Yes. Good in bed. You bet. But still a babe in the woods. Apparently. And she'd gone to ag school, for God's sake. Not the sharpest crayon in the box. But he wasn't going to make the same mistake he'd made with Dana, thinking of her as a daughter, worrying about her, losing his, um, focus. And he had some insurance with him just in case. The little blue pill.

The tigers, he sudden realized, referred to the big midnight show at the Midas Touch, the great Popolopalous and Greco. It was part circus, part magic, total spectacle: flaming rings, leaping tigers, dancing elephants, just feet away from a crowd of spectators. Popolopalous, a large bald man who looked ridiculous in his skintight teal costume, provided the comedy, and what passed for magic in the act. Greco, a seventh-generation animal trainer, was his physical opposite. Compact, muscular, with a lacquered pompadour and a handlebar mustache, Greco was a tight package of concentration. The duo had a whole team of backstage handlers, who lurked unseen behind the curtains with tranquilizer guns.

Barstad and Jessie took a taxi to the Midas and got to Mega, the hotel's cavernous theater, right as the show was about to begin, but Barstad knew that they always reserved a table or two up front in case a VIP showed up, and when he slipped the maître d' a crisp hundred-dollar bill from his evening's winnings, he was proven correct. They walked down the stairs, past rows of gamblers and sightseers packed tight into vinyl banquettes, and Jessie's magnetism seemed to kick in again. True, with her sequined dress she could have been onstage herself. But Barstad had a feeling this bombshell would unsettle a room even in jeans and a T-shirt.

The problem came right at the show's most celebrated moment, a hammy bit of buffoonery from Popolopalous, in which he appeared to have locked himself inside a tiger's cage and was shaking the bars, desperate to get out. The cage was surrounded by eight drooling Bengal tigers, and Greco, all spandex and muscles, had to pass the tigers to release Popolopalous. Normally, it worked like magic. Presto chango! The tigers were in the cage, and Popolopalous was out, taking a stagy bow with his partner.

But not tonight. Greco advanced toward the locked cage, but the tigers turned around and headed in the direction of the audience. Headed, in fact, right to the table where Barstad and Jessie were seated.

It must have been Jessie's animal magnetism, those unfathomable sparks of electricity that she kept discharging, Barstad decided later, after the tranquilizer darts had all been fired, the Mega had been evacuated, the maître d' had apologized, returned his hundred-dollar tip, and offered them a free weekend at the Midas. Barstad hoped that, in all the commotion, Jessie wasn't swift enough to notice that he'd sat there the whole time frozen, not so much as lifting a finger to protect her. Or even worse, that during the moment when it appeared they would become so much cat food, he'd stained his boxer shorts.

Chapter Twenty-Four

One of the things the decorator had talked Heather into was a built-in kitchen desk, with the same dark cherry cabinetry and granite countertop that she'd chosen for the rest of the room. "Mother's little workshop," the decorator had said, outfitting it with fifteen hundred dollars' worth of organizational accessories from Hold Everything, all cleverly designed to hold everything but show nothing. At first glance, all you could see was a magnetic board bearing a few photographs of Connor. But that was just camouflage. Carefully hidden inside the desk unit were a full-size bulletin board, ten cubbies, a stapler, a cordless electric pencil sharpener, a file drawer, and a laptop computer with wireless Internet access.

Now it was her war room.

Heather had moved into the little cubicle as soon as she'd unpacked her suitcase and asked Kevin to throw in a wash. She hadn't used it much before—just for paying bills and keeping her class-mom lists—but now it was the hub of her two-front war. Heather was mustering every ounce of her considerable resolve for the struggle of her life: she had to beat her endangered-species rap in court and fight Galapagos Estates' effort to cast her and her family out of the house she had worked so hard to, well, make into a home.

She'd spent most of the weekend there, and for the past hour she'd been rummaging through the file drawer, looking for every piece of paper she'd ever received on the subject of Galapagos Estates. There was the original ad she'd torn from the newspaper, the sales brochure, the contract, and the community's bylaws. She wore a pair of magnifiers and a deep scowl as she scrutinized all the fine print she'd never read before. It wasn't just that the language was legalistic. She'd expected that. But it looked like Jack Barstad had employed teams of attorneys and locked them in a hotel until they came out with a document so lop-sided that it protected him from every single negative outcome, no matter how arcane or unexpected, leaving his buyers with no recourse whatsoever.

"Certain laws do not allow limitations on implied warranties," the fine print read. "If these laws apply, some or all of the above disclaimers, exclusions, or limitations may not apply to you. You agree that any action relating to these terms and conditions shall be filed only in state or federal court located in Burlington County, New Jersey, and you hereby irrevocably and unconditionally consent and submit to the exclusive jurisdiction of such courts over any suit, action, or proceeding arising out of these terms and conditions."

Kevin walked into the kitchen, opened the refrigerator, and asked, "What's for dinner?"

"God, I hate lawyers," Heather muttered.

"Thanks," said Kevin, pulling some two-week-old drumsticks out of the refrigerator.

"You know what I mean," she said. " 'You hereby irrevocably and unconditionally consent.' When did I do that?"

"When we bought the house," said Kevin. "So. Are you cooking?"

"So. Are you watching football?"

"Connor's hungry."

" 'Connor's hungry,' " she mimicked. "Connor's always hungry, if you haven't noticed."

"Well, I'm hungry too."

Heather stood up and turned around to face him. "Can't you see I'm working here?" she said. "When I'm in jail, who's going to cook for you then?"

Silently—and squeezing every bit of drama he could out of the situation—Kevin opened the cabinet under the sink and dropped the congealed drumsticks into the hidden wastebasket. Then he washed his hands very slowly and deliberately, and dried them. Finally he spoke. "If you hold that scowl for another hour, you're going to have permanent wrinkles," he said. Then he shouted in the general direction of the TV: "Connor! We're going to McDonald's."

Fine. Let them go to McDonald's. Let Kevin clog his arteries. Maybe Connor could be the first kid in third grade to tip the scales at a hundred pounds. What did she care? She was just trying to keep a roof over their heads.

She heard the door open and close and Kevin's car engine start. Only then did she allow herself to reach up and touch her face. Wrinkles? She willed herself to stop frowning, but she could only hold a smile on her face for a second at a time.

Finally she turned back to the piece of paper with the fine print, boring into it with all her intelligence. That bastard thought his lawyers had taken care of everything. But he'd never seen the likes of Heather Peters.

Every nerve in Heather's body was stretched taut, so when she heard the tiniest sound on the floor behind her, she knew instantly what it was.

She turned around, flexed her foot, and kicked the rat in the general direction of the garage door. Kevin could deal with it when he came home.

Jessie was a good-luck charm. Jack Barstad was sure about that. His little gambling trips to Atlantic City had never been more lucrative, and he was feeling so good physically, due to Jessie's ministrations, that he thought his fee to the escort agency should qualify as a medical expense.

His accountant would never go for it, of course, but he'd found a way to legitimize his whole sex-and-gambling junket for the zoning board—and to write it off. The New Jersey League of Municipalities was holding its annual convention next month in Atlantic City, and Barstad Enterprises would host a hospitality suite. And what hospitality he would offer! Unlimited booze and canapés, and—for decoration—some pretty faces from the same agency that had furnished him with

Jessie. Of course, officially, he'd hire the escorts for something legit—passing trays of hors d'oeuvres around—but then he'd let his buddies know (nudge, nudge, wink, wink) that these beautiful young vixens were available for other favors. It was brilliant, if he said so himself. It could even stand up to the scrutiny of the IRS—or Barbara.

Lately, he'd worked something out to put Jessie on a retainer. Rather than paying by the night, he paid by the week. That afforded him a serious discount and also allowed him to have her nearby more often. He'd put her up at a motel in the middle of the Pinelands, nothing fancy, but she didn't care. She liked being outside of Atlantic City, and near farms. You could take the girl out of animal husbandry, apparently, but you couldn't take animal husbandry out of the girl. When she was "off duty," she told him, she liked to take walks down country lanes, past pastures and rolling hills.

Sometimes, driving around to his various construction sites, Barstad would find himself taking country roads, rather than the highways, on the lookout for a tall, lanky blonde, wearing slim jeans and hiking boots. If he found her, he'd slow down, pull over to the side of the road, flash a big smile, and offer her a ride. And, of course, being on his payroll, she'd always smile back and get into the car.

Coming upon her like that, of course, turned him on in a way that even staying at the Borgata couldn't. Once, on a warm day, he'd left his car on a little side road and joined Jessie on her walk. They found an old abandoned barn and had a roll in the hay. Literally. It was the best sex he'd had in decades, Barstad decided. A little itchy, yes. But basically teenage-quality, hormone-crazed sex—not the desperate humping of a middle-aged man. After he'd zipped up and dropped her off at the motel, he congratulated himself on money well spent. It was important for a man in his position to feel virile, masterful, confident. It wasn't just sex. It was potency—something a builder needed, whether he was driving a nail or hammering out a deal.

After dropping Jessie off, Barstad quickly glanced at all his mirrors, side and rear, making sure that he didn't recognize any cars. You couldn't be too careful. But he was safe. Nobody he knew hung out around here. It was farm country, a future site for Barstad to build on, a few years down the road. But for now it was as remote as an Iowa cornfield. Besides, Barbara never spent any time in the country. Why would she? There were no nail salons or Saks Fifth Avenues there.

Kevin hadn't been too surprised when he woke up to find that Heather had never come to bed. She'd been pretty pissed. That is, more pissed than usual—pissed being his wife's default state of being. He looked in the mirror, shaving, and saw that he was frowning. It was, he realized, his guilty frown. Well, okay. Maybe she had been right. Why had he demanded that she make dinner? She had been working and he had been watching football. He could have defrosted a few burgers.

He walked down the hall toward the kitchen to make coffee. He'd probably find her in the guest bedroom. Or on the couch. He'd give her a gentle little kiss on the forehead—a sign of affection and contrition—and remind her that she'd have to get Connor up for school pretty soon.

But he found her right where he'd left her when he and Connor went out to McDonald's. Hunched over the kitchen desk. She wasn't even asleep. There was a sheaf of papers in the printer, evidence that she'd been up all night, researching things on the Internet, printing them out. She was online now, reading what looked like a newspaper article, hunched toward the screen in complete concentration.

Kevin walked over and touched her lightly on the shoulder. "Good morning," he said softly.

Heather jumped. "You scared me," she said. Her eyes were puffy, her makeup smeared.

"I didn't mean to. Look, about last night—"

Heather's expression turned from surprise to glee as she cut him off: "I'm going to get that fucker!" she said triumphantly.

"What, um, fucker?" Kevin asked.

"Jack Barstad, of course," she said. "Just wait till you hear."

"I'd love to, hon," Kevin said. "But I've got a deposition at nine. You'll tell me everything tonight, okay?"

He leaned down to give her a kiss, but she'd already turned back to the computer. He smiled as he grabbed his jacket and walked to the door. He was no longer at the top of Heather's shit list. Jack Barstad was.

Chapter Twenty-Five

Nobody had bothered to tell Connor that childhood was supposed to be fun, and that American childhood's crowning event, its Mardi Gras, the annual recompense for homework and broccoli and picking up one's toys, was the festival of Halloween. It was the one day of the year when none of the regular rules applied. Regulations regarding sugar intake and bedtime were suspended. Parents could be talked into throwing fistfuls of dollars away on purple spiderwebs and plastic welcome mats that made ghoulish sounds. Math and spelling were replaced by parties and parades. Kids were free to express their inner demons, to sneer at death, to dress inappropriately, and to maraud through the neighborhood, pounding on doors and demanding candy. For the normal, well-adjusted child, Halloween was practically the life force itself.

And then there was Connor, who regarded Halloween as a fast-approaching opportunity for utter humiliation.

Maybe if his mom hadn't screwed up, it wouldn't be so bad. But for the past few days, at the end of school, when it was time to line up at the door before the final bell, Miss Kindermack would tap him on the shoulder, pull him aside, and ask him to remind his mother to call her. He had done this, dutifully, but had his mother even listened? Now whenever Miss Kindermack touched his shoulder, Connor drew back in horror, as if he'd been touched by the exposed metacarpals of a graveyard skeleton.

And then there were the kids—on the playground, in the cafeteria, on the school bus, anywhere a teacher wasn't nearby—hissing at him over the fact that their class didn't have a chance of winning the pizza party, to be awarded to the class in Pine Hills Elementary that, in the opinion of Mrs. Gupnick and the two office secretaries, had the best costumes. All because Miss Kindermack's class didn't have a theme! And why didn't Miss Kindermack's have a theme? Because they couldn't do *If You Give a Mouse a Cookie* after all the rats had been dropped off on Connor's front lawn! And because Connor's mom had, in the words of Thomas Kobel, the arbiter of all things male, cool, and third grade, "dropped the ball."

Miss Kindermack's class was doing the unimaginable: they were going themeless, leaving the costuming of the children up to the children themselves.

Connor had gotten so used to being taunted about his mother that it had almost become background noise, like a radio station that was on so much you didn't notice it. What really bothered him, as he listened to the other children on the school bus bragging about masks and wigs and fake blood, was that he didn't have a costume. It was the night before Halloween, and he didn't even have an idea for a costume.

Ever since they'd moved out of the hotel, Connor noticed that his mother spent all her time at her desk. He wasn't sure what she was doing there. All he knew was that she wasn't on the sidewalk waiting for him when he got home from school, and there were no milk and cookies, or even cut-up fruit, laid out on the kitchen table. In fact, his mother didn't so much as turn around from her computer when he got home. She didn't even ask if he had homework.

On the weekend, she paid even less attention, as there weren't even any alarms to set or lunches to make. It was Sunday and he'd spent all day eating potato chips in front of the TV and his mother hadn't even noticed. Well, he thought, she was going to have to pay attention to him, whether she wanted to or not. He needed a costume. And if he had to have a temper tantrum to get one, he would.

Connor began with a loud sigh, and when that didn't get her attention, he turned it into a whimper, which was also ignored. He increased the intensity of the whimper until it became outright sobbing, and when that didn't work, he began stomping his feet. Within minutes, what had begun as a premeditated, and somewhat staged, cry for attention had turned into a full-fledged fit. The tears and the screams were real now, and still nothing from the lady at the desk.

He was, at this point, fully involved in his tantrum, his blood coursing hotly through his veins and his face wet with tears. He was, as the worry doctor would have said, "beyond reason and beyond reach," a swirling vortex of distress. But even in this state, Connor had a good idea. He walked into the living room, the room that he was expressly forbidden to enter without permission, went over to the coffee table, picked up a large but particularly delicate glass vase, and smashed it against the wall.

The sound it made was thrilling. It hit the wall not with a thud but with the sound of firecrackers. It didn't just break, it exploded. Thousands of shards erupted on impact, flying in amazing patterns and landing everywhere. One piece, in fact, lodged itself into the chubby flesh of his hand, but in Connor's adrenaline-charged state, he felt no physical pain. All he felt was anger, justifiable anger, the anger of the righteous avenging injustice, and so Connor took his bloody hand and swiped it in one long motion against his mother's prize possession, the white living room sofa.

Now it looked like Halloween.

His mother came running in. Her eyes popped wide and she howled, like an animal in pain. "What the hell is going on?" she screamed. "Are you insane?"

Connor mustered his courage and his dignity and faced his mother like a little man. "I need a Halloween costume," he said. "And you need to call Miss Kindermack."

It was the day the clocks were turned back and daylight savings time officially ended, and it was Agnes's least favorite day of the year. True, it had been darkening for weeks, since the end of June actually, but it never seemed as dark as the day the clocks turned back. It was as if a veil of darkness fell over everything, including her mood. It made her think of Greek mythology, of Hades, the underworld, of animals hibernating: that half of the year when you would leave the office and have to navigate your way home through utter blackness.

To ward off the darkness, she spent this day outside each year, breaking down the garden, harvesting any remaining vegetables, composting. It kept her in the light all day, let her soak up the available hours of sunshine like a battery absorbing energy. Being in the garden helped tame her mood. The garden took on a ragged beauty this time of year, and some of the weeds had actually attained a kind of towering majesty. There hadn't been a frost yet, so there were actually a few edible tomatoes left. The fall vegetables—cabbages, broccoli—sat in crisp rows, ready to be sacrificed for slaws and stir-fries. Gold and crimson leaves littered the yard like oversized confetti.

It was a great time of the year for birds, which were flying south, sometimes in such huge flocks that they momentarily blackened the sky, and as Agnes noticed them, it made her think of bird issues, things she worked on at the nature center, like the roundups of the Canada geese in July. That made her think about hunters. And thinking of hunters made her think again of Harlan.

A long time ago, as kids, they were part of the same crowd. Harlan had been her brother's best friend, and she used to tag along when they hiked through the woods, crossed the creek on rocks, and caught frogs with their bare hands. Harlan was there, of course, the day that Kit had been bitten by the rattlesnake, and Kit's death had been the end of everything, the end of playing in the woods, the end of Harlan coming over for dinners at their house, the end of her childhood, really. After that, Agnes had only seen Harlan when she passed him in the hallway in school, and she'd ignored him, deliberately, as if everything had been his fault, because fairly or unfairly, she would always associate him with that ill-fated day in the woods.

Later, after high school, when she saw him buying worms at the general store or wearing orange hunting vests, she knew that he'd gone over to what she considered the dark side. She had no sympathy for animal killers, no sympathy whatsoever. This was the way she'd classified him for years, except that he was the egg man too, and she'd admired the fact that he'd gone organic, although she didn't altogether trust him.

But now, for some reason, she felt a little sorry for him. Something had happened to his egg business, and she might be partially responsible. His phone was disconnected. Why? And all those times she'd seen him hanging out on the bench in front of the general store, he'd looked a little sad, lonely, like a person left behind at a bus stop. Then it occurred to her. The last few times she'd been to the general store, she hadn't seen him. That was probably the most troubling sign of all.

And so it occurred to her to take some of her vegetables over to Harlan's house and check on him.

By the time Agnes got organized, changed out of her dirty jeans, washed the broccoli and the cabbages and put them in a towel-lined basket, it was dark. It was just a little after five, but it looked like midnight. When she got to Harlan's, she could barely see the driveway. Well, that was the country for you. The strange thing was that the driveway didn't seem to end. She drove through blackness, slowly, her tires crunching the gravel, until suddenly her headlights were illuminating the house. One moment she was in an inky field in the middle of nowhere, and the next she'd practically driven into the side of Harlan's house. There was no porch light, no glow of a lamp from anywhere.

Strange. Well, maybe he had gone into town, and his front-porch lightbulb had burned out. Or maybe he was such an old codger that he'd already gone to bed. She'd leave the vegetables on his porch anyway.

Agnes got out of the car, grabbed her basket, and walked cautiously in the direction of Harlan's house, taking small steps to make sure she didn't trip over anything in the darkness. Her eyes were beginning to adjust to the darkness, and she thought she saw a light glow coming from inside. But it could be her eyes playing tricks on her. Carefully, she climbed the steps, and she was just about to knock on the door when it opened slowly. It was just as dark inside, but suddenly Agnes discerned the outline of a long, hard object pointed toward her. A bit of moonlight glinted off what must be . . . a barrel.

A shotgun.

"Jesus!" she screamed.

"Agnes?" Harlan said softly. He put the gun down.

"What the hell are you doing? You could have killed me!"

"Well, if you hadn't been you, that might have been the general idea," he said.

"What's wrong with you?" She was ranting now, not even the thinnest veil of civilization hiding her rage. "No lights! No phone! No eggs for the past week! I come here, with vegetables from my garden, to see what's going on with you, and how do you greet me? By pointing a gun in my face!"

"I'm sorry," Harlan said. "Really. Come in."

She shuddered, trying to shake off the adrenaline that had surged through her body. "Okay." She followed him into his living room.

The first thing she noticed—she would have noticed it sooner had her heart not been pounding so hard—was the smell of kerosene. Harlan had three old-fashioned kerosene lamps set up, and they were flickering with an eerie orange light. Then she noticed a fire going in the woodstove. Sitting on top of the woodstove was a big black kettle, which emitted a horrible, gamy smell. Finally, after Harlan offered her a seat and took his own, she could make out Harlan himself. He sat down in a great big easy chair, and pulled up a wool blanket that had fallen to the floor. That's when she noticed that, despite the woodstove, it was cold. Her teeth chattered, and she pulled her jean jacket tighter.

"Here," Harlan said, handing her the blanket.

"What in the world is going on with you?" she asked.

He explained. Explained about the bills, about Barstad, about the land offer. Then he told her about all the strange things that had happened to his egg business, the break-ins, the rumors of salmonella, and finally the desecration by cow manure that had put him out of business. How he'd had to let his hens run free to prevent their asphyxiation.

"And so," Agnes said.

"I'm living off the land."

"No phone . . ."

"Or electric. Or grocery bills. Nothing."

"And what's that smell?" she said, gesturing toward the pot on the stove and wrinkling her nose.

"Squirrel stew," he said.

"Squirrel?" She was appalled.

"Well, skunk, actually," he admitted. "It's pretty good. Want some?"

She shook her head violently. It was pathetic how low he'd sunk.

Maybe that was why Agnes felt the need to give him something, something besides vegetables, and so she confessed about that last ill-fated meeting of the Friends of the Fauna, about that new girl, Dana, and her plans for exposing conditions in his henhouse, and that led to a confession about Leroy and what she suspected—no, knew—was his act of larceny and ecoterrorism in the release of fifteen hundred laboratory rats in the front yard of Heather Peters. She let out a sigh—it felt good, getting this all out—and waited for Harlan to condemn her.

Instead he laughed. "Heather Peters," he said, shaking his head, as if it were the funniest thing in the world.

"What?" said Agnes.

"Heather Peters, the little gal that killed the rattlesnake," he said. "Only she didn't."

Agnes narrowed her eyes. He couldn't possibly mean what he was saying. "I don't get it," she said.

"I said, news reports to the contrary, Heather Peters didn't kill any rattlesnake."

"But, Harlan," Agnes said, "I was there. At her house. In her garage. I found the thing. I was the one who turned her in."

"Yes," Harlan said. "And guess who put it there? Who killed it? Cleaned up the mess? Hosed off the patio? Bagged it all up? Told her to get rid of it? Informed her, even, that it was an endangered species. And by the way, the way she was carrying on screaming, I didn't have any choice."

"No," Agnes whispered.

"Yes."

"Don't tell," she said. "Don't tell anyone."

Heather was exhausted. It wasn't enough that she had a court date the next morning, that her community was trying to cast her out, that she had dark shadows under her eyes from working so hard over the past week, learning everything she could about endangered-species law, property law, and the shenanigans of one Jack Barstad in the planning, zoning, and building of Galapagos Estates. It wasn't enough that she'd been trying desperately to hold on to her house and her freedom, all while being henpecked continuously by Miss Kindermack, and that she'd done it all under warlike conditions, with rats running through her kitchen, for God's sake. Or that she'd chewed down her nails, neglected her aerobics routine, and was eating carbs in the middle of the night. Now she had to deal with Connor going ballistic and taking her living room down with him.

She'd found Kevin working out on the treadmill right after the meltdown and they drove Connor to the emergency room together. Connor was bleeding like a red shirt in a white wash, and it had taken three stitches to staunch the flow of blood, after which two residents from the psych ward came down to interview them. There'd been a frantic call to the worry doctor, both for reassurance and to convince the psychiatric residents that Connor did not need to be admitted on the night before Halloween, that Heather was not an unfit mother, that the Division of Youth and Family Services did not need to be called. Yes, the child was under his treatment. Yes, he was seen regularly and was taking medications. Yes, the parents were fit parents, respected members of the community and blah blah blah. There had just been a bit of stress in the household lately.

When they left the ER, Kevin had taken Connor to a party store to pick out a costume, and Heather had rushed home to work on the stain. She'd tried cool salted water (she'd looked it up on the Internet), but in the time they'd spent in the emergency room, the stain had begun to set. So she'd moved on to hydrogen peroxide. She had a little bit in the medicine cabinet, but not nearly enough, so she called Kevin on the cell phone to tell him to stop and get some on the way home. While she waited for him to return, she took what peroxide she'd found, diluted it, just the way they said, and the stain had turned from a hideous red to a repulsive pink. Well, it was progress, she supposed.

The costume that Connor chose, against Kevin's wishes, was that of a news reporter. It came with a Dick Tracy–style trench coat and fedora, a microphone, a laminated "official press" card on a chain, and a little spiral-bound reporter's pad. Whether Connor was trying to be ironic, or just hoping to rattle his mom, Kevin couldn't tell, but there was no talking Connor out of it. At least it was only $36.99. When they got home, Connor had run right into the living room, bumping into the bucket of diluted hydrogen peroxide, and stuck the mike in his mother's face. "Mrs. Peters," he'd said, "how did this bloodstain get on your couch? Are you ready for court tomorrow? Is it true that you hate snakes?"

"No comment," Heather had said wearily. "Go to bed."

Now Connor was finally in bed, and Kevin, still in his workout clothes, had come into the living room and slumped into a chair.

"How's it going?" he asked.

Heather, who was down on her knees scrubbing, turned around. From her vantage point, at carpet level, all she could focus on were Kevin's sneakers, encrusted with the viscous mess of decaying leaves. She shuddered. "Please," she said, "take off your shoes."

Kevin reached down and began to untie them. "Look," he said. "You want me to take over? So you can go back to the case? Or maybe you want to run some stuff by me, as a lawyer?"

Heather sat down on the stained sofa. What the hell. It was only blood. "Well," she said, "there is something I wanted to talk to you about."

"Shoot," he said.

"The snake."

"Yes?"

She paused, leaning down to put her rag in the bucket and squeeze out some blood.

"Yes?" Kevin prompted.

"Never mind." She returned to scrubbing.

"Heather?"

"I didn't kill it."

"What?"

"The snake. I didn't kill it."

Kevin stood up and began to bellow. "Oh, I heard you," he said. "I just don't believe what I think I heard."

"Sshhh," Heather said. "You'll wake up Connor."

But Kevin didn't sshhh. If anything, he got louder. "You didn't kill the rattlesnake?"

"That's right. I didn't."

"Then who did?"

“The handyman, Harlan White. He was here, helping out.”

Kevin sat down, folded his arms, and glared. He started to speak a few times but was only able to sputter. Finally, he took a deep breath, rubbed the back of his neck, and composed himself. “What about all that press? Those stories? The *Today* show? The little lady who killed the rattlesnake? Are you telling me you were lying?”

Heather looked down at her lap. “I prefer to think of it as stretching the truth,” she said.

“Stretching?” Kevin was getting loud again. “We have reporters staking us out twenty-four hours a day, we both spend a night in jail—”

“I didn’t tell you to speed,” she said quietly.

“There’s a New Orleans–style jazz funeral for the snake, a nut drops three cases of laboratory rats on our front lawn, our neighbors hate us, Connor is ostracized in school, you’ve spent days hooked up to a computer, ignoring us, not making a single meal—”

“So this is what this is all about,” Heather said. “You’re not getting good-enough service?”

“I’m just saying that maybe all of this could have been avoided if you simply had . . . told . . . the . . . truth.”

“Well, I don’t know what I can do about it now,” she said. “It’s too late.”

Kevin stared at her. He was a lawyer now, talking to an adversary across the table at a deposition. His eyes bore into hers like lasers, his voice was icy, his attention concentrated, precise. “It’s too late for what?” he asked.

“If I admit that I was, um, stretching, well, I’ll be the laughingstock of Galapagos Estates.”

“I hate to tell you this, honey, but you already are the laughingstock of Galapagos Estates.”

“And they’ll feature me again as that funny story at the end of the newscast. And, and . . . my credibility at Pine Hills Elementary School will be shot.”

“Not a single thing you’ve said has any bearing on this case,” he said. “Have you thought about what you have? You’ve got an out. A loophole. A way to prevent yourself from going to prison. And if you have to get down on your belly and slither through that loophole like a . . . like a snake, that's exactly what you're going to do."

"I don't know whether I can do that," she said.

Kevin stood up. If there was one thing he had perfected, after all his years in litigation, it was the power of a strong exit. He fired his last shot as he crossed over toward the entrance of the living room. "You will," he said. "If you want to stay married to me."

Chapter Twenty-Six

It was unseasonably warm for Halloween. That's what the radio said. It was sixty-two degrees first thing in the morning and was expected to go up into the seventies—great weather, the announcers couldn't help saying, for all those little ghouls and goblins out trick-or-treating.

If it wasn't for the fact that she had a court appearance at nine, Heather herself might have even enjoyed it. She did plan to go to Pine Hills Elementary following her plea hearing, after all, and do whatever it was a class mom had to do on this weightiest of class-mom days. But her mind was not on ghouls and goblins or trick-or-treating. She had more momentous things to consider, like whether to rat out Harlan White.

She sprang out of bed and, hands on hips, squinted in the direction of the wool suit hanging on the back of her bedroom door. It had been so chilly just a few days ago, when she'd bought this suit, but in the current weather it looked absurd. Like dressing up in polar fleece for a July Fourth picnic.

She looked at the clock: 7:08. She had less than an hour to get showered and dressed before she had to leave for the courthouse. At least according to Kevin, who believed in always allowing time for traffic, parking, and unexpected roadwork. She entered her walk-in closet and began plucking out possible outfits, holding them up, looking in the mirror, and then laying them out for further consideration. The charcoal gray summer-weight wool was perfect—except for that large grease stain, in the shape of Africa, on the lapel. Where had that come from? The navy blue pinstripe pants suit would do—but when she tried it on, the shoulder pads, which hailed from the early 1990s, made her look like a linebacker. When she clipped out the pads with nail scissors, the fabric puckered and sagged. Then there was the pink Chanel, wrapped in dry-cleaning plastic, which she'd worn on the *Today* show. Well, at least it was clean. And the style was current.

She tried it on, modeled it in front of the full-length mirror, and walked into the bathroom, where Kevin was shaving. "What do you think of this?" she asked.

"Like Lawyer Barbie," he said.

That smarted.

"I thought you'd planned what you were wearing. Isn't that what I told you to do?"

"I did," Heather said. "But who knew we were getting global warming?"

She'd taken the suit off and was standing around in panties when Connor barged in. Heather grabbed her nightgown off the bed and held it up to cover herself. Jesus! It didn't matter how many times she told him to knock, he never did.

"Mom," he said. "I've changed my mind about the costume."

"What do you mean you've changed your mind?"

"Global warming strikes again," Kevin muttered.

"Dad made fun of me," said Connor.

"No, Dad wasn't making fun of you," Heather said, trying to hurry him along. "He was making fun of me."

"No, before. Last night. He said that reporters were stupid."

Heather glared at Kevin.

Kevin looked at her, his eyebrows arched. A challenge. "Reporters are stupid," he restated, for the record. Connor let out a wail, sounding something like a monkey in distress.

"Thanks a lot," Heather said. "Then you may handle this."

She grabbed the summer-weight gray wool suit and a bra and locked herself in the bathroom. She would wear a scarf to cover the stain. Even though scarves were so . . . so . . . Mary Tyler Moore. She hooked her bra, scrubbed her face, brushed her teeth, assumed the pucker she always assumed to put on her lipstick. Beyond several sets of closed doors, she heard the sounds of males fighting. Kevin boomed, Connor screeched. Pleasant. Just what she needed, today of all days, the day of her court appearance.

When she stepped out of the bathroom, Connor practically fell on top of her. He'd been pushing against the door, which she'd locked. There he was in his Halloween splendor: wearing an old pair of Spider-Man pajamas, the kind with footies, which had been through the wash so many times it was shiny at the knees and elbows and seriously pilled everywhere else. Heather sighed. He was going to be made fun of. That was a guarantee. You could tie it up and put a ribbon on it. And there went thirty-seven dollars—for that reporter costume—down the drain.

Connor's face began to fold into a horror mask as he read hers. "You hate it," he said.

Be maternal, Heather told herself. Anything to prevent another meltdown. She reached over to Connor, drew him into her arms, and patted his back. "That's not true," she lied. "I was just thinking about my court case. You look great."

Really, what difference did it make what Connor wore for Halloween? He was going to eat too much candy and run around like a maniac no matter what costume he chose. And the children were going to hate him no matter what he did.

From outside came the blast of a horn. Kevin was already in the car. He continued to hold down the horn, just like an obnoxious teenager. Great. If there'd been anyone left on Giant Tortoise Drive who didn't already hate them, there wasn't anymore. The plan was to drop Connor off at school—there wasn't time to wait for the bus—and then drive to court. Even though she'd insisted on representing herself, Kevin planned to sit next to her, just in case. But now, as the horn insistently demanded her presence, she wished she hadn't even accepted that offer of help. She still hadn't picked out a scarf. She released Connor. "Get your backpack," she said. "And tell Daddy I'll be right out."

Finally, Heather found a checked swath of silk that seemed marginally appropriate with the gray suit. She picked up her briefcase, grabbed a chocolate-peanut-butter PowerBar, in case she got hungry later, and opened the front door. The weather struck her as even warmer than the news reports had said. And what was that smell? Like sulfur, used matches, rotten . . . eggs. She scrunched her nose, following the odor to its source, turning around until she discovered it. Smashed eggshells, glued to the front of her house. Egg yolks congealing in the morning sun. Toilet paper too, in loopy strands, some of it mixed with the eggs.

Any other day, she would have cried. Stomped her foot. Yelled to the heavens. Insisted that they call someone immediately to power-wash the house. She looked at her watch: 8:12. Already behind schedule. She opened the car door and took her seat. "What the hell?" she said, gesturing at the house.

Spider-Man, in the backseat, provided the explanation.

"It's called mischief night," he said. "I heard some kids on the bus talking about it."

She thought about calling Harlan White from her cell to ask him to come clean it up, but her stomach lurched. She realized she hadn't even decided whether she was going to finger him as the real snake-slayer. It was hard to decide what was more important, holding on to her dignity or keeping a reliable handyman.

It wasn't bragging, Barstad told himself, just general expansiveness. Bragging was rubbing your opponent's nose in his loss. Expansiveness was merely walking the earth with your chest full. And what a day for it. It was glorious. The brilliant coloring of fall, the maples blazing orange-red, all wrapped up in the warmth of August.

He'd been out picking up some Halloween candy, because Barbara surely hadn't bought enough. True, their custom-built house, situated at the end of a remote cul-de-sac, rarely got more than a handful of trick-or-treaters. But with weather like this, there was sure to be more foot traffic than usual. He'd gone into CVS and bought chocolate, only chocolate. Why bother with anything else? He hadn't been able to resist opening a few Hershey's Kisses as he drove off. They'd dissolved in his mouth, a melting sweetness wrapping around his tongue, and all he could think of was Jessie, lovely Jessie, barely older than a trick-or-treater herself. He was supposed to have gone to the gigantic new Home

Depot that had just opened, to check out prices on their kitchen cabinets and maybe negotiate a volume discount, but he'd found his car heading toward Jessie's little motel. Strange, he'd thought, how cars sometimes seemed to have a mind of their own. He'd let himself in with his own copy of the key and found Jessie asleep, her bird's nest of blond hair spreading in every direction. She'd looked all the sexier for it.

Now they were at the edge of the woods, just Barstad, Jessie, and an open bag of Hershey's Kisses, and he was making sweeping gestures, pointing out the future site of Galapagos Estates 2. "Two hundred homes," he said. "Eight hundred thou apiece. Do the math." Then, not waiting for her calculations, he supplied the answer himself. "A hundred and sixty mil. And it all belongs to yours truly." It occurred to him that he'd never have said such a thing to Dana, who could have done the math in the middle of an orgasm.

Barstad took hold of Jessie's elbow and walked her into the woods, as if he were escorting her into his own private castle. Already his dick was pressing against the front of his pants. Was it thinking about the money? The next outpost of his mighty empire? The chocolate still on his tongue? The lovely young lass on his arm? The unseasonable weather? Or perhaps the combination of all of these things?

He noticed, out of the corner of his eye, the edges of Harlan White's property, the rickety and weathered chicken coop just visible through the pine trees. A small voice in his brain reminded him that it was not his. Yet. But on a day like today he had no doubts. He knew that White's property would soon belong to him. And the price was falling every day.

Barstad breathed deeply and steered Jessie further into the woods.

The judge pounded his gavel and declared the plea hearing over. The silence of the courtroom was broken by a hundred small noises: the sound of chairs scraping backward as the prosecutor and his assistants stood up, lawyers representing other cases moving toward the front of the room, cell phones awakening with their musical little chimes. The courtroom was in motion. The case of *New Jersey* v. *Heather Peters* was finished, for the day at least.

Heather was done. She was free to go to Pine Hills Elementary and be a class mom.

She was elated. She'd done it. She'd represented herself, stood before the judge, entered her own plea: not guilty. It was as simple as that. Kevin, sitting silently next to her at the defense table, hadn't had to utter a single word. And now the wheels of justice were set in motion. She could handle it.

The assistant prosecutor walked over to Kevin and whispered something in his ear. "Thanks," Kevin said. Then he told Heather. "There's an elevator down that hallway. We don't have to take the courthouse steps."

"I don't mind walking," Heather said brightly. "It's a nice day."

"The press," Kevin muttered through clenched teeth.

"I don't mind the press," Heather said.

She slid her papers into her briefcase, opened her purse, took out a small compact, reapplied her lipstick, and walked out of the courtroom.

When she got to the steps, they were there. Dozens and dozens of them. More than at the jazz funeral, more than after the rats, more than had staked out the hotel.

Several of the television reporters were already doing their standups. They stood, framed against the courthouse's old-fashioned entrance, speaking to oversized cameras. The radio reporters ran toward her as soon as they saw her, their microphones festooned with square mike flags bearing their stations' call letters. The photographers, hefting lenses the size of rocket launchers, were the most aggressive of all. They were the big-game hunters of the press corps. They'd trample any fool who dared get in their way.

A shadow suddenly cast itself over the courthouse lawn, and the sound of rotors whipping furiously filled the air. Heather looked up. A news chopper was recording the scene from above.

Kevin took Heather's elbow, as if to lead her protectively down the stairs. But she shook it off and stopped, signaling to the crowd that she was, indeed, available for their questions. She sucked in her breath, composed herself, and smiled.

Two dozen reporters shouted her name simultaneously. She nodded toward one, to get the thing started.

"Mrs. Peters, why did you plead not guilty?"

"Because I'm not guilty," she said.

"But everybody in America knows that you killed that snake!"

"But I didn't kill the snake," she said.

Suddenly everyone was shouting questions. Shutters snapped furiously. Microphones were thrust closer. The TV reporters turned away from the cameras and ran toward her. Heather could only hear snippets of questions. "But you said—"

"The *Today* show—"

"—in your garage—"

"—didn't kill—"

Heather held her hand up to silence the crowd, signaling to one and all that she was prepared to explain, once they quieted down. It worked. A hush descended on the courthouse steps. Heather looked at all the expectant faces, then took a deep breath.

"I regret to have to tell you that I misrepresented myself before," she said. "I didn't kill the snake."

"But the snake was dead!" someone shouted. "In your garage."

"I, however, was not the one who killed it," Heather said. "It was someone else."

The crowd, as one, had a single question. Who, if not Heather Peters, had killed the snake? Again, a cacophony of voices rose, and Heather raised her hand for silence. Again, it worked.

"I must protect that person's identity," she began. "But I can tell you this. There's a good story here, a better one than the one you've been covering. My house was built on a snake sanctuary. And the builder of Galapagos Estates, Jack Barstad, knew it all along. Go back to the public record. And you'll find an environmental impact statement that was falsified, a herpetologist paid off . . ."

The great news-gathering machine pressed in. A Medusa of cables and cords, the press corps moved like a single organism, closing in on the little blonde on the courthouse steps like a monster ready to swallow its victim alive.

The first thing he felt was a flush of shame. He, Rodney Campbell, had created this story. He'd been the one to discover Heather Peters, to put her on the front page, with her hands spread in that ludicrous "so big" pose, showing the length of the rattlesnake she had supposedly killed, single-handedly, on her patio. And now she was saying, to him, his colleagues, his competitors, and his editor, that the whole story had been a fake.

Rodney Campbell was toast.

Heather Peters had lied and he had bought it. Where was his bullshit detector that day? Why hadn't he seen through her? What a bitch!

But then, he realized, everybody had bought it. If she was a con artist, she was a master con artist. She hadn't tricked just him. She'd tricked Katie Couric and Brian Williams. And she would have tricked Oprah too, if her appearance hadn't been pulled for that of the woman with the botched mastectomy, according to what he'd read in the *Drudge Report.*

And then a third realization came to him, and it was this one that caused him to tuck his reporter's notebook into his jacket and run down the courthouse stairs. A rattlesnake was dead, and somebody had killed it. If it wasn't Heather Peters, it had to be someone else. And that someone else would be, yes it would . . . the handyman!

Campbell thought back to his standing interview with Harlan White. There'd been something funny about the whole thing, something the guy was holding back. And then he remembered, like he was watching a movie, a funny little thing that had happened that day he was standing on Harlan White's front porch. When Campbell had mentioned Heather Peters, the lady who killed the snake, the farmer had laughed. Now he understood.

Even better, he understood that he was the only one who understood. The other reporters standing on the steps had followed the Heather Peters story, staked out her lawn, her hotel. They'd been there for the New Orleans jazz funeral for the snake. The story about the rats, from the TV point of view, had been like manna from heaven. They'd analyzed everything from her haircut to her footwear. But he was the only one who'd really dug around, the only one who knew about Harlan

White. Investigative reporting. It was still something newspapers could do better than anyone else.

Campbell got into his car and turned on the radio, so he could hear the rest of what Heather had to say. And then he headed in the direction of Harlan White's farm.

Chapter Twenty-Seven

Harlan had been hunting turkey since he was nine, but he'd never quite had the taste for it like he had this year. His dad had taught him all he needed to know: the legalities, logistics, and pleasantries. Having the permits, getting permission of property owners when you hunted on someone else's land, making sure you could always see exactly what you were shooting at, and of course the safe and proper cleaning, handling, and carrying of a shotgun. Harlan knew, of course, that hunting turkey was dangerous. Everybody used turkey calls—little whistles and boxes and other thingamajigs that made gobbling sounds—and it was all too easy to confuse one of these contraptions for an authentic gobbler. Or the converse: some asshole could shoot you. Harlan knew all these things as well as he knew how to turn on a TV or wash his hands. They were second nature.

The fall turkey season in New Jersey was a mere six days, and it ended tomorrow. He'd bagged a tom every day this week—one a day, that was the legal limit, and he was still operating within the law—but he needed to bag two more, one today, one tomorrow, to make it a perfect season. After all, he wasn't grocery shopping these days and getting coupons for a free frozen turkey. He was sick of squirrel, and he had seen from Agnes's reaction that skunk stew was beyond the pale of civilization. He'd been losing weight too. His pants were getting loose, and he'd had to tighten his belt a notch.

Harlan was mad that it had taken him so long to wake up. It had just been so damn cold lately, and he'd developed a cough, what with the temperature and the smoke from the woodstove. Mornings were the roughest, the fire always having died overnight. Harlan was still in bed, covers to his chin, hacking away, unaware that the weather had changed, that it was going to be the warmest Halloween in eighty years. When a house has been chilly for close to a month, it hangs on to that chill—even when the temperature outside warms. It was the sound of gunshots from the woods that finally roused him.

Harlan didn't discover how warm it really was until he walked outside to check the abandoned henhouse for salvageable eggs. As he felt the heat, he shed one jacket, then another, enjoying the sun's radiating warmth through his flannel shirt. He felt momentarily like a baby chick in an incubator. Maybe there was a God after all. Then in one corner of the coop, under some straw, he found two eggs, one cracked. In better times, he would have thrown the cracked one out. But these weren't better times.

As he walked back, he heard voices coming from the woods. His woods. Well, that explained the gunshots. Damn. He had signs posted, and nobody had come asking for permission to hunt. But he was still going to have to be extra careful, and he'd have to wear some bright orange just to make sure some asshole didn't confuse him for a turkey. Which, unfortunately, would give the turkey warning too.

Campbell was still listening to Heather's impromptu press conference on his car radio. It was amazing, really, this little brat of a woman, suddenly spouting all kinds of accusations against Jack Barstad. He could picture the whole scene in his mind—he'd just come from there, after all–but it still was strange, Heather Peters taking on a whole battalion of reporters, talking about a falsified environmental impact statement, a corrupt zoning board, and the fight for survival of the poor, indigenous rattlesnake. Had he heard that right? Heather Peters worried about rattlesnakes? Now he wished he hadn't left so soon, while she was just winding up. Maybe he'd missed the story after all. Maybe going to White's farm would be a wild-goose chase. Well, he'd already made the commitment when he headed to the parking lot. If he went back now, it could all be over.

His hunch about Harlan had better be right. That's all. And the guy better be around too. He rolled down the driver's side window and let in some air. It was amazingly warm for Halloween.

Agnes let out a deep disgusted sigh as she placed the glass cage containing her two corn snakes in the backseat of the VW. Not that there was anybody around to witness her annoyance. It was too bad she led such a solitary life, that Oliver wasn't here anymore, that she had nobody but the animals to hear her sighs and whines and moans and to commiserate with her about the general stupidity of the world.

Moving the snakes hadn't been easy. The cage—actually a seventy-five-gallon glass aquarium—weighed a ton, and she was no spring chicken. She'd had to wheel it out, using a rolling cart, which of course had to be emptied of all the reports and office supplies that were currently camped there. At least, given the weather, she didn't have to worry too much about the heat lamps being disconnected for the car trip. Her main concern would be keeping all those sugar-crazed children at Pine Hills Elementary from pounding their grubby little fists on the glass.

The principal, Mrs. Gupnick, had promised that the children would be well behaved, or at least well supervised. That they were looking forward to Agnes's visit, had all been taught "herp etiquette," and would be kept a minimum of four feet away from the cage, unless she invited them closer. And Agnes would be giving some of them a chance to pet the snakes, wouldn't she? Agnes sighed again, as she took her position behind the steering wheel, imagining sticky fingers stroking Corny and Cobby—that's what she called them in front of school groups—and leaving disgusting deposits of Reese's Peanut Butter Cups on the snakes' skin. It was all too much. If it weren't for the twenty-five hundred dollars, which might help in her campaign for the nonmigratory geese or some other doomed species, she wouldn't have even considered putting up with it.

It was a pleasant drive, a mere ten minutes, and she was leaving on time. Some classical music would be nice. Agnes pushed the button for the radio, always set to the local public station, but instead of the civilized strains of Mozart or Debussy, she was surprised to discover the discordant sounds of a live news conference. What country is the president bombing now, she thought disgustedly, and she was about to turn the radio off when she heard the name that the reporters were shouting. "Mrs. Peters! Mrs. Peters!" Could it be . . . *her* Mrs. Peters? Heather Peters, of Galapagos Estates? The sonorous voice of a public-radio announcer confirmed it. "We're outside the Burlington County Courthouse," he said. "Live with Heather Peters, the lady who killed the snake."

Agnes flinched—thinking of Corny and Cobby in her backseat—and though she knew they couldn't understand English, she felt annoyed to have snake killing mentioned in their presence. Just then, a squirrel darted across the road, and she had to slam her brakes and swerve to avoid hitting it. A Ford Explorer, which had been following too closely, blasted its horn at her.

Agnes took a breath, put her foot on the accelerator, and began again, vowing to stay calm and watch more closely for small animals. Then she heard Heather say, "I, however, was not the one who killed it. It was someone else."

Someone else!

Agnes had to go warn Harlan. Right away. She veered to the right, in order to make a quick U-turn, and the commentary from the Explorer this time made the previous horn blast sound like a friendly toot.

No matter. She executed her turn without killing any animals, though the Explorer wound up in a ditch. As she sped by in the opposite direction, toward Harlan's farm, she saw the driver angrily flash the middle finger. It was a shame, she thought, that people had such bad manners these days.

It had started with a single Hershey's Kiss. Jessie had put one in her mouth, and had closed her eyes in an expression of rapture. When Barstad inserted his tongue, she pressed the Hershey's Kiss into his mouth, and they'd exchanged the candy back and forth until all the chocolate had melted and their tongues and mouths were coated with the fat little chocolate globules. Barstad was sure he saw Jessie's nipples prick up against her stretchy T-shirt then, that the chocolate, the kissing, the woods, the day—all of it—was doing the same thing to her that it was to him. He pressed her up against a tree and inserted another candy kiss in her mouth. She took it eagerly and wrapped her right leg around him.

As the chocolate dissolved, Barstad began to have other ideas, imagined other places where chocolate could be deposited, places where chocolate could melt. He took off his jacket, threw it onto the ground, and then nudged Jessie there. He took the button of her jeans in his mouth, trying to undo it with his teeth. But it was harder than he thought, and he had a morbid fear of dental work. So he abandoned the button and moved his mouth to the edge of her waistband, inserting his tongue between the stiff denim and her flat belly, tracing a wet chocolate trail as he went. He would have her right here, in the woods, like Adam had Eve, with only God watching. Like Adam and Eve, only with chocolate.

Chapter Twenty-Eight

It had started off fine, even better than fine. The fabulous weather made for a successful parade. Each of the classes, except for Miss Kindermack's, had come to school in theme, linked to the master theme, "All Creatures Bright and Beautiful." And it could not be denied that this year the class mothers—with, of course, certain notable exceptions—had outdone themselves. It was a shame, Mrs. Gupnick thought, that it was such a transient affair, over in less than an hour, recorded only by amateurs. She fantasized about a TV documentary and could even picture the camera angles, starting with a bird's-eye view that would capture the entire parade. And if not that, she should at least be accepting a "best practice" award at the New Jersey teachers' convention in Atlantic City next week. If only there were a special session on Halloween practices! "My fellow educators," she would say, blushing slightly. "The credit really shouldn't go to me but to the dedicated class parents who work so hard . . ." It always sounded good for an elementary school principal to deflect praise back to the parents.

But the splendor of the parade and the creativity of the class moms was not to be denied. Miss Gentilly's second-grade class had all dressed up as Beanie Babies, and Cynthia West, their class mom, had actually driven into New York City's garment district and walked door to door until she struck a deal on remainder rolls of plush fabric. All the children's oversized "Ty" tags looked adorable, and there was even the poignant touch of having the Beanies marked on sale. The theme for Mrs. Rambol's kindergarten class was Animal Crackers, and it was amazing the effect that had been achieved just using tan-colored felt. But that wasn't all. Mrs. Rambol's class mom, Jane Perfido, had a brother-in-law who designed sets for TV commercials, and this talented brother-in-law had built, as a prop, an oversized Animal Crackers box, which looked exactly like the real thing. Of course, it was a little scary—*What Ever Happened to Baby Jane?* came to mind—to see the ancient Mrs. Rambol in a wig of blond ringlets, tap-dancing alongside her class, pretending to be Shirley Temple. But Mrs. Gupnick couldn't concern herself about that. Halloween did bring out something twisted in certain people; she only hoped that the cuteness of the younger children would provide an antidote to whatever excesses naturally emerged.

Truly, the only sour note in the whole parade was Miss Kindermack's class. After the superintendent's office had requested that they scratch the *If You Give a Mouse a Cookie* theme, the class had floundered. Heather Peters had never come up with anything else, never even returned calls, according to Miss Kindermack. The poor third-graders and their parents had therefore been left to their own devices. Mrs. Gupnick tried to make the best of it, smiling and praising the students as best she could. But she'd never had much of a knack for pop culture, and the array of unthemed costumes befuddled her. She thought one boy, with darkly drawn sideburns and a white satin pants suit, was a stock-car driver. "Elvis," he said, rolling his eyes. She mistook a Zorro for Sherlock Holmes, Hermione Granger for Nancy Drew, and, worst of all, she thought that the pathetic little Peters boy, dressed in footie pajamas, was just pretending to be a toddler. When she discovered that he'd really been going as Spider-Man, it was too late. The boys nearby started to tease him relentlessly. "Baby want his bottle?" they sneered. "Where's your pacifier?" The boy's tears merely notched up the fun for his tormentors.

It was in the cafeteria, at the Halloween feast, that Mrs. Gupnick's perfect Halloween began to unravel.

One of the mothers had apparently not gotten the memorandum about nuts, and unfortunately Mrs. Gupnick didn't discover this until she was surveying the sweets table midway through the festivities and discovered a half-consumed batch of walnut brownies. True, it hadn't been peanuts. But everybody knew—at least everybody should have known, by now—that walnuts are frequently packaged in the same factories where peanuts are packed and could therefore be contaminated by microscopic particles of peanut dust. Mrs. Gupnick knew she was in for a reprimand from the school district's lawyers; they'd sent her a video on this very subject. But it wasn't her fault. She'd sent a memo to every parent in the school! What was next? Forbidding any treats from home, ever? No cupcakes for birthdays? An outright ban of brown-bag lunches?

Mrs. Gupnick quickly dispatched a teacher's aide from one of the special-ed classes to run down to the school nurse, so she could pull the files on student allergies and rush down with an epinephrine kit, just in case. It was all she could do, given the circumstances, and yet she could not possibly have foreseen that half the special-ed kids, sugared up on candy, would jump from their seats and chase the aide down the hall or that this would set off a chain reaction among the rest of the kids, who were sugared up as well, and getting tired of sitting in docile groups waiting for the costume contest to begin. In the commotion, the nurse misheard the aide and thought that one of the children was already in anaphylactic shock, so she quickly dialed 911 before setting off to the cafeteria. Within minutes the rescue squad, a fire truck, and three police cruisers were on the scene. The police—recently drilled in how to secure a school threatened by deranged gunmen—ran into the cafeteria, SWAT team–style, guns drawn.

It took half an hour to straighten everything out. The kids with allergies were all checked, and though one boy was practically in diabetic shock from ingesting fistfuls of candy corn, it was confirmed that he hadn't consumed any of the errant brownies after all. Mrs. Gupnick tried to pretend that the police, firefighters, and ambulance workers had all come to the school to make the event that much more festive. "Why, it's the Village People!" she said, proud to have remembered the group's name. She popped up to lead the whole cafeteria in "YMCA."

While Mrs. Gupnick swung her arms around, forming *y*'s and *m*'s, one of the cafeteria ladies, on instructions from the school superintendent, wrapped up the remaining walnut brownies and stuck them in the freezer. The lawyers wanted them available for a laboratory analysis, in the event of a lawsuit.

And the day had started out so well!

In the back of the cafeteria, a surly group of fourth-grade boys leaned against the wall, their arms folded, looking like thugs. Mrs. Gupnick glanced quickly at the clock on the wall above them. Where was the lady from the nature center? She should be here by now. Mrs. Gupnick needed something to entertain these kids, and she needed it quick. She was in danger of losing control of the cafeteria.

Making love in a barn had been thrilling, but it paled beside doing it in the open woods. Barstad marveled at how completely animal the experience was, like dogs mounting. Pure bodily need, stripped bare of the frills of civilization.

Sure, it must be a little uncomfortable for Jessie, who was on the bottom, with just Barstad's thin jacket for protection from the brittle leaves and twigs. But he was paying good money, wasn't he? And by the sound of things, she was enjoying it as much as he was.

Barstad felt triumphant, the only way a man could feel while he was taking a beautiful young nymph in the middle of the woods. He now knew that he was over Dana, over any shame he'd felt that day in the hotel room in Atlantic City. He came, thunderously, like Zeus, and as he did he felt more than the mere pulsations of physical pleasure. He was reborn, revitalized, his virility restored.

They lay in a postcoital heap, their jeans kicked off and forming a puddle of blue at their feet, panting, catching their breath. Barstad's heart had been hammering, every muscle, synapse, cell of his body in a state of overdrive. Now the tension began to melt, like the Hershey's Kisses, and he closed his eyes, willing the euphoria to linger, when Jessie suddenly clutched his arm. "What?" he said.

"Listen."

At first Barstad couldn't hear anything. When he finally did, it sounded like the *glug-glug* of an old-fashioned water cooler. But that was impossible. No, it wasn't a machine; it was a voice. Not quite human, but a voice nonetheless.

Jessie, suddenly getting it, burst out laughing.

"What?" he said.

"A tom."

"A tom?"

"A turkey."

They relaxed again, and Jessie draped a coltish leg over his torso. She wasn't ready again so soon, was she? His heart raced, half in expectation, half in alarm. She couldn't expect him to get hard immediately, could she? Even James Bond took a little while to reload. Jessie reached down and gently took hold of his balls. "Gobble, gobble," she said. "Gobble, gobble." Barstad turned to her with a mock pout. It was the closest she had ever come to making a joke. But it was true. The essential male apparatus did bear a certain resemblance to a turkey.

He lay back again, trying to reestablish his state of bliss, but the universe seemed set on disturbing him. A huge blast rang out in the distance, followed by an unmistakable report. This time Barstad didn't need Jessie to call his attention to the sound, or interpret it. It was a shotgun, loud and clear. "Shit," he said. "Hunters."

He began to reach for his jeans, but Jessie grabbed his wrist so hard she could have been a dominatrix.

"Don't," she ordered. Her voice was low but strong.

"What?"

She pointed. And there, tangled with their jeans, he saw it.

The thing was several shades of brown, and it matched the leaves and the dirt so perfectly it was as if it had been designed by a decorator. The colors formed a pattern of two-inch diamonds, darker against lighter. The texture was hard, oily, and scaly, and it reminded Barstad of an old pair of boots his North Carolina grandpa used to wear. The object of Jessie's interest was coiled like a gardening hose, except that unlike any gardening hose Barstad had ever seen, it pulsed. It was muscular, strong, writhing, and in a truly upsetting way it reminded Barstad of a gigantic penis, even to the slightly bulging shape of its head.

"Timber rattler," Jessie said. "I took herpetology at Penn State." Then, even more violently than she had grabbed his arm, she reached over and covered his mouth with her hand. "Listen," she whispered.

At first Barstad thought it was leaves or pine needles rustling in the wind. Then it sounded more like insect shells, the hard casings of June bugs or Japanese beetles, smashing up against one another like they were being shaken in a martini pitcher. Then suddenly he remembered a similar sound, one that he hadn't heard for years, since his children were very small. A baby rattle. And it was that idea—rattle—that informed him of the danger. After all, he had read all the newspaper accounts. Like everyone else, he knew all about the infamous rattle of the infamous snake in the infamous Heather Peters's backyard.

It was one sound you really didn't want to hear. You didn't want to hear it in your backyard, and you sure as hell didn't want to hear it out in the middle of the woods with your pants down and your gobble-gobble sitting there all exposed and vulnerable.

Harlan set out with his shotgun and his turkey call and the determination that he would bag his fifth turkey that week, even if he had to be more careful than usual. The gunshot he'd heard earlier, and the voices in the woods, had unnerved him. At least, he thought, he still had his woods. It was better to have your woods, and have to share it with some asshole who didn't have the common courtesy to ask permission to hunt there, than to open your back door and see a hundred houses that all looked alike.

It occurred to Harlan, as he passed his henhouse, that it was about time for Halloween. Having lost track of the dates, he wasn't sure. Was it coming up? Or had it passed? His farmhouse was too remote for trick-or-treaters, but he'd always gotten high school kids the night before, sneaking into his henhouse to pick up ammunition for mischief night. Well, he wouldn't be underwriting their mischief this year. No chickens, no eggs, no need to lock down the coop. And that, in a way, was the saddest thing about the turn his life had taken, sadder even than having the power and phone turned off and eating skunk stew. He didn't have anything to lose. Though he'd had little regret over the fact that he'd never taken a wife or reared a family, he had to acknowledge that it was a quiet, lonely existence. But now, without even the clucking of the hens, Harlan's life was as desolate and parched as the surface of the moon. The only thing he'd had, since his parents died, was his little business and the sense of belonging to a place. But now the business was gone and Hebron Township bore little relation to the small rural community he'd grown up in. He had his land. That was all.

Harlan walked slowly through the woods, more alert than usual, listening for footsteps, for the rustling that might indicate another hunter. He put his turkey call to his lips and heard its ridiculous gobble, then thought better of it. Too dangerous, he decided. Another hunter might just take aim.

A small commotion in the distance focused his attention.

At first the sounds were indistinct, but as he got closer Harlan could make out grunting, snorting, and flesh slapping against flesh, a sound that reminded him of pigs rutting. Well, that happened in the woods all the time, he thought. Maybe not pigs, but other animals. Then he realized the grunting sounds came not from an animal but from a man, and sure enough, through the trees, he caught a glimpse of what was certainly human skin. He stood absolutely still, beholding the scene from about fifty feet away, until he heard a final massive grunt from the man and what sounded like a moan of ecstasy from the girl. Kids, he thought disgustedly, and started to walk away.

Then he thought again. What if that sound, the female sound, had not been a cry of pleasure but of distress? Was he so detached from human society that he could walk away from a rape and not even try to help?

It was the middle of the woods, the middle of the day, and though he didn't really know whether or not it was a weekday, when kids should be in school, he supposed it didn't matter. Two human beings having sex in the woods wasn't exactly normal under any circumstances. He needed to check it out. It wasn't just prurient curiosity, he told himself, moving toward the sound, but a genuine desire to do the right thing. Besides, this was his property.

Harlan walked in the direction of the naked couple, taking care to move so cautiously that he barely displaced a twig. If the girl appeared to have been willing, he would turn back, and nobody would be the wiser. The thought of finding a used condom in his woods was disgusting enough. He didn't really want to come face-to-face with fornicators if he could help it.

Then, for the second time that day, Harlan heard the distant boom of a shotgun. Instinctively, he lifted his gun and squinted, scanning the distance. Nothing. But you could never be too careful.

His attention returned to the naked pair, who seemed awfully quiet for people who'd just made whoopie. No cooing, no giggling, no pillow talk—or whatever passed for pillow talk out in the woods. Maybe the shotgun blast had frightened them. But as he moved closer still, Harlan could tell something else was wrong. They were as naked as people in a French painting, but their faces revealed no pleasure. They were staring at something, and the man looked just as scared as the girl. Maybe more.

Then he saw it, a timber rattler, which had taken up residence right on top of the lovers' blue jeans. Shit, what was it about him and rattlesnakes? How many could a person come across in one season? Had they bred in greater numbers this year? Was the warm weather bringing them out?

It was with the first real pang of pleasure he'd had in weeks that Harlan realized he recognized the man, the ugly grinning face he'd seen a million times on the billboard that cast an offensive shadow over Route 381. It was none other than his nemesis, Jack Barstad, the real estate developer, with his pants down, a rattlesnake on top of them, and a bimbo clutching his arm.

Harlan aimed his shotgun directly at Barstad's head. He ought to shoot the bastard right now and get it over with.

Rodney Campbell parked his car, ran up to Harlan's door, and started pounding on it. Nothing. He tried again. Still no response. That was strange. There was a light blue rusted-out pickup in the driveway. It had to belong to the old guy. Campbell knocked again, and when he failed to get a response, he walked over to the truck and looked in the back. He saw the regular stuff you'd expect to see: old coolers and plastic buckets, fishing rods, a black metal tool kit, badly dinged, and a few coils of rope. He stuck his hand through the open window and pulled the registration out of the glove compartment. It was registered to Harlan White, all right.

Shit. This wasn't getting him anywhere. He winced, thinking about the Heather Peters press conference he'd run out on, and about what the managing editor would say when he found out he missed the big story on his beat. So much for hunches, for getting out ahead of the crowd. He'd had to be a hero, to get the big scoop. Now he was going to have his sorry ass handed to him.

Campbell walked back to his car and leaned against it for another minute, refusing to give up, when a bumper sticker on the back of the pickup caught his eye. IT'S MORE THAN GUNS, IT'S FREEDOM, it said, and Campbell noticed the circular logo of the NRA. A small clue, but maybe, just maybe . . . The man was a hunter, and it had to be hunting season for . . . something. There were woods right out back; maybe the guy went hunting in his own backyard. Hence, no need for his truck. It was a long shot. Those were big woods, and it was probably not wise to waltz into them in the middle of hunting season. But if he missed the Heather Peters story and didn't come back with something, he was as good as dead anyway.

He ran into the woods the way only a desperate journalist could, not taking any time for stealth, because he didn't know how much territory he'd have to cover before he either found the farmer or gave up. He ran without a plan, unsure of his direction, not knowing whether he was doubling back on his path and covering the same ground twice. He stumbled several times, though he always managed to regain his footing. But in short order, his sedentary ways and his nights hanging out at bars, bumming cigarettes off waitresses, caught up with him, and he was wheezing. He had to stop and catch his breath.

He stayed in that position for several minutes, holding on to a small tree and bending down to clear his pitiful lungs of the film of phlegm that had accumulated during his sprint. While he waited for his breathing to slow, he began to become aware of . . . something. But what? He willed himself to stop his gasping, so he could hear, but even when the rasp of his lungs subsided, he heard nothing. Yet he knew something was there, just beyond a big clump of pines. The hairs on the back of his neck bristled, the involuntary reflex of a central nervous system registering an invisible threat. He wasn't sure if he'd found what he'd come into the woods to stalk, or if something was stalking him.

Campbell began to move slowly, toward what he didn't know, taking care now to make as little noise as possible. And after just a few feet he was rewarded with a scene he could not have invented were he a reporter for a supermarket tabloid. There was Harlan White, dressed in hunting garb all right, and pointing a shotgun, right at a man and woman lying buck naked on the floor of the woods. The woman was young and beautiful, with large, perfectly shaped breasts, a thin waist, and tousled blond hair. The man, who looked red from overexertion, looked to be in his fifties. Campbell's eyes widened as he recognized him. It was Jack Barstad, president of Barstad Enterprises, the real estate developer who'd built Galapagos Estates and half a dozen other subdivisions nearby, and whose face, topped by a horrible comb-over and blown up several hundred times its natural size, grinned down from billboards all over the southern half of the state.

Hot damn!

But there was more. Campbell stared as the farmer aimed his shotgun away from Barstad's face toward a point near the developer's feet. There, of all things, was a snake, coiled on top of a pair of blue jeans.

Campbell couldn't help congratulating himself. So his instincts, after all, had been right. He'd found a story, a better story, than the one he'd left on the courthouse steps. Another rattlesnake—it had to be. Along with the original rattlesnake killer. And, as a bonus, the biggest developer in the country, caught in flagrante delicto, in the woods, for God's sake, with a woman certainly not his wife. Campbell reached into his jacket to take out the small digital camera he'd bought for his own birthday, and prayed silently that the batteries in it still held a charge. He was relieved when the power switch worked, but when he brought the viewfinder up to his eyes, he discovered there were worse things than dead batteries or even botched assignments. What he saw, through the lens, was the business end of Harlan White's shotgun.

Campbell dropped the camera and slowly raised his hands in the air, just the way he'd seen in dozens of movies.

It was probably the thud of the camera that caused the snake to strike; and the reactions of the naked developer, his paramour, and the farmer were equally swift. The lovers sprang to their feet just as the shotgun discharged.

It sounded to Campbell more like a hand grenade than a shotgun, although he'd never heard either in real life, and as he had just seen the gun aimed directly at himself, he assumed at first that he was dead. He waited for blood to spurt from his forehead, and when none did, he reached up and touched his own head. It was still there, dry and intact. What luck! Harlan White must have turned the gun on the snake at the last minute!

But the relief was temporary. White had missed. The reptile wasn't on top of the jeans anymore, but a flash of movement through the leaves and brush indicated it was still around.

Campbell scuttled backward, trying to give the snake as wide a berth as possible, and the blonde did exactly the same thing. Barstad took the opportunity to run, but given that his feet were as bare as his wobbling white ass, his retreat turned quickly into a comic hobble. Only Harlan stood his ground. He steadied his shotgun and aimed again, squinting into the brush and following the path of the snake with the barrel of his weapon.

"Wait!"

Out of nowhere, a white-haired woman had arrived on the scene, and she seemed, oddly enough, to have a special regard for the snake. But it was too late. The shotgun exploded again. And this time Harlan White hit his mark.

Chapter Twenty-Nine

Kevin held his hand up and said there would be no more questions, and like the Red Sea responding to Moses, the press parted. They ran, actually. The radio and television reporters ran to file their stories, and the newspaper reporters and the stringer for *People* magazine ran off to Barstad Enterprises to confront the developer with the allegations Heather Peters had just made.

It was extraordinary how fast a mob like that could clear out, and soon Heather stood alone, but for Kevin, in front of the courthouse. She sighed deeply.

The press was gone. Her moment in the sun was over. One minute, the whole world was interested in her ordeal, the next she was a has-been. There'd be no more invitations from the *Today* show or from Oprah. If she was remembered at all, it would be by those second-tier news shows that specialized in fabulists and frauds. She'd played her hand, and if Kevin was right, the fact that she hadn't killed the rattlesnake would keep her out of jail. He was still pissed that she refused to name the actual rattlesnake killer, but he'd come up with the idea of having her undergo a polygraph. That way she could prove she hadn't violated any endangered-species law. They'd get a good lawyer and work out some kind of deal to get them to drop the assault charges stemming from her arrest. She'd been in a state of shock, after all, when they'd barged in on Back to School Night and dragged her off in handcuffs. No wonder she'd tried to bite the police officer.

But Heather also understood the downside of her confession. She had lied, flat out. She'd trumped up her own bravery and importance from the start, so that now, as soon as the news got out that she hadn't killed the snake after all, she would be the laughingstock of Galapagos Estates, of Pine Hills Elementary, of Hebron Township and Burlington County. Heck, she'd be the laughingstock of all New Jersey! Why she'd told that first fib, she didn't know, but once she had, it had become harder and harder to take it back. It had almost gotten to the point where she believed she had killed the rattlesnake. And, she had to admit, she'd enjoyed the limelight. Enjoyed the phone calls from reporters in Japan. Enjoyed having limos whisk her to New York at 4 A.M. Enjoyed buying her cute little Chanel suit. Enjoyed snacking on smoked salmon and rice crackers in the greenroom. And now, after the press chewed her up and spat her out one last time, it would all be over. She'd be just another housewife with a wash to do and a brat to ferry around.

"Well," Kevin said.

"Well," said Heather.

"What next?"

She sighed. That was a good question. She still had to fight the Homeowners Committee and—in addition to the legal research she needed to do on resident covenants—she was planning to take her campaign door to door. It was time for the rehabilitation of Heather Peters, and if that meant making industrial quantities of fudge to hand out to every single resident of Giant Tortoise Drive, well then, that's exactly what she would do. But first . . . first, she had some unfinished business at Pine Hills Elementary.

"Drop me at the school," she said. "It's Halloween. I'm still class mom."

After he was sure that the snake was dead, Barstad, who'd been hiding behind a stand of pines a safe distance away, came skulking back to pick up his jeans. He turned away from the small crowd as he stepped into them, trying to pretend that a nude man getting dressed in the middle of the woods surrounded by onlookers was perfectly natural, happened every day. For their part, Agnes, Rodney Campbell, and Harlan cooperated in this little charade, looking down and drawing small patterns in the dirt with their shoes. The man was disgusting, cowardly, and clearly a letch. He'd raped the countryside and defiled a young woman, and in the moment of danger, he'd run off without concern for anyone but himself. Still, there was no use going out of their way to humiliate him.

Campbell, who'd heard Heather Peters's accusations against Barstad, knew that he would have to confront the guy—but he could at least wait for him to zip up. Harlan, who was absentmindedly rubbing the metal handle of his shotgun, wondered why he hadn't just taken the bastard out in the first place. Agnes looked solemnly at the rattlesnake, deciding whether to take it back to the Rutgers lab for a full workup or to leave it in the woods for nature to dispose of in its own way.

When he was finally dressed, Barstad tried to put his arm around Jessie, who had slipped her clothes on while he was still hiding. But when Barstad touched her, she shook him off, as if his hands had been coated with slime. Something had changed when the snake appeared and the gun went off and Jack Barstad had hobbled away as fast as he could to save his own fat middle-aged ass. Jessie had begun to undergo a transformation. What was she doing selling her companionship? She peeked up at Agnes from underneath her long eyelashes, appealing to the older woman. Although Agnes had never been a mother, she took the girl under her wing. Agnes nodded to Harlan as she walked out of the woods, the young lady nestled protectively under her arm.

Harlan waited for Agnes to leave before he bent down and wrapped the snake in his jacket. He'd heard of rattlesnake stew; the colonists had eaten it during hard times. He'd just have to go to the town library and look up how to get rid of the venom before cooking it. After everything that had happened, he didn't feel like hunting turkey—at least not today. The snake was certain to contain some protein.

Barstad was stalking off in the opposite direction from Agnes, Jessie, and Harlan. Campbell ran after him, and when he caught up he pulled out his New Jersey press card. "Rodney Campbell, *South Jersey Eagle,*" he said, catching his breath. "I've got a few questions. About Heather Peters, that is. And some allegations she made this morning after court—"

"Fuck off," Barstad said.

"Okay," Campbell said to himself. "Have it your way."

Campbell had to ask for Barstad's side of the story, of course. That was protocol. But he didn't need Barstad's quote to make a story. He'd memorized the scene and could describe it precisely. Moreover, there'd been three other witnesses. Campbell took out his camera and shot Barstad's retreat. The picture surely wasn't as good as a staff photographer could have taken, but it would do.

Running back and overtaking Harlan White was a good deal easier than catching up with Barstad. The farmer was in his seventies. Campbell walked silently beside him for a while, sensing that not talking would be the best way to establish rapport. "So," he said finally. "Were you the one who killed the rattlesnake?"

"You just saw," Harlan said.

"No, the other one. Heather Peters's rattlesnake. Today, outside court, she said she wasn't the one who killed it."

Harlan nodded.

"And I remembered that you'd worked as her handyman."

"I suppose," Harlan said with a small smile, "you could say that killing rattlers has become my specialty."

Campbell took out his notebook, asked a few more questions, and jotted down White's replies. The farmer was droll, matter-of-fact. He didn't go out of his way to kill rattlesnakes, he said, but he did go out of his way not to be killed by them. Sometimes you didn't have a choice.

"Thanks," Campbell said. "By the way, what are you going to do with it?"

"Eat it," Harlan said.

That was one way, Campbell supposed, to get rid of the evidence.

It was time, now that he'd had his little scoop, to rejoin his colleagues in the fourth estate, and by the time he got to Barstad Enterprises, the rest of the press was in full-ambush mode. Mikes were thrust out on the ends of long poles, television cameras stared out like huge cyclopes, thick cables snaked hazardously underfoot. The press corps had Barstad pinned between his car and the front door of his building, and to Campbell, the man had the same panicked expression as a squirrel caught midway across the road with a car coming, frozen in indecision. And Barstad seemed to have picked up a nervous tic. His hand kept slipping down to check his fly.

Heather rang the buzzer at Pine Hills Elementary and waited to be let in. Nothing. She smiled up at the little video camera perched above the door, protection against homicidal maniacs and pedophiles. "Heather Peters!" she said, pressing the buzzer again. "I'm here for Halloween!"

Nothing.

She turned around. Kevin had already pulled away. Well, this was strange. In the past, the secretaries had always answered the buzzer and let her right in. She wasn't being frozen out, was she? She'd only confessed herself as a fraud half an hour earlier.

Well, she'd just have to try some of the other entrances.

She walked around the school, and frankly that wasn't very comfortable in the heels she'd chosen in order to look authoritative in court. But finally she found an unlocked gym door around the back. As she clicked down the hall in the direction of the cafeteria, she was suddenly reminded of her ill-fated Back to School Night. Why was it that whenever Pine Hills Elementary was concerned, she was always late? Heather Peters, the most punctual person in the world! More than punctual—early, usually! But when it came to this place, she was always running in after the last minute. Well, with any luck, she hadn't missed everything.

She began to hear the commotion when she was rounding the corner at the music room, which was a whole corridor away from the cafeteria. It sounded like the angry chanting of a mob, and the first image that popped into her head was one of those foreign protests you sometimes saw on the news, with signs written in crazy languages and burning effigies of George W. Bush. Well, that was strange! As she got closer, other images came to mind: Times Square on New Year's Eve, soccer riots, Chuck E. Cheese.

When Heather finally swung open the lunchroom door, she could see why nobody had been there to let her in. Everybody, it seemed, was in the cafeteria. The secretaries were both there, as were the janitors, the librarian, all the lunch ladies, the teachers, and a row of class moms, and for the first time Heather noticed how they all seemed to look alike:

streaked hair tucked neatly into their headbands, tasseled loafers on their feet. In the center of it all, of course, was poor Mrs. Gupnick, who looked like a missionary about to drop into a stew pot. She was doing that clapping thing that usually brought the kids to attention—*clap, clap, clap-clap-clap*—but the only people clapping obediently were the class moms. The children, most of them dressed as little animals, were dancing on the tables, arm wrestling and throwing food against the walls. In one corner, two boys from Miss Kindermack's class, who'd dressed as pirates, were fighting with plastic swords. Candy corn was everywhere: on the floor, on the furniture, smashed into children's hair. Some of the more single-minded kids were standing dull-eyed next to the food table, stuffing cupcake after cupcake into their mouths. About a dozen were now astride the oversized Animals Crackers box that had so carefully been constructed by Jane Perfido's brother-in-law. It was wobbling violently, a lawsuit waiting to happen.

Heather stood there, her mouth open, when one of the class mothers grabbed her arm. "Are you the snake lady?" she asked.

"Why, yes, I mean, no," Heather sputtered. "Not anymore."

"Well, why not?" the woman said. "There are 425 children in this room who have all been waiting a whole hour for you to show us your little snakes. And you show up late. Without them."

"Oh, I'm not . . ." Heather stammered. Why was the woman so angry? What little snakes? Then suddenly she understood. The class mom had been referring not to her but to that other snake lady, the one from the nature center, who was going to do a reptile demonstration for Halloween. Heather had seen the notice about it, from Connor's backpack. That was to be the afternoon's entertainment. But for reasons unexplained, the snake lady had never shown. It didn't quite clarify the pandemonium going on in the cafeteria, but coupled with all the sugar and the costumes, it was a start. Well.

Heather turned away from moms and teachers and began searching for Connor, but the scene was like a painting by Hieronymus Bosch. It was hard to pick out a specific demon. Finally she saw him, sitting alone in a corner of the cafeteria, wearing his worn-out Spider-Man pajamas, rocking back and forth in a fashion that struck Heather as autistic. "Self-comforting," wasn't that the term the worry doctor had used? Connor was rocking to try to stave off the madness around him, and suddenly Heather was filled with rage. What was wrong with these people? The grown-ups, that is. How had they let things get so out of control? It was all because of this school's ridiculous tradition of over-doing Halloween, of having to control every single little detail and make everything perfect. Why a themed parade? Why couldn't the kids just wear whatever costumes they wanted? What was it with the huge Halloween feast? And what idiot picked this day, of all days in the school calendar, to bring a nature expert into the mix?

Heather blinked, and she suddenly had the feeling that she'd just had LASIK surgery. Never had she seen so clearly. Look at every single class mom: identical, uniform, as if their hairdos and footwear had been mandated by Mrs. Gupnick too. Why were there so few brunettes? Why didn't any of them have short hair? Or wear Converse sneakers? Why wasn't a single one fat?

Everything had gone wrong since she'd moved to Galapagos Estates. She should have figured it out when the window treatments didn't fit. She should have figured it out after the snake. Why? Why had it all gone wrong? She'd just wanted everything nice. A nice house. Okay, a nice *big* house. And a good school system for Connor. And look at him now, practically catatonic with his rocking and not even noticing that she'd come in.

It occurred to Heather that this was the perfect opportunity to be the hero, the real hero, to take charge and rescue all the hapless adults in the room. She could do it too. She knew she could. Nobody in the world had a will like Heather Peters. Not even 425 sugar-crazed brats. She could stand up on a table, click her heels, and force the room to pay attention. And if they wanted snakes, she'd give them snakes. She'd regale them with snakes. She'd have them all wide-eyed in wonder with the story of the rattlesnake in her backyard. She'd tell them how she'd . . . but what would she tell them? How she stood on the lawn chair and screamed for her handyman? How she'd lied to Rodney Campbell, and pretended to have killed the snake herself? How she'd been led out of this very school in handcuffs?

Well, then, maybe she wouldn't tell them the real story. She'd make up a story. About snakes. Or—she looked around—candy. Candy houses. She'd tell them the story of Hansel and Gretel, and she'd hold them spellbound. Mrs. Gupnick would practically fall on her knees, thanking her. The Galapagos Estates Homeowners Association would hear about it, and beg her to stay. And Connor . . .

She looked at him again, a sad boy in footie pajamas who'd suffered one humiliation after another since they'd moved here. No, of course she couldn't be the hero, any more than Connor was really Spider-Man. Heather couldn't bring the room under control—it was just a stupid fantasy—and even if she could, Connor would then have to live it down for the rest of his life. He'd develop phobias so bad she'd have to take him out of third grade, home-school him.

Something in her softened, and she walked across the room to the corner where Connor sat, picking up a handful of candy corn on her way. She sat down next to her son, and for once she didn't even worry about the dirt on the floor and how it was going to ruin her suit, which needed dry cleaning anyway. She held her hand out. Connor took three pieces of candy corn, and the rest of it she plopped in her mouth. Then, taking his little hand in hers, she began to rock.

Chapter Thirty

It was spring, and the world was that tender color of green, the color of buds and new growth on the tips of shrubbery. A hammer struck nails with a rhythmic precision, a tinny *tap-tap-tap* like the sound of pennies clanging together, followed by the deeper thud of wood finally swallowing each nail. Over and over, the sound repeated, and from this alone you could tell that the person wielding the hammer was patient and methodical.

Agnes walked over an open field in the direction of the hammering. She was carrying a mug of peppermint tea, and she carefully covered it with her hand so that it wouldn't spill. The steam from the tea rose and warmed her fingers. It was spring, but the chill of winter still clung to the air.

She walked into the open structure and held the mug up to Harlan. He put down the hammer and took the mug, cupping it in his hands to capture the warmth before putting it to his lips. His arthritis always kicked up during a wet spring, and his fingers were stiff and achy. "Peppermint," he said.

"Yes, your favorite," Agnes answered.

Harlan had come around slowly to the idea of herbal tea. Agnes had worked on him all winter, serving him teas made of cinnamon bark and cloves and anise, sweetened by honey and served alternately in rough earthenware mugs and in shiny mugs advertising various shows on public radio. At first Harlan had grumbled, but slowly he'd taken a liking to it. Perhaps it was less the tea than the experience of drinking it with Agnes in front of the fire.

"How's it going?" she asked.

"Good," he said. "Foundation's almost done."

She nodded.

Harlan was building a new henhouse. It was going to be a demonstration project for the new Rolling Hills Nature Center, a state-of-the-art organic henhouse, the centerpiece of the center's much-expanded new home. The entire arrangement had been Agnes's idea. Harlan had willed his land to the nature center, with a stipulation that it would never be developed commercially. An estate attorney recommended by someone on Agnes's board arranged the rest. The gift went through immediately, Harlan's personal debts—which represented a mere pittance of the value of the land—had been paid, and in exchange for his gift, he was given a lifetime contract as the center's live-in caretaker. The henhouse would replace the one Harlan had lost both to vandalism and to the fact that he'd slowly disassembled it over the winter and used the wood to keep his stove burning. It would also be a living monument to the humane treatment of animals and a field-trip destination for schoolchildren.

"So?" Harlan asked. "What's for dinner?"

"Lasagna," Agnes said.

"Vegetarian lasagna?" he asked, pretending to cringe.

"I'm afraid so," she said. She'd put an end to Harlan hunting skunks and squirrels.

They both smiled.

Agnes still kept her little bungalow on Route 381, but recently, she'd been spending several nights a week at Harlan's house. After all the papers had been drawn up and signed, she had insisted, of course, that Harlan get his lights and the phone turned back on. She was paying for it, she pointed out, and the caretaker for Rolling Hills Nature Center had to be reachable in case of an emergency. Plus, she needed somewhere to plug in her laptop when she spent the night.

Barbara spent hours at the nickel slots, carrying her plastic cup of nickels from machine to machine and keeping her eyes alert for any coins twinkling up from the casino floor. People did drop them sometimes. Barstad looked at her with disgust. She was lumpy and pale like everybody else who played the slots. And the people who played the nickel slots, the old saddlebag included, were even lumpier and paler than the people who played the quarters. His wife was deluded, just like the rest, giddy every time a machine spilled out a pile of nickels, acting like she'd just pulled off some feat of financial wizardry. Well, maybe it looked that way, and even sounded that way when you jingled your plastic cup. Ten dollars was an awful lot of coins. But it was still just ten bucks, and anyway, within an hour, Barbara would give it all back to the house—and then some. What an idiot.

Atlantic City. How had he wound up here? With her?

Well, he knew how. Of course he knew. He'd bargained away his chips. Traded them, in the form of an enormous check made out to the State of New Jersey—it was called a civil penalty—to have the criminal charges against him dropped. It was, he thought ruefully, like buying a "Get Out of Jail Free" card during a game of Monopoly—it was hard not to think in Monopoly terms when you lived on Mediterranean Avenue—only it wasn't free, and it wasn't a game. They had him on falsifying government filings because of the stupid environmental impact statement he'd had written in order to get approval for building Galapagos Estates. It was, in any objective sense, ridiculous. So what if he'd claimed there were no endangered species and hired a phony herpetologist? What exactly was the harm in that? They were rattlesnakes, for God's sakes. Why shouldn't they be endangered? The world was better off without them. Who could have predicted then that some skinny little bitch named Heather Peters would come along and turn the presence of a few rattlesnakes into a federal case?

And then there was the matter of one Miss Jessie Gabrowski, who, it turns out, was just seventeen. Yes, she'd gone to Penn State, but she'd dropped out after her freshman year. Even though Jessie was past the age of legal consent in New Jersey, the prosecutors had threatened Barstad with an aggravated sexual-assault charge anyway. Something about the fact that Jessie was on Barstad's payroll, which meant that he had "supervisory power" over her—and therefore she didn't have the wherewithal to resist his advances. Since she was under his supervisory power, they said, the fact that he'd had sex with her was the same as statutory rape. Especially since she was under eighteen.

A royal mess, is what it was. There was only so much that lawyers, even a whole team of them, could do. But Barstad really wanted to sue the ass off that escort company, which, by the way, said he still owed them money for the private party he'd booked, and had to cancel, for the week of the League of Municipalities convention. In any event, an agreement had been worked out by which Barstad divested himself of all of his assets and "contributed" them to the state's million-acres initiative, a program to preserve open space. A program that was also always short on funds. Voluntary civil penalties: a brand-new governmental initiative for meting out justice and whittling down the state deficit at the same time. Why give the likes of Jack Barstad a free thirty-eight-thousand-dollar-a-year meal ticket to the state penitentiary when you could skin him for every cent he had? It was brilliant, Barstad had to admit. Well, at least it kept him from getting fucked in the ass in the state pen.

The transaction had left Barstad with his house. Singular. One house. Not a dozen subdivisions. Not even one subdivision. Not even a single goddamn street. The family dwelling, that was all—and that was mortgaged up to the roof. When Barstad had to sell his Lincoln Navigator, it was the last straw. He couldn't show his face in front of the neighbors anymore. Somehow, he managed to talk Barbara into Atlantic City, where real estate was cheap. Not in the heart of the casino district, maybe, but there were plenty of run-down blocks, and Barstad would have a chance of growing his empire again, from scratch. His son, Will, a senior in high school, hadn't been happy about the move. But then, who was? And a little toughening up was going to be good for him.

"Listen," Barstad said to Barbara. "Don't bet every fucking nickel, okay?"

"But, Jack," she said, hurt in her voice. "I'm winning."

"Yeah, and I'm a millionaire," he said before turning around and walking out. He went over to his rickshaw, which had a sign on it advertising the Borgata. "Thanks," he said to a fellow named Joe, who'd watched it while he went inside to get some coffee.

It was three o'clock, half an hour until the Legends show over at the Claridge, which had just hired an Ella Fitzgerald imitator and a new Madonna. It was starting to drizzle. That was always good for business. If Barstad was lucky, maybe he could get a ten-dollar fare—and a three- or four-dollar tip—to push someone down the boardwalk. He just hoped that his next fare wasn't too fat.

Then, out of the corner of his eye, he saw something that made his heart lurch. Walking out of the casino, on the arm of a distinguished-looking man with silver sideburns, was a tall girl who walked like she owned the entire boardwalk. She had juicy lips, blunt-cut hair the color of ebony, legs that went on and on.

Oh, fuck, the last person in the world he wanted to see.

Dana.

Fuck oh fuck oh fuck.

"Joe," Barstad said quickly to the guy next to him. "I've got to go take a leak. Can you watch the rickshaw again?"

Barstad handed the guy a twenty and ran off to hide under a pier.

Heather was the teensiest bit relieved when the school bus had disgorged them at the camp and she saw the facilities where she would be spending the next two nights. At least they were staying in cabins. Not that it was the Ritz. Far from it. But there were cots, with lumpy little mattresses, and the place was built out of logs, and actually had a ceiling and walls, which was, Heather thought, a lot better than having to stay in a tent. She didn't even want to imagine what it would be like to try to sleep on the ground with just one thin layer of canvas to protect her from everything . . . out there. There were even bathrooms in the cabins, though they were very, very rustic. Well, it was better than a latrine. Thank God for minor miracles.

This camping trip was a major component in the Rehabilitation of Heather Peters, her plan to woo back the mothers and teachers and administrators at Pine Hills Elementary, and its auxiliary mission, the Rehabilitation of Connor Peters. Heather didn't want to be here, that was for damn sure, but she knew she couldn't afford to pull a prima donna act either. She knew her role like it was a part in a play. To be a sunny, cheerful, helpful kind of mom, the kind of mom who would say, "Oh, I'd love to organize the children to find kindling" or "Potatoes need peeling? That's my specialty!" She had vowed, before stepping on the bus with Connor and all the other rapacious monsters of the third grade, to be exactly that kind of mom, or at least to play one, no matter what happened.

Heather had managed to cling to her job as class mom. A shift had occurred in her public relations, and it had started on Halloween, in the cafeteria, when she'd gone over and sat beside Connor and taken his hand. It was the smallest thing, really, but the other mothers had noticed. Heather hadn't been trying to get their attention or win their praise. She'd simply responded to the sight of Connor, sitting there so pathetically.

But, she was beginning to understand, the relationship between a mother and her offspring was one of those things that the other mothers watched. They kept score, actually, even though nobody would ever admit it. They were everywhere, watching, like Big Brother. In the checkout line, on the playground, at the movies. Whenever a child fell off the swings, the mothers standing nearby would hold their collective breath, silently judging what happened next, how the mother of the screaming child handled it. Some mothers made too much of a fuss, acting as if each little scrape was the end of the world—until the whole thing became like an episode of *ER* and you wanted to vomit. And then there were the other mothers—just as bad—who kept right on talking. They'd put a hand on their sobbing child's shoulder but not look down or wipe away their tears, all the while keeping up their end in the playground conversation without missing a beat. This was noted with equal disdain.

When she'd first moved to Galapagos Estates, Heather had thought it was the visible things that mattered. What kind of car you drove, what kind of furniture you had, even what kind of shrubs you planted. And sure, those things still mattered. But it was the invisible things that mattered even more. Otherwise, why would Elsie Roberts, whose taste was entirely in her mouth, be president of the PTA?

They had forgiven her lie. That was the surprising part. It had been the most embarrassing thing in the world to admit that she'd been a phony, that she'd never killed a snake, much less a rattlesnake. She'd been a phony through every single interview, from the *South Jersey Eagle* to the *Today* show. And on Halloween, on the courtroom steps, the truth about her lying had finally come out. Luckily for Heather, however, the sordid truth of Jack Barstad's lies had also come out that same day and overshadowed her own. That had been what had put her back in the good graces of the Galapagos Estates Homeowners Committee, which now had somebody else to blame for everything that had happened since the first rattlesnake appeared on the scene.

Now Heather was a nobody again, like everyone else. But guess what? That appeared to be the very reason they had begun to accept her. Because she was a nobody, and because she had been brought down a notch. It took Heather a long time to figure it out, but she finally had. There was nothing like success to make people hate you, and nothing like being disgraced to make people feel sorry for you. Which was almost as good as being liked, and just as useful.

The Rehabilitation of Heather Peters was also working in regard to Kevin Peters. The rattlesnakes had been in hibernation all winter, the press had forgotten her, and the laboratory rats were, for the most part, gone too. This had freed up all kinds of time. Heather could actually go to the grocery store and cook dinner. She could supervise Connor's homework. She could even suggest that he invite a little friend home from school for the occasional playdate. As order descended upon the Peters household, its lord and provider started coming home from work a little earlier. He eased up on the sarcasm. Gradually, he even began to compliment her on her cooking, on little odds and ends she'd bought for the house.

For weeks, for months really, she hadn't been interested in sex. She'd simply been too exhausted. Then one Thursday morning, right after Connor had gone to school, the doorbell rang and two thick-armed delivery men arrived with the new white love seat that Heather had been coveting since September. A surprise! From her dear, dear Kevin. And that evening after Connor's bedtime, Heather, well, Heather gave thanks.

Occasionally, she looked at the built-in desk in her kitchen, where she'd worked so feverishly in the days leading up to her court date, and felt a kind of loss. Now the desk was littered with fabric samples and cookie recipes. So ordinary. She knew she had no cause to complain. She had everything: a beautiful house, a good provider, a fine son—well, a son anyway. Everything, that is, except a suitable target for moral outrage.

The job Heather had been assigned when they got to the camp was to give the bathrooms a quick cleaning. Nothing much, the mother in charge of the third-grade field trip explained, just a "lick and a polish," to make sure they didn't all get some horrible disease from sitting on the seats.

"Of course," Heather had said with a fake smile. "Happy to."

She was down on her knees, wiping the surface of a wooden toilet seat and trying her best to ignore the odor, when she heard the sound of footsteps running into the cabin. She could tell by the speed and the weight of the footsteps, and by the huffing that accompanied them, that it was Connor. "Mom!" he said. "Mom! Mom! Guess what?"

She stepped out of the toilet stall and, without thinking, put her hands on her hips. Then she realized she was still wearing those yellow rubber gloves. Disgusting. God knew what germs were on those gloves. She'd have to change her jeans, and make sure she didn't get her other pair dirty by falling in a creek or letting Connor smear s'mores all over her. She looked up to see her ruddy-cheeked son, out of breath, standing at the entrance to the bathroom. "Yes, dear?" she said.

"Mom, we found a snake! And I told all the kids and Miss Kindermack and everybody that you could identify it, that you were an expert on snakes."

She stood, facing him, her mouth forming a little *o*.

"The other mothers were afraid," he said. "One of them even screamed. But I told them: not my mom."

"That's touching, Connor," she managed. "It really is."

He pulled on her arm and started dragging her in the direction of the cabin door. "Come on!"

"Really, sweetheart, the only kind of snake I could identify would be a rattlesnake," she said, trying to pull back.

Connor broke his hold on her arm and then crossed his arms, frowning. He stared at her yellow gloves, then looked up at her face. "Really!" he said. "I didn't think you were the kind of mother who was meant for cleaning bathrooms. I thought you were meant for bigger things."

Well, certainly that was true.

She sighed, and tugged off her yellow gloves. "Okay, Connor," she said, resigned to her fate, whatever it might be. "Show me the snake."

Heather let Connor take her hand and drag her in the direction of the snake. Then, for the benefit of the other mothers, she arranged her mouth into a credible approximation of a smile.

Author's Note

In 2002, I wrote a column about endangered timber rattlesnakes in the state of New Jersey. Part of the story was about a new housing development that had been built on a rattlesnake habitat. The situation and the setting stayed in my mind, and a few months later, I began developing this novel. But the real story served as only a spark for my imagination. This is not that story: Galapagos Estates is not the development I wrote about and the characters in this book aren't the people I wrote about, either. The story is farce—it's all made up, although the state (New Jersey) and the species of snake (timber rattlesnake) remain the same.

1. Most people describe Heather as vain and domineering, but she sees herself as just looking out for her family's interests. What was your reaction to Heather? Do you recognize her qualities in people you know, or in yourself? How do you feel about a main character whose qualities are so unattractive?

2. In *Rattled,* newcomers to the countryside threaten the rural lifestyle of characters like Harlan White, the chicken farmer and handyman. Do similar tensions exist where you live? Do you find yourself rooting for Harlan?

3. Heather is described by some characters as living in a McMansion. McMansions have become a flashpoint in culture wars about home, community, and aesthetics. How does *Rattled* contribute to this debate?

4. One of themes of the book is the contrast between the two basic creation motifs—Darwinism and the Garden of Eden. Heather lives in Galapagos Estates, but as in Eden, it's the sudden appearance of a snake that gets her ejected. How do you think these themes contribute to the novel?

5. Pine Hills Elementary School is a stewpot of anxieties, especially for Connor. Discuss Connor's difficulties finding his place in the cafeteria and on the playground. What do you think about his "worry doctor"? How might his parents contribute to his maladjustment? Why is Halloween such a trial for him?

6. The mothers at the school have their own pecking order, and Heather disregards this invisible hierarchy at her peril. Her attempt to pick Connor's teacher similarly backfires. Do you see similar dramas playing out in schoolyards today?

7. The Friends of the Fauna are frustrated by the fact that timber rattlesnakes are not a "cute" enough species to garner public sympathy. How do you feel about the rights of reptiles?

8. Harlan and Agnes are both old-timers in the New Jersey countryside, and although they both have contempt for Heather, that doesn't make them friends. Discuss what these characters represent and how their relationship changes over the course of the novel.

9. Do you think that Heather becomes a better mother at the end of the book? Is her change believable? Why do you think Heather is shown on a camping trip in the last chapter?

A Reading Group Guide

For more reading group suggestions, visit www.readinggroupgold.com

St. Martin's Griffin